Some Kind of Devotion

GRACIE BANKS

SOME KIND OF DEVOTION

First Printing, 2025

Your presence was my light when I couldn't find my own.
This book exists because of you.

This book contains depictions of domestic abuse, alcohol abuse, smoking, and sexual content, as well as themes of emotional neglect, trauma, mental health struggles, and dysfunctional family dynamics. Reader discretion is advised, especially for those sensitive to these subjects.

CONTENTS

~ 1 ~

CHAPTER ONE

Weighted Silence

When I think back to the days of elementary school, the memories feel faded. They appear in fragments and always seem to lack color—until I close my eyes and truly focus. I have to imagine my entire life, like a film being rewound, diving deeper and deeper into the deluge of memories that shape who I am. Inevitably, my thoughts drift back to *her*. I hated her—with all my being. Despised everything about her for as long as I could remember.

I met her when I was young. Really young. Back when the world was new and I was blissfully oblivious, when life made sense. She was unremarkable at first—black hair, brown eyes, skin a shade too pale, like she was allergic to the sun.

She was totally ordinary. But her gaze—it held something. Something that made my stomach twist and my throat tighten. Not a sparkle of joy or childish innocence. No, it was something darker. Something deeper than the rest of the children. A gleam of intelligence? Or maybe something I recognized without understanding. Something I'd seen before, though I couldn't place where. I wasn't sure back then. Maybe if I knew what I do now, things would've turned out differently.

At first, it was little things—she was taller, faster. Silly competitions that carried the weight only childhood could give them. When the world was small and victories felt monumental simply because we didn't know any better. But in the gray world of youth, she was the only thing that stood out—a smear of color against the bland. I competed with her in my head, always trying to outdo her. But she always won. It wasn't the speed that got to me. It was her smile.

It wasn't really a smile. Just an uptilt of her lips, one side higher than the other, like she was trying—and failing—to repress it. To me, it looked like a display, something meant just for me. A silent laugh. Not with me, but at me. That's how I read it—like she knew I was losing, and she wanted me to feel it. Maybe she didn't mean anything by it. Maybe it was just her way of existing in the moment. But back then, that curve of her mouth felt like everything.

"Couldn't catch up again?" she'd mock. I hated it. For eight-year-old me, it was the ultimate insult. A girl beating me? It felt unfair. So, I made it my life's mission—dramatic, I know—to beat her.

But I was average, and despite appearing average too, she was better. Maybe it was just a game to her. I don't know. Maybe I was just a classmate to outpace. Maybe she found it funny.

One winter, we played King of the Hill on a snowbank carved by the plows. We weren't supposed to, but the teachers never really stopped us. "We" was a loose term—we knew each other's names from roll call, but beyond that, we were strangers brought together by play. I usually sat out, but that day, I must have been feeling bold. None of us were roughhousing. It wasn't that kind of game. Just harmless fun—until it wasn't. I slipped on ice, scraped my knee, and felt her grip the back of my jacket, pulling herself past me with a cheer that sliced through the air. Shrill. Not just in pitch, but in tone—bright and victorious. I flinched at the sound, not from the volume, but from what it meant.

I guess I was just sick of constantly losing. Watching her at the top, carefree and triumphant, something ugly clawed up inside me. My head buzzed—no, roared. The air around me thickened, my vision wavered, edges blurring as if the world couldn't hold its shape anymore. Her face vanished in the noise. Even her smile—gone. All I could feel was the pressure, the heat rising to my ears, the distorted sound of everything being too much. I didn't care about the rules. I didn't care about her.

I didn't just push her—I ripped her by the jacket pulling her toward me like I was tearing away at something fragile and whole. My hands were shaking. But I didn't let go. The buzzing didn't stop, it only grew louder. She landed hard against the snowy ground, solidified from dozens of children's feet packing it down, which probably hurt. I remember hesitating for a moment, before deciding that I didn't really care, more focused on the feeling of accomplishment, of victory, and recognition. I had finally beat her at something.

A small cluster of students surrounded her. Perhaps she was actually hurt. I remember a teacher yelling at me, causing any sense of victory to vanish. As I got pulled down by the teacher by my wrist, I glanced her way. She wasn't crying. Her face was blank as she stared back at me, and that made it worse. It wasn't twisted in pain or fury. It was just... nothing.

Her eyes—they were *so* familiar. Like I'd seen them in places I'd rather forget. Places where silence pressed down heavier than words, where staring was defense. Her gaze burned into me. For a moment, I wondered if she'd always been watching, waiting. The familiarity twisted something deep inside. Her smile was gone. As if it had never existed—swallowed by her gaze, leaving only emptiness behind.

After recess, I was dragged to the principal. Her voice was sharp and unforgiving, each word designed to pierce through my skull and settle in the hollow space where guilt was supposed to live. But I didn't really hear her. I kept my head down, nodded when I thought I should. Pretended the scolding was doing more than making noise. She said my mom couldn't pick me up. I'd have to walk home.

Outside, the cold slapped me. The kind of cold that cuts through layers and leaves your skin raw, your breath sharp. My boots sank with each step, the sky darkening to that dull winter gray. The wind carved lines across my face, but I hardly noticed. I should've felt miserable. But I didn't. Not really.

My mind was still back there—on the hill, on her eyes. Right before she hit the snow. There was something deeper than surprise in them. A flicker of something I wasn't supposed to see. I kept trying to decipher it. Was it recognition? Resignation? Accusation? The knot in my chest only tightened with every attempt to name it. Her stare clung to me, sharp and silent, refusing to let go. Cold. Empty. More painful than any bruise. It filled the space where guilt should've been.

At the apartment, I saw my mother standing outside the door. She looked like she could barely stand, her body a weight she didn't want to carry. Her face was ghostly pale. The lines around her eyes too deep for someone so young. She had me at seventeen. She was twenty-five then. I remember hesitating, unsure if I was even allowed to feel angry, unsure if I was allowed to feel anything at all.

She didn't look at me. Didn't speak until I touched the doorknob. She opened her mouth. I paused.

"Your school called." She said, her voice quiet, like she was speaking through a fog. There was no anger in her voice, no judgment. Just a quiet acceptance, as though this was a daily occurrence. I said nothing. There was nothing to say, she didn't need me to explain myself. She already knew. The silence stretched for a moment, my hand growing more numb by the second from the chilled metal. "We won't tell your father."

I didn't respond. It wasn't a question. Just something I was supposed to agree to, to just nod. Pretend nothing happened. I didn't know if it was the silence between us—or the weight of being acknowledged, barely, and only because the school forced her to—that made my chest tighten. I tried to swallow the lump in my throat, but it stuck.

She didn't look at me when she spoke again. Her voice was barely loud enough to hear, her tone distant—almost like she was voicing a thought aloud rather than speaking to me.

"You'll have to find something to do during the day."

I wondered if anyone else ever felt this way—if they too, were just living through the motions. Pretending that everything was okay, when in reality they were drowning—and all they wanted was for the waters to recede enough for a single breath. Feelings and thoughts no child—or adult—should have to experience.

My dad always said boys shouldn't cry. That it was loud. Annoying. I think Mom learned that too. So, I just breathed deep—cold and heavy, like I was dragging it from beneath the surface. But it didn't help. It wasn't enough. I was still drowning, still choking on everything I couldn't say. Tried to swallow the knot in my throat. It remained regardless.

I pushed into the apartment. Quiet. Dark. The air was thick—stale and unmoving, like even it had given up. A wilted plant sat by the window, leaves curled and brown, forgotten and gasping for light. It hadn't been watered in weeks, maybe longer. Just like everything else in the apartment, it was surviving by accident, not care. The windows were always covered, as if hiding the world might make it disappear. Mom followed but said nothing more. She stood there, swallowed by shadows.

"There's leftovers in the fridge," she said, her voice thin and mechanical, barely parting the silence. She drifted toward the bedroom, the door clicking shut with a finality that seemed to seal her away. I stood there, the stillness pressing in, looking for something—anything—to pull me out of my head. But all I could think of was her. The girl with those eyes.

The silence was suffocating. There was nowhere to go. I stood frozen, willing myself to move. My fingers itched for purpose, but everything felt lifeless. I didn't want to eat. Didn't want to think. Didn't want to exist. Perhaps I wanted to drown.

Mom stayed silent. She always did. I couldn't remember the last time she asked how I was—if she ever did. The last time I mattered enough to be noticed. To be seen. Her eyes didn't meet mine anymore. At some point, they'd stopped looking at me and started looking through me. Like I was a piece of furniture, something she had to step around but didn't really register. Like I wasn't even there.

The silence dragged on, thick as fog. I glanced at the kitchen, where the fridge door was ajar, the dim light from the bulb inside casting a faint glow on the floor. There were leftovers, but I had no appetite. Still, my legs carried me toward it. I wasn't hungry, but I didn't know what else to do.

The refrigerator hummed as I opened it. The sound folded into the thrum in my head, just another layer of noise I barely registered. Last night's dinner sat in plastic containers. Half-forgotten. Waiting to be consumed. I stared at them like they were abstract art—shapes and colors that meant nothing. I wasn't hungry. I hadn't been hungry in a long time. I was just going through the motions, my body moving because it had to, not because I felt anything at all.

I grabbed one container without looking. Closed the door. The room felt colder, despite the heater running. I stood still, holding plastic, staring at nothing.

Her eyes flashed again in my mind—their blank emptiness. I didn't know what it meant, this sense of recognition. The feeling gnawed at me, twisting inside my gut. It wasn't just that she was familiar. No, it was something deeper, darker. A kind of silent accusation.

My fingers gripped the plastic tighter, and I realized I hadn't been breathing.

I exhaled slowly, turning toward the living room, where the shadows seemed to gather tighter, deeper, as though they were trying to swallow me whole. There was nowhere to hide, no way to escape the feeling that something was terribly wrong. Something I couldn't understand, something I didn't know how to fight.

I brought the container to the table and sat down, the chair creaking under my weight. I peeled the lid back and took a bite, expecting nothing. But then—taste. Salt, warmth, the texture of something real. It hit too hard, too suddenly. My throat clenched. Tears sprang up before I could stop them—not from comfort, but from the shock of it. The taste was a reminder. Of my body still working, still reacting, still tethered to this place. I wasn't crying for the food. I was crying because it meant I was still here.

They were for the fact that I could feel it at all.

And her eyes were still there, imprinted behind mine, like she'd reached into something hollow and left her mark.

But there was one thing I was sure of: I couldn't shake her from my mind. Not now, not ever.

~ 2 ~

CHAPTER TWO

Through Her Eyes

The days after the King of the Hill incident dragged on like a sentence with no end. Something had been sparked in me—something sharp and restless. I had seen her in a way I couldn't unsee, and it left everything else dulled in comparison. The hours moved slower. The air felt heavier. Every step I took felt like it echoed louder. Her image lingered, not just in memory, but in every inch of space I passed through. I couldn't escape it. I couldn't escape her.

She was everywhere. In every hallway, every classroom, every silence. Always just ahead. Always watching.

She was everywhere. In every hallway, every classroom, every silence. Like a reflection in a warped mirror—familiar, but untouchable. Always just ahead. Always watching. And in her presence, I felt myself fading. As if the more I saw her, the less there was left of me. I couldn't compete with her shadow—I couldn't even find mine.

Before the incident, it always felt like I was just a step behind her—close enough to believe I might catch up, if I just worked harder, ran faster, thought quicker. But that illusion shattered. Now, it felt like she was pulling away on purpose. Every move she made, every answer she gave, felt deliberate. Calculated. Like she wasn't just trying to win—she was trying to make sure I knew I'd already lost. And somehow, I kept playing the game, even though I never agreed to the rules

It wasn't just about being better anymore. It was about the constant reminder, the suffocating awareness that no matter how hard I tried, I would never escape her.

Then, one day in class, the teacher called on me—something about a passage we'd read, or maybe it was a math problem. It didn't matter. My thoughts scattered like broken glass, sharp and irretrievable. My chest tightened. My heart thudded against my ribs, faster than it should, each beat a jolt that echoed in my ears. My palms were slick with sweat, and my fingers trembled against the edge of the desk. Breathing felt like a task I had forgotten how to perform. And then, I felt her gaze.

It was like a pressure on my chest, invisible but immense. She wasn't looking at me like a rival, not even like a person. Her eyes were blank, analytical—eyes that didn't seem like they should belong to a child. Too knowing, too distant. As if I were just another data point in her day. Something to be observed. Measured. Filed away.

The worst part was, it wasn't just that I was struggling or faltering—I had failed before. That wasn't new. I could live with being wrong, with being slow. But this was different. This was about her. She didn't even seem to care whether I got it right or not. Her gaze wasn't invested—it had already moved past me. As though my answer didn't matter because I didn't matter. Like I'd already been dismissed before I'd even spoken. I wasn't her opponent. I wasn't anything at all.

I froze. My mind went blank, words dissolving before they could reach my tongue. My throat tightened like a vice, sealing off air, sealing off sound. My hands began to tremble, fingers curling against the edge of the desk in a desperate search for grounding. The minutes dragged on like hours, each second stretching unbearably. My vision blurred at the edges, my body stiff and cold, and I became painfully aware of the eyes on me—her eyes, sharp and inescapable. I was drowning again, not in water, but in heat and noise and silence all at once. And there was no one there to pull me out.

Then she smiled.

That crooked, cold tilt of her lips. A familiar motion, one I'd seen a hundred times before—but now there was something unreadable in it. Something that didn't fit. Not warm, not teasing. Just strange. It struck me as mocking, and maybe it was. Or maybe it wasn't. I didn't know. I only knew how it felt—to me, in that moment. Like dismissal. Like a quiet confirmation that I would never measure up.

I wanted to scream. I wanted to throw something, to break something, to run away. But I couldn't. Not in front of her. So, I dug my nails into the wood of the desk, my heart aching. I forced myself to stay still, refusing to let her see the chaos in my mind. I couldn't let her know. I couldn't let her see the effect she had on me.

The bell rang. I didn't move. Her smile stayed with me long after the classroom emptied.

I was frozen. Not because I was unsure, but because I mattered so little in that moment. Her eyes weren't cruel—they were empty. Detached. I was an object, not a peer. I hated how familiar it was.

Summer dragged on like an echo with no end. For other kids, it was a season of freedom—sunlight, games, ice cream. For me, it was just more time. More hours stuck in a sweltering apartment that smelled of mildew, cigarette ash, and something acrid I couldn't name. My father was always there—loud when he was drunk, louder when he wasn't. His voice cut through the walls, his anger always directed at my mother unless I gave him a reason. My mother never fought back. She drifted like smoke from room to room, eyes unfocused, limbs slow.

The apartment felt like a tomb. I stayed in my room with the fan on high, but it didn't matter. The heat was a blanket I couldn't peel off. The silence was a lie—underneath it was tension, like a wire pulled too tight. I barely left. What was the point? There was nothing out there for me. And even inside, I couldn't escape her. Her image haunted the blank spots on my walls, the corners of my mind. In every idle moment, in every stale breath, she lingered.

It wasn't freedom. It wasn't reprieve. Just heat, pressure, and the memory of her.

When school started again, I noticed something: I was taller. Not by much. But enough. For years, she had always been the one who looked down on me—taller, quicker, just out of reach. It had been a constant, one small but sharp reminder of the gap between us. Now, that advantage was mine. I should have felt something—pride, relief, maybe even victory. But I didn't. It felt wrong. Unnatural. Like the balance had shifted without permission.

I expected her to care. To flinch, to falter, to acknowledge it. But she didn't. If she noticed, she gave no sign. Still untouchable. Still perfect.

She just smiled that smile—the one that reminded me of my place. Beneath her.

I joined the basketball team. Not because I liked it—I didn't. I hated every practice, every drill. But I needed something. Anything. A win I could claim. Proof that I was capable, that I could matter.

And I was good at it. I worked hard, got noticed. Teammates cheered my name. Coaches nodded in approval.

But she didn't flinch. Didn't react. She came to every game, sat in the stands with a textbook on her lap, barely looking up. And when she did, it was with that same infuriating smile—cool, detached, knowing.

She still existed in a world where nothing I did could ever touch her.

I quit the team. Basketball hadn't been enough. It hadn't made her flinch, hadn't drawn her gaze the way I needed. So I doubled down. I studied harder. Pushed further. Sleep became irrelevant. Friendships fell away. My world narrowed to one point: her. I wanted to win, not just compete. To beat her at something, anything, and claim a single inch of ground. I didn't care what it cost.

But it was never enough. No matter how many equations I solved or essays I perfected, she remained ahead—distant, quiet, unreachable.

High school arrived, and the grind continued—studies, assignments, the same relentless pace that had kept me afloat for years. But beneath the surface, something felt different. My habits hadn't changed. My parents remained the same. But the halls felt narrower, the weight of expectation heavier, like the space between each moment had contracted. High school amplified everything—the pressure, the stakes, the sense that something vital was slipping just out of reach.

The popularity I once clung to in middle school had faded, dissolving into the background noise of shifting social hierarchies. I wasn't lonely, exactly. Just unanchored. Like a shadow walking through someone else's life.

Some girls noticed me. Whispered confessions in the halls. I didn't care. My eyes were locked on something else.

Her.

Always there. A constant, ever-lurking presence at the edge of my vision. Even as I drowned myself in study, she kept surfacing, a quiet reminder of everything I couldn't figure out. At first, it was the rivalry that gnawed at me, but now, something about it felt... different. In a way I couldn't understand—or wouldn't let myself.

Still a constant. Still just out of reach. Our rivalry had changed. It wasn't about grades. It was about something unspoken, something I didn't dare name.

We got paired for a science project. I told myself I didn't mind—she'd pull her weight, and I wouldn't have to carry anyone. But when I saw her name beside mine, my chest tightened with something I didn't quite understand. My fingers fidgeted, tapping against the desk without rhythm. It was easier to call it relief than to ask what it really was.

The first time we met in the lab, I wasn't sure how I felt. She sat across from me, tapping her pen rhythmically against the table—a habit she's had for years. That all-too-familiar smile tugged at her lips. It wasn't mocking. Not exactly. But it lit something in my chest. My blood felt too warm, prickling under my skin.

"You're not planning to outdo me again, are you? Like back in eighth grade?" Her tone danced the line between teasing and probing—light and casual, like she was trying to draw me out. Friendly, even. But all I could hear was challenge. All I could feel was heat rising under my collar.

"You know," she added, tapping her pen with a small grin, "I figured you'd be the science guy. You study more than I do—and that's saying something."

It should've stung. But it didn't. I forced my eyes back to the assignment, willing my focus onto the measurements in front of me. Anything to drown the heat rising in my chest, to silence the flutter that threatened to betray me.

She watched me. Closely.

"You look tired. Staying up late again?" Her voice was quiet, almost casual—but the way her eyes scanned my face said otherwise. She had noticed. She had been noticing. And the realization unsettled me more than the words themselves.

I flinched. Her concern hit something I wasn't ready to acknowledge.

"Yeah," I said flatly, the words more defense than response. I hadn't expected her to notice. I wasn't sure how I felt about the fact that she had.

For a fleeting moment, I saw something in her expression—something close to pity. She stepped back, just a fraction, and the air between us seemed to thicken with unspoken words. I hated it. I hated that look in her eyes. "Maybe you should take a break sometime," she suggested casually, flipping through the textbook. "Relax a little. You can't keep pushing yourself like that. You'll burn out."

Her voice, soft but earnest, wrapped around me like a quiet threat. I could feel the tension in my shoulders, but I refused to let it break. Instead, I clenched my jaw, trying to ignore the faint pulse of something stirring inside me—something that wasn't anger. Something more insidious.

"I guess," I said, forcing a casual tone, "But I don't really know how to stop."

She didn't respond immediately, her eyes tracing over the data we had collected, a quiet understanding passing between us. It unsettled me. How could she understand? I didn't want her to. It felt like she was seeing through the walls I'd carefully built around myself. It scared me.

Weeks passed. We worked—efficient, focused, like clockwork. But somewhere in the repetition, I found myself anticipating our sessions. Her presence dulled the edges of my solitude, numbed the ache I refused to name. I hated that it helped. Hated more that I noticed when it didn't. She was steady, patient, and the rhythm we settled into became its own kind of silence. I didn't trust it. I didn't trust myself.

Then she came to my house.

The air inside hit like a wall—thick, heavy, and sour with the scent of old beer, sweat, and something rotting. The kind of smell that clung to your skin, that settled in your lungs and never quite left. My father was sprawled across the couch, shirtless, his chest rising and falling in uneven heaves. The television played to no one, flickering blue light over his slack features. My mother sat at the kitchen table, motionless. She didn't look up. Her eyes were fixed somewhere just past the wall, as if she'd found a way to be somewhere else without moving. She didn't blink. She barely breathed.

She stood in the doorway behind me, silent. I could feel the weight of her gaze pressing against my back, dragging across the wreckage of my home. Her eyes scanned the disarray—my father's collapsed form, my mother's vacant stare, the stench-soaked furniture—and her presence felt too real, too close. Intrusive. I hated how exposed I felt, how small. Shame curled in my stomach, hot and unrelenting. I wanted to disappear.

"I didn't realize it was like this."

The words landed like a slap. I didn't want her to pity me. Not her. Not anyone.

"It's fine," I said. "Just how it is."

She looked again. Something shifted in her eyes.

"I should've known," she said quietly.

"Don't," I snapped. "Don't act like you understand."

For a second, her gaze hardened, but then she stepped closer, her voice steady. "I wasn't trying to," she said. "I'm just *trying* to understand."

I wanted to say something, to push her away, but the words stuck in my throat. I swallowed, anger surging within me, before muttering, "Forget it. Let's just get started. My room's this way."

She didn't push. She just... stood there, her gaze lingering, but not pressing. She understood in her way—without saying a word.

But in that silence, I felt her slip in. She'd made it. Through anger. Through the noise. Past my walls. I didn't know how to keep her out.

~ 3 ~

CHAPTER THREE

Fractures

As the project continued, I noticed a strain between us growing. She'd smile at me like she always did, but now there was something behind it—something I didn't want to acknowledge. It was subtle at first, but it was unmistakable. The easy, playful teasing that once peppered our interactions had faded. She wasn't trying to one-up me anymore. Instead, her smile was softer, more hesitant, as if she was waiting for something—waiting for me to notice whatever it was.

One afternoon, we were at the library, surrounded by piles of notes and textbooks, going through the final details for the project. I was buried in my work, but I couldn't ignore the distance growing between us. She wasn't as talkative as before. The air was heavy with unspoken things, things that she seemed to be pushing toward me—wanting me to see, wanting me to understand—but I wasn't ready to acknowledge it.

"Hey," I said one afternoon, my voice breaking the silence more abruptly than I intended. I didn't look up right away, afraid of what

I might see in her expression. "What's going on?" It was the first time I reached across the gap, the first time I tried to understand instead of retreat.

She didn't look at me right away, and when she did, there was that same sadness in her eyes. She opened her mouth, but the words seemed to catch. "Nothing. Just... tired." Her voice was thin, hollow, as though she didn't believe it herself.

I felt the sting of her words, a strange weight in my chest. She was holding something back. Something about me.

"I don't want to make you feel... like you're not enough." She stopped herself, her eyes searching for the right words, but I could see the way she curled into herself, her shoulders hunching slightly. "I just don't know how to fix things."

I didn't respond right away. The tension between us pulsed, heavy and inescapable, and I hated the way it settled in my chest. I wanted to push her away, keep her at arm's length where she couldn't touch the raw, untended parts of me. But at the same time, there was a pull—quiet and insistent—that begged me to reach across the space, to close the distance. A part of me was burning to pull her closer, even as another part screamed to keep her out.

"You don't need to fix anything," I said, trying to sound casual, but the lie sat heavily on my tongue. "We're just doing a project. That's all."

But even as the words left my mouth, I knew they weren't true. She had always been more than just a project partner to me, and I resented that. I resented the way she made me feel seen—like I couldn't hide anything from her. The way her stare would always burn into me.

The next few days blurred together in a haze of failure and frustration. Her presence still lingered with me—not as a rival with a mocking smile, but as something heavier. Different. She wasn't just an ideal to chase anymore, not someone to beat at tests or assignments. She had become something else entirely—an untouchable part of my world that only reminded me of everything I wasn't. The way she walked through the halls, steady and self-assured, made it feel like she existed just slightly out of reach. Like she had already moved on from whatever game I thought we were playing, and I was the only one left still clinging to the rules. I felt forgotten, for some reason.

I remember seeing her one afternoon, just outside the school gates. It wasn't anything special at first—just another passing moment in the flow of the day. But then I saw him—her boyfriend.

I didn't recognize him at first. Some guy from the other class. Tall, confident, with a swagger that made my stomach tighten. They were standing there, talking, laughing. I don't know why it hit me so hard, but it did. She was leaning into him, her hand resting lightly on his arm, and he was looking at her like she was everything. And then I saw it—her smile. It wasn't the same. It wasn't the one I remembered, the one she used to wear around me. It was softer, brighter. It was for him. And for some reason, that made me angry. Not because she was his, not because she had someone—but because she had changed, and I hadn't.

I couldn't look away. I felt like I was suffocating, like there was this pressure building in my chest, and all I could do was watch. She laughed, a light sound, carefree, and it made something inside me twist. It didn't make sense. I had no right to feel this way. We weren't... anything. I was just the guy she used to compete with. She didn't even see me anymore.

And yet, there it was—a jagged, burning feeling that I couldn't place. Jealousy? Was that what this was? It didn't feel like jealousy, not exactly. I wasn't in love with her. But watching her with him... it felt like betrayal. Like she had quietly stepped off the battleground and into something else—something better—and left me behind still clutching a sword for a war she no longer acknowledged. I had no rulebook for what we were anymore. I didn't even know if we were still anything at all.

I turned away before I could feel it too much. Before I could let myself realize what it really meant, what it said about me.

I wasn't supposed to care. But I did. And that made it worse.

~ 4 ~

CHAPTER FOUR

Prom

The gym was a mess of colored lights and pounding bass, a haze of sound and motion that made my head spin. The punch tasted like watered-down cough syrup—spiked, probably—but I found I didn't care. The heat from the crowd pressed in from all sides. I hated everything about it—the noise, the chaos, the fake cheer of it all.

I was standing off to the side, leaning against the bleachers. I hadn't come to enjoy the night or the music or even the temporary illusion of teenage freedom. I came because it gave me an excuse to not be home. The noise, the crowd, even the spiked punch—they were all better than the silence that waited behind my front door. And I definitely didn't come hoping to see her.

"Enjoying yourself?" Her voice cut through the noise, sharp and teasing, like it always was.

I turned my head just enough to glance at her. She was wearing a pale blue dress—simple, understated—but it clung to her frame in a way that made it seem like it had been made just for her. Her hair was different too, pulled back from her face, revealing the sharp line of her jaw and the soft curve of her neck. She looked like something from a different world, like she didn't belong in this place of sweat and strobe lights and sticky floors. Not in a way that made her seem better—just... apart. Distinct. My breath caught for a second before I could stop it. She looked...

I stopped myself before the thought could finish.

"No," I said flatly, looking back at the sea of dancing bodies.

"Shocking," she said dryly. "You're the life of the party as always. Did someone have to drag you here, or did the gym's fluorescent lighting just call to you?"

I didn't respond, and for a moment, she just stood there, watching me. Then, to my surprise, she extended a hand.

"Come on," she said.

I blinked at her. "What?"

"Dance with me," she said, like it was the most obvious thing in the world.

I stared at her, waiting for the punchline. "Why?"

She rolled her eyes, but there was a flicker of something in her expression—nervousness, maybe, or hesitation. "Because it's a dance. That's what people do here. Or are you too busy sulking to participate?"

I wiped my palms against my pants, suddenly too aware of the way they were starting to sweat. "No thanks," I said, maybe a little too quickly, folding my arms like a shield.

She didn't move her hand. "Scared you'll embarrass yourself?" she asked, her tone turning playful.

"I just don't want to," I said, my voice edging toward annoyance.

Her smile shifted, turning into something sharper. "What's the matter? Afraid you can't keep up with me?"

That did it. I knew what she was doing, and it worked anyway. With a sigh that was more irritation than anything else, I pushed off the bleachers. "Fine," I said. "One dance."

Her smirk softened into a real smile, and then she reached for my hand. Her fingers closed around mine—warm, certain—and it was like the floor shifted beneath me. Just for a second, everything inside me twisted: surprise, confusion, something dangerously close to wanting. Before I could untangle any of it, she was already leading me toward the floor.

The music shifted to something slower, a song I vaguely recognized. She stopped in the middle of the crowd, turning to face me. For a moment, I didn't know what to do. Then she placed one hand lightly on my shoulder, the other sliding into my hand.

It was awkward at first. I wasn't sure where to step, and the closeness felt strange, like stepping into a space I wasn't supposed to occupy. But then something shifted. Her hand in mine steadied me, the press of her palm grounding. For a moment—just a moment—I found myself actually enjoying it. The sway, the rhythm, the illusion that maybe this wasn't completely foreign. And then, realizing that, I pulled back internally, the comfort itself making me uneasy.

For once, she wasn't talking. She just looked at me, her expression unreadable. Her hand was small and warm in mine, and the smell of her shampoo—something floral and soft—hit me in a way that made my stomach flip-flop. It was disarming, unexpectedly intimate, and I hated that it affected me at all.

"You're not as bad at this as I thought you'd be," she said finally, her voice quieter than usual.

"Thanks, I guess," I muttered. "What, thought I'd crush your toes?"

Her lips quirked into a faint smile. She giggled lightly, a sound that felt too soft for the noise around us. "Maybe," she said, still teasing, "but you're doing surprisingly well." I raised an eyebrow. "If you were so worried, why'd you ask me?" She didn't answer—just gave me a coy smile that made my mouth go dry. I swallowed hard, trying not to let it show.

For a moment, it felt like the rest of the room faded away—the noise, the lights, the crowd. It was just us, swaying awkwardly in the middle of the chaos.

Then I opened my mouth.

"So, where's your boyfriend?"

Her hand tensed slightly against my shoulder, and her expression shifted—defensive, like I'd touched a nerve she hadn't expected to be exposed. "Why do you care?"

"I don't," I said quickly, but as soon as the words left my mouth, I realized how they sounded. The sharpness in her tone hit harder than expected, and I faltered, awkwardness settling over me like a second skin. "Just figured he'd be the one you'd want to dance with," I added, trying to sound casual and failing.

She pulled back slightly, just enough to put space between us. Her gaze was colder now, the softness from a moment ago gone.

"Maybe I didn't want to dance with him," she said, her voice low and a little too quick, like she hadn't meant to say it aloud but couldn't stop herself in time.

"Why not?" I pressed, even though I didn't know why I was pushing.

She let out a short, bitter laugh, her voice laced with frustration. "You're unbelievable," she snapped, shaking her head. "You spend all this time pretending not to care, and now you act like it's some mystery why I didn't want to dance with him."

Her words hit harder than I expected, but I didn't let it show. "I didn't think it mattered," I said, the defensiveness in my voice betraying the confusion I couldn't quite name.

She shook her head, stepping back completely now. "You don't get it. You never do."

"Then explain it," I snapped, though the anger in my voice wasn't really aimed at her.

Her eyes narrowed, and for a moment, it looked like she might. But then she just shook her head again, the frustration clear on her face.

"Forget it," she mumbled, dropping her hands from mine and turning on her heel, walking toward the exit of the gym.

I stood there, the music and the crowd rushing back in around me. My chest felt tight, like I'd missed something important, but I didn't follow her.

I told myself it didn't matter. That the feeling in my gut wasn't screaming at me to chase after her. Instead, I turned back toward the refreshment table, grabbed a red solo cup, and downed the rest of the spiked punch in one long gulp.

But the look on her face as she walked away told me otherwise.

~ 5 ~

CHAPTER FIVE

Cost of Victory

The midterm finals were days away, and I was drowning.

The library was suffocating. Not because it was crowded—there were maybe ten people scattered across the room, their whispers blending with the scratch of pens and the faint hum of the air conditioning—but because every time I looked at the thick textbook in front of me, my brain refused to cooperate.

My notes were gone. I didn't know where they were, but that didn't matter now. They could've been sitting in the gutter outside for all the good they'd do me. I rubbed the heel of my palm against my temple, the tension building with each moment wasted.

A chair scraped nearby. I ignored it until her voice cut through the fog in my head.

"You look like you've been through a war," she said, eyeing the mess of papers and the way I was gripping my pen like a lifeline.

I looked up sharply. It was her, standing there with her bag slung over one shoulder, the light behind her catching on the strands of her hair. I hadn't seen her in the library much lately, not since prom. She wasn't supposed to be here—not anymore. And definitely not alone. She was supposed to be with him—her boyfriend. Or at least, she used to be.

"What do you want?" I snapped, too tired to mask the irritation in my voice.

She raised an eyebrow, her smirk tugging at one corner of her mouth. "Friendly as ever, I see."

When I didn't respond, she shifted her weight, dropping her bag onto the chair across from me. "I was passing by and figured you'd be here. I don't know, call it a hunch." Her tone was casual, but there was a flicker of hesitation in her eyes, quickly masked by her usual confidence.

"You guessed right," I said flatly, looking back at the textbook, though the words blurred together.

She didn't sit. Instead, she leaned against the table, her fingers drumming lightly against the edge. "Shouldn't you be studying?"

"I am," I muttered, gesturing vaguely at the book.

"Really? Because it looks like you're just trying to set it on fire with your mind."

My jaw tightened, but I didn't look at her. "If you're here to waste my time, don't bother."

There was a pause, long enough that I thought she might actually leave. Instead, she reached into her bag, pulling out a neatly organized stack of papers. Her handwriting—precise and annoyingly perfect—lined every page. She slid them across the table.

"Here. You can use these."

I glanced at the notes but didn't touch them. "Why?"

She shrugged, but her gaze lingered on me a little longer than it should have. "Because you're obviously struggling. And because if you fail, who am I supposed to beat?" Her smirk returned, but it felt forced, like she was trying to patch over the cracks left from prom—like she was pretending nothing had happened, even though we both felt the weight of it. That night lingered between us like unfinished business, a fragile silence waiting to be broken. she didn't know how to talk about that night without shattering whatever fragile connection remained between us.

I didn't move.

She sighed, her tone softening just slightly. "Look, I know you think you're too good for help, but I figured you might appreciate it. Or not. Whatever."

Her words didn't make sense. Had she always thought I was too proud for help? Too unreachable? I stared at her, wondering if the smirk she wore was just a mask for the same confusion I couldn't seem to escape since prom.

"What about him?" I asked abruptly, the question slipping out before I could stop it.

Her smirk faded. "Him?"

"Your boyfriend. Shouldn't you be helping him instead?" I tried to keep my tone neutral, but something bitter seeped in anyway.

She rolled her eyes. "He doesn't need my help. And besides, he's not... we're not together anymore." Her voice faltered for a second, not with regret, but with something else—a quiet vulnerability, like admitting it out loud still stung. Her voice wavered slightly on the last part, and for the first time, I caught something—an almost imperceptible crack in her usual composure.

"Why not?" I pressed, though I didn't know why.

She hesitated, her fingers brushing over the edge of the notes. "Maybe I just figured... I wanted to help someone who actually needed me. Someone who might notice."

Her words hung between us, heavier than they should have been.

I finally picked up the notes, flipping through them without really reading. "Thanks," I muttered, though the word felt foreign in my mouth.

She watched me for a moment longer, and I thought she might say something else. But instead, she grabbed her bag, slinging it over her shoulder.

"You're welcome," she said quietly, and for the briefest second, I caught the faintest trace of something on her face—a mix of hope and disappointment, like she had been expecting more from me.

As she turned to leave, she glanced back, her gaze lingering on me just a moment too long.

"Oh, and... for the record," she added, her voice almost playful, "not everything I do is about beating you." Her eyes met mine briefly, and for a flicker of a second, I saw the same vulnerability from prom—like she was still waiting for me to understand something I kept missing.

She walked away before I could respond, leaving me with the notes and a strange, hollow feeling I couldn't place.

I told myself it didn't mean anything.

A few weeks later, midterm final grades were posted—something our school didn't usually do, at least not in such a public way. I scanned the list taped to the wall outside the main office, my eyes tracking the names I knew, until I saw hers—sixth place, a position I'd never seen her in before. My stomach twisted. I was second, just a few spots ahead of her. It hit me harder than I expected. For years, she had been the top, and I had been the one trailing behind. And now, the tables had turned.

The feeling wasn't satisfying, like I thought it would be. It was something worse—anger, frustration, and confusion. I glanced at her, but she was already looking at me, a small, almost resigned smile on her lips. It wasn't the same confident smile she used to wear when she was on top. No, this one was softer, filled with something I couldn't quite place.

I couldn't hold it in anymore. The frustration bubbled over.

"What the hell is your problem?" I shot across the room, the words coming out harsher than I'd meant.

She blinked in surprise, her face blank for a moment before she looked back at me. Her voice was calm, unnervingly so. "What do you mean...?"

I stalked over to her, not caring about the growing crowd watching us. "Why aren't you in the top five? What the hell happened? You're always on top. Always. And now I'm ahead of you?"

Her eyes narrowed, her lips pressing into a tight line. For a brief moment, I saw something I hadn't expected—disappointment.

"So this is about my grades?" she asked, her voice low and cutting, far sharper than I'd anticipated.

"Yes!" I snapped. "It's always about your grades! Why aren't you trying? Why don't you care?"

Her eyes didn't waver from mine, and for the first time, I saw the cracks in her icy exterior. "Maybe I don't care because it's never been about that," she said quietly, almost to herself. "It's about you. It's always been about you."

The words hit me harder than anything she had ever said to me before. My breath caught, a sharp, involuntary intake that felt like I'd been struck. My mind scrambled for a retort, something to reassert control, but all I could feel was the echo of her voice ringing in my ears, raw and final. It cracked something open inside me

I wasn't ready to face.. They knocked the air out of me, and for a moment, I stood there, speechless. I wanted to say something, anything, but the words stuck in my throat.

Before I could recover, a hand landed on my shoulder, and I jerked away, seeing one of the other guys from the crowd trying to intervene. I shoved him off, my mind still racing, but all I could do was stare at her. Her face was a mask again, but there was something behind it, something real.

She didn't say another word. Her eyes lingered for just a moment longer, as if trying to memorize my face or search for a last trace of understanding. Then she turned away from me, and with that, the weight of her words hung between us like a silent accusation. I wanted to say something back, something to make it right, but all I could do was retreat into myself, burying my thoughts in my work again.

The tension didn't go away. It festered, twisting in the back of my mind, gnawing at me like a wound I didn't know how to heal.

A few months later, the end of year finals came. I had poured myself into studying in the weeks prior, losing track of everything outside my textbooks. It was the only way I knew to quiet the noise in my head, the only control I could grasp. So when I finally looked up—when I finally allowed myself to scan the board for her name—my heart hammered in my chest. But this time, there was nothing. No sign of her anywhere in the top fifty.

I felt panic rise in my throat. Had they made a mistake? Maybe she was absent. Maybe there was some kind of error.

I rushed to the school office, frustration swelling inside me with every step. I had to know. Had to make sure there was a mistake.

The staff looked at me with pity as they explained. She'd dropped out. Family issues. They were sorry, but it had been over a month now.

But I knew. I knew exactly what had happened. She hadn't dropped out because of family problems. She'd done it to get away from me. To leave me with this feeling. She had won, and there was nothing I could do to change it.

The hollow feeling inside me deepened. It wasn't just her grades anymore. It was everything. It was us.

The rest of high school passed in a blur. I kept up with my studies, but the motivation had evaporated. What was the point of competing when there was no one to compete against? The scholarships had already been secured. I was already on my path. But with every passing day, it felt emptier.

I had nothing left to prove anymore. No rival left to outpace, no gaze to chase. She had already won—not by climbing higher, but by walking away first, leaving me behind with the silence, the questions, and the echo of everything unsaid.

~ 6 ~

CHAPTER SIX

Smoke and Silence

The rest of high school blurred by. I stuck to my studies out of habit more than anything else. The grades came easily, but they felt empty—like ticking off boxes on a list I no longer cared about. Each A felt less like a victory and more like a reminder of what I'd lost. A routine without meaning.

She had won. Not just our endless rivalry, but something deeper—something foundational. With her absence, it was as if she'd taken the very fire that fueled me, the reason I woke up and tried. My victories were ashes now, and standing at the top felt like shouting into an empty void. She had been the axis my world turned on—and without her, everything spun aimlessly.

I went through the motions, applying for colleges and collecting scholarships like trophies I couldn't bring myself to care about. On paper, I was everything I was supposed to be—successful, promising, bound for great things. Inside, I was crumbling.

When the acceptance letter came, it felt more like a formality than an achievement. Moving to college was supposed to be a fresh start, but as I packed my bags, I couldn't shake the feeling that I was running away.

The night before I left for college, the house was eerily quiet except for the faint hum of the refrigerator and the muffled sound of a late-night infomercial droning from the living room. My father lay slumped on the couch, one arm dangling off the side, a half-empty bottle of whiskey clutched loosely in his hand. A few amber pill bottles rolled across the floor, their caps missing, the labels worn and peeling. The sour smell of stale liquor and urine clung to the air, suffocating and unyielding.

He wouldn't lift a finger to help me. He didn't even acknowledge I was leaving. I doubted he even remembered.

My mother lingered by the doorway, her hands clasped tightly together, her lips parted as if to speak. I waited, my duffel bag slung over one shoulder, for her to say something—anything. But she didn't. Her mouth closed with a soft click, her gaze flickering between me and the luggage at my feet.

I didn't expect her to stop me or even wish me luck. That wasn't who she was anymore, if ever. She stood there, pale and drawn, her hollow eyes watching as if she were already mourning something.

"I'll call," I lied, just to fill the silence.

She gave a faint nod, though it felt more like a dismissal than a response. No hug. No parting words. Just the echo of my footsteps down the hallway and the dull thud of the door closing behind me.

As I stepped into the night, the weight on my chest didn't lift—it shifted. The thought of leaving them behind should have felt like freedom, like a fresh start. But it didn't. It felt like running, and the shadows I was running from were tethered to me, no matter how far I went.

My apartment was a one-room shoebox with faulty lights and a leaky faucet that never stopped dripping. The landlord hadn't bothered to fix it despite my complaints, and I stopped asking after the second week. The walls were thin, letting in the muffled sounds of my neighbors—arguments, laughter, the occasional crash of something breaking. It all blurred together, background noise for my descent into routine.

At first, I tried to convince myself I was adjusting. I threw myself into studying because it was the only thing I knew how to do. But without the constant push and pull of competition, even that felt aimless. I'd sit at my desk, staring at textbooks and notes, lighting cigarette after cigarette just to fill the silence. Smoking became a crutch, something to occupy my hands and dull the edge of my thoughts.

The first time I lit one, it was out of curiosity—something I'd always seen my dad do. The acrid taste burned my throat, but the rush of it, the way it made my chest feel heavy, was grounding in a way I hadn't expected. Soon, it was a habit. A cigarette in the morning to wake up. Another after class. One more before bed, sitting by the open window as the smoke curled into the night.

I made one friend, if you could call him that. He wasn't much more than an acquaintance, a guy who remembered me from high school. I couldn't recall his name at first, but he seemed determined to stick around. He was loud, carefree, and airheaded in a way that both annoyed and distracted me. He treated life like a series of jokes, never taking anything seriously, and for reasons I didn't fully understand, I let him stay in my orbit. Maybe because his easy demeanor was a contrast to my own heaviness, or maybe because I was too tired to push him away.

I wasn't sure why I tolerated him. Maybe it was because he did most of the talking, filling the silences I would have otherwise been left alone with. Or maybe it was because his constant chatter acted as white noise, drowning out thoughts I didn't want to have.

He wasn't subtle in his efforts to pull me out of my self-imposed isolation. Ethan made it a point to cross paths with me whenever he could, offering a casual nod or a joke in passing that I never responded to. If he noticed my lack of enthusiasm, he didn't seem to care.

It was after one of my late-night study sessions, the kind where the hours slipped by unnoticed, that I first found him waiting outside the building. I didn't realize it was him at first, not until the glow of my cigarette lit up his face.

"You know, I had this feeling you were a smoker," he said, pushing off the wall when he saw me. "You always looked like you were one bad day away from picking up the habit."

I didn't answer, just lit the cigarette and took a slow drag, letting the smoke settle in my chest before exhaling.

Ethan smirked. "You know, you don't have to do this alone. I could be your wingman in this—bring you the good stuff, show you the ropes."

I gave him a flat look, flicking the ashes off my cigarette. "I'm not here for socializing," I muttered, barely looking at him.

"Eh, that's the thing," he said, ignoring my tone as usual. "You act like you've got it all figured out, but you don't, man. You're cooped up in this little room, chain-smoking like it's the answer to all your problems, but it's not."

I took another drag, my eyes narrowing on him. "What do you want, Ethan?"

He didn’t seem bothered by my indifference. "I don’t know. I just thought we could hang out. You seem like someone who could use the company."

I didn’t know how to answer that, so I just stared at him, still trying to figure out if I actually wanted to talk to him or if I just didn’t have the energy to push him away.

“You’re weird,” I said finally, shaking my head, but I could feel the slightest pull of something in me, a reluctant curiosity about the guy who wouldn’t leave me alone.

He grinned, sensing the shift. “I’ll take that as a compliment.”

The conversation drifted off after that, and I went back inside, but I knew he wouldn’t be far behind. Ethan was relentless, in a way that was both irritating and oddly... comforting. Ethan didn’t follow me right away when I went back inside. For a moment, I thought he’d finally taken the hint—or given up. But as I reached my apartment door, the faint sound of footsteps trailed me down the hallway. I didn’t need to turn around to know it was him.

“You should quit those things, you know,” he said, his voice light, almost casual.

I unlocked the door and paused, glancing over my shoulder. “I’ll quit when I feel like it.”

He shrugged, shoving his hands into his pockets. “Fair enough. Just don’t make me carry your sorry ass to the ER when your lungs give out.”

I snorted, more out of disbelief than amusement, and opened the door to my dim, cluttered apartment. “I’ll keep that in mind, Ethan. Thanks for the concern.”

“Anytime,” he said, and for once, there wasn’t a hint of teasing in his voice.

I lingered in the doorway, half-expecting him to push his way in, to keep talking, to keep being... him. But he didn't. Instead, he offered me a small, two-fingered salute and turned to leave.

"See you around, man."

I watched him disappear down the hall, his footsteps echoing faintly as the silence swallowed him up. For the first time, I realized how quiet my apartment really was. No voices, no laughter, just the low hum of the fridge and the distant sound of traffic filtering through the window.

The cigarette I'd been holding had burned down to the filter, the acrid scent of charred paper and tobacco wafting into the room. I crushed it into the ashtray on the counter, staring at the gray stub for a moment longer than I should have.

Ethan wasn't wrong. About the smoking, about the isolation—about any of it. But acknowledging that would mean acknowledging everything else too: the reasons I was here, the emptiness I couldn't seem to shake, the weight that sat on my chest every time I tried to breathe in this new life I'd built for myself.

I turned off the light and let the darkness settle around me like an old, worn blanket. Tomorrow, I'd get up, go to class, bury myself in textbooks—because that's what I did. And Ethan would probably show up again, grinning like an idiot, throwing off my rhythm with his ridiculous optimism. A crack in the monotony I wasn't ready to admit I needed.

For now, I let the silence stretch. It wasn't comfortable, but it was mine. The same way the ache in my chest was mine.

I closed the door behind me, locking the world out for another night.

~ 7 ~

CHAPTER SEVEN

Midnight Snack

The night wasn't cold enough to justify the jacket Ethan had thrown on, but he didn't seem to care. He leaned against the edge of my desk while I jotted down notes, his usual grin plastered across his face.

"C'mon, man, you've been cooped up in this room all day. It's criminal."

I didn't look up from my notebook. "It's called studying. You might want to try it sometime."

He scoffed. "Oh, I've tried it. Didn't take. Now let's go. Snack run. My treat."

"Pass."

"Nope." Ethan pushed off the desk and snatched the pen from my hand, holding it above his head like a trophy. "You're coming with me. You've been sitting here all day, probably inhaling more nicotine than oxygen. Time to get some real sustenance."

I glared at him, half-considering grabbing the pen back. But his persistence had already worn me down, and I knew he wouldn't leave until he got his way. With a heavy sigh, I grabbed my coat. Might as well—my stomach had started sounding like a broken engine three hours ago.

The streets were quiet, the city easing into its nighttime rhythm. Ethan walked a few steps ahead, hands stuffed into his jacket pockets. I kept my pace slow, my thoughts trailing behind like shadows.

"You know," Ethan said after a while, breaking the silence, "for someone who doesn't like people, you sure tolerate me pretty well."

I shrugged. "Tolerating you is easier than trying to get rid of you."

"Flattering," he said, smirking. "But I'll take it. So, what's the deal? Are you always this fun at parties, or is this just a special brand of brooding reserved for me?"

I didn't answer right away, eyes fixed on the cracked pavement. The streetlights cast long, flickering shadows, and for a moment, I thought about telling him the truth—just the plain, unfiltered kind that never makes it past the teeth. weight I carried, the emptiness that followed me like a second skin. But the words caught in my throat.

"I don't do parties," I said instead, clipped.

Ethan didn't press. He just nodded, his gaze lingering a moment longer than usual. "Well, I guess this snack run is the next best thing."

The convenience store buzzed under fluorescent lights. Ethan grabbed a basket and started loading it with snacks like a man starved.

I lingered by the door, watching him. He was a strange mix of energy and ease—someone who could make even a mundane errand feel like an adventure, or at least less like a chore dragged out by my reluctance to leave the apartment.

"You gonna grab anything, or are you just here to judge my taste in junk food?" he called over his shoulder.

I sighed, picking up a pack of gum just to avoid looking entirely out of place.

At the register, Ethan paid without hesitation, brushing off my half-hearted attempt to pitch in.

"I told you, my treat. You can pay me back with your sparkling personality."

Outside, he tore into a bag of chips and offered me one. I declined, lighting a cigarette instead.

"Seriously though," Ethan said, his voice softer now. "What's your deal? Are you always this closed off, or is it just a defense mechanism?"

I froze mid-drag, the question hanging in the air. "Why do you care?"

He shrugged, munching on a chip. "I don't know. Maybe I like a challenge. Or maybe I think there's more to you than the chain-smoking hermit act."

I exhaled slowly, smoke curling into the night. "Don't read too much into it. I'm not your pet project."

"Fair enough," he said, though his tone suggested he wasn't convinced.

We walked in silence, his question lingering between us like the smoke of my tabacco.

"So," Ethan said eventually, voice tinged with mischief, "about that girl from high school..."

I tensed. He noticed.

"I already told you—there's nothing to talk about," I muttered.

Ethan smirked, walking backward to face me. "Come on. I remember her. What was her name? Annie? Andrea?"

"Drop it."

"Can't. It's too interesting," he said, grinning. "You two were what—rivals? Friends? Frenemies? Sounds like a bad teen drama. Let me guess: she was the overachiever who kept beating you in class, and you were the brooding underdog who secretly liked it."

"She didn't beat me," I said—too quickly. Even I could hear the edge in my voice.

"Uh-huh. But you were close, right? In that competitive, flirty sort of way?"

"She wasn't flirting," I snapped, more defensively than I meant to.

Ethan gave me a knowing look. "You sure about that?"

"Yes," I said firmly, though the knot in my stomach begged to differ.

He shrugged, casually opening another bag of chips. "Could've fooled me. From the way you talked about her—and the way you react now—it sounds like she was trying to get your attention."

"That's called being annoying, not flirting."

Ethan chuckled. "Man, you really don't get it, do you? Girls don't put that much effort into someone they don't care about. Especially not smart ones like her. She was trying to reach you."

"Yeah, sure," I muttered, flicking away my cigarette. "Because mocking someone is the pinnacle of affection."

"Mocking, or trying to pull you out of your shell?" Ethan countered. "Maybe she thought you were worth the effort. Just a theory."

I scoffed. "You're reading too much into it. She didn't care about me like that."

"Okay," Ethan said lightly, though his smirk was infuriating. "If you say so. But riddle me this—why'd she drop out after you two had that big blowout? Coincidence?"

My chest tightened. "That had nothing to do with me."

"Right," he said, dragging out the word. "Just like snapping at her didn't totally crush her or anything."

I clenched my fists. I hated this—hated that Ethan was poking at something I thought I'd buried.

"She probably just got bored," I said flatly. "Moved on to something better."

"Yeah, that sounds like someone who was totally indifferent to you," Ethan said, still chewing thoughtfully.

I glared at him. He just shrugged, popping another chip into his mouth. "I'm not saying she was your soulmate or whatever. But maybe stop pretending she didn't matter. Just a thought."

His words stuck with me more than I expected. A voice in the back of my mind whispered, *What if he's right?*

But I shoved it down. "You done psychoanalyzing me, or should I start paying for these sessions?"

Ethan laughed. "You're a tough nut, but I like a challenge. And hey—if you ever want to revisit the whole 'what could've been' thing, I'll be here. With snacks and terrible advice."

I shook my head, letting out a dry chuckle to mask the unease. "I think I'll pass."

As we reached my building, Ethan paused, giving me a look. "By the way, a couple of us are hanging out tomorrow night. You should come."

"What's the catch?" I asked, narrowing my eyes.

"No catch," he said, though his grin said otherwise. "Just people. Normal college stuff. Fun, remember that?"

I hesitated. The instinct to say no was strong—but something about his invitation tugged at me.

"I'll think about it," I said, brushing past him to unlock the door.

"That's the spirit," Ethan called, triumph in his voice.

I didn't look back, but as I climbed the stairs, I caught myself almost smiling—annoyingly, begrudgingly, like a reflex I couldn't stop.

He's obnoxious.

~ 8 ~

CHAPTER EIGHT

Unspoken Truths

I hadn't planned to say yes to Ethan's invitation, but there I was, driven by a quiet pull—maybe guilt, maybe loneliness, or just the vague sense that declining would mean admitting something I wasn't ready to face. It wasn't that I felt compelled by camaraderie or excitement—those were foreign concepts at this stage of my life. No, it was something else. Maybe it was the small voice in the back of my head whispering about the inevitability of nights spent alone. Or maybe it was the baser instinct, the one that promised fleeting distraction wrapped in soft skin and a warm smile.

I said yes, though I told myself I didn't care either way.

By the time classes ended, the dread had settled like a rock in my stomach. I found myself standing outside the bar Ethan had chosen, feeling the low hum of bass from within and watching the glow of neon signs bleed into the evening sky. The door swung open, releasing a cacophony of laughter and music, and I knew there was no backing out now.

Inside, Ethan was easy to spot. His grin widened when he saw me, and he waved me over to a table near the back. There were eight of us in total—four girls and four guys, all seated in a loose, mismatched formation.

"Glad you made it," Ethan said, clapping me on the shoulder as I sat down.

I nodded, glancing at the group. A muscular guy with an overly polished charm was already leaning into a conversation with a girl who seemed more interested in her drink than him. Another girl was absorbed in her phone, and the third was laughing loudly at something a guy with a big chin was saying. I didn't know any of them.

It was the fourth girl who caught my attention, though not for any reason I'd have liked. She was seated directly across from me, nursing a glass of something amber, her fingers tapping idly against the table. Black hair framed her face, and when she glanced up, the air seemed to shift between us.

Her.

Of course it had to be her. But she didn't look exactly how I remembered. The soft edges of adolescence had sharpened; her hair was longer now, more deliberately styled, and she carried herself with a calmness that hadn't existed back then. In high school, she was all fire, sharp wit, and snarky remarks. Now, there was something quieter, more self-assured in the way she sipped her drink, in how she held my gaze. Familiar, yes—but changed. Changed enough to make me wonder who exactly was sitting across from me.

She held my gaze, not with hostility but with something softer. My chest tightened, and I had to resist the urge to look away too soon, like flinching from sudden light. Familiar. It felt as though she was studying me, like I was a puzzle she hadn't yet solved. Then, just as quickly, she looked away, her expression neutral as she took another sip from her glass.

For a moment, I considered leaving. It wasn't too late—I hadn't even ordered a drink. But then Ethan's voice cut through the haze.

"Hey, don't just sit there like a statue. Let me get you a beer or something."

Before I could protest, he flagged down a waitress, and I resigned myself to staying. The idea of bolting now, with her watching, felt more humiliating than whatever the night had in store.

As the drinks flowed and conversations meandered, the table began to fragment. The muscular guy and his girl left first, their departure as obvious as their intentions. The girl with her phone followed soon after, leaving the rest of us in an awkward shuffle to fill the empty spaces. I ended up next to Ethan and the girl—her—who now seemed focused on the remnants of her drink.

Ethan, ever the instigator, leaned back in his chair with a calculated smirk—like he knew exactly what he was doing and was waiting to see how we'd react. "So, you two know each other, right?"

I didn't answer. My eyes stayed on the condensation pooling at the base of my glass.

"You were in the same high school," he pressed, clearly enjoying himself. "Bet you've got stories, huh?"

Her lips quirked into something that wasn't quite a smile, but there was a glint in her eyes when she replied. "Maybe a few."

My chest tightened, unsure if it was the jab I expected or something else entirely.

Ethan laughed, oblivious. "Come on, you have to give me more than that!"

Her gaze drifted toward me again, slower this time, and I felt pinned under it. "You haven't changed much," she said, her tone lighter now. Not friendly, but not unkind either. There was something in her eyes—curiosity, maybe, or the kind of recognition that made my skin prickle.

I swallowed, unsure how to respond, and settled for nothing at all.

Ethan took the lead after that, talking enough for both of us while I sat still, hyper-aware of her presence and the words I wasn't saying. But the longer I sat there, the more I felt the air between us crackle with something unspoken. It wasn't warm exactly, but it wasn't icy either.

As the group thinned, the din of the bar quieted. It was just Ethan, her, and me now, though she seemed preoccupied with the last sips of her drink.

Ethan stretched in his chair, looking far too pleased with himself. "Well, this went better than expected. See? Not so bad to get out once in a while, huh?"

I glanced at him, then at her. She was looking at her phone, the faint glow illuminating her face. "How'd you even set this up?" I asked, keeping my voice low.

Ethan grinned, leaning forward on his elbows. "Ah, a little magic, a little fate."

"Try again."

"Fine, fine. I ran into her a couple of weeks ago." He nodded toward her, lowering his voice conspiratorially. "We got to talking, and—surprise, surprise—you came up."

My stomach knotted. "Why?"

His grin widened as if he were savoring some private joke. "Because she brought you up, man. She was the one who mentioned you first. Said some things that made me curious."

The knot tightened. I glanced at her again, but she didn't seem to be paying attention. "What kind of things?"

"Relax, nothing bad," he said, shrugging. "Actually, it was the opposite. She talked about you like you were..." He paused, searching for the right word, his gaze flicking to me. "Important."

The word landed heavier than I expected. "Important?"

He nodded, his grin softening into something more genuine. "Yeah. Like she respected you or something. Said you were smart—always challenging her, keeping her on her toes. And there was something in her tone that seemed... sad. Wistful, almost."

I barked a quiet laugh, though it came out more bitter than amused. "That's what she said?"

Ethan shrugged. "I'm just telling you what I heard. She didn't have to bring you up at all, but she did. That's what made me think, you know... maybe it's worth seeing what would happen if you two ran into each other again."

The words left a sour taste in my mouth. Part of me recoiled, unsure if it was bitterness, disbelief, or some twisted sense of regret rising up from old wounds I hadn't realized were still open. I couldn't reconcile the version of her Ethan was describing with the girl who had stolen every victory out from under me, who had laughed at my missteps and pushed me past my breaking point.

"She's good at putting on a show," I muttered.

Ethan raised an eyebrow but didn't argue. Instead, he leaned back in his chair, crossing his arms. "Funny thing is, though—there's something else I remembered after we talked."

I didn't respond, but he continued anyway.

"Back in high school, after she left, there was this... thing." He waved a hand vaguely, as if trying to draw the memory out of thin air. "You remember those girls? The ones who used to talk trash about everyone? They were on the cheer team?"

The memory came back in jagged fragments. The sneering faces, the low whispers that carried through the hallways like poison.

"They were going off about her one day, real nasty stuff," Ethan said. "And you—you just lost it."

I stiffened, the knot in my stomach unraveling into something sharper. "I don't know what you're talking about."

"Come on, man. You don't remember telling them off? I swear, it was the loudest I'd ever heard you talk. You went all in, called them out right there in the middle of the hallway. It was like something out of a movie."

"I didn't—"

"You did," Ethan cut in, his voice quieter now. "And they shut up after that. I think they were too shocked to argue. But, dude, it wasn't just what you said. It was how you said it. Like, there was passion. Seemed like you actually cared about something."

"I didn't care," I snapped, too quickly. The words hung in the air, unconvincing even to me.

Ethan tilted his head, studying me with a mix of curiosity and amusement. "Sure. Whatever you say."

His tone was light, teasing, but it didn't stop the weight of the memory from settling in. I avoided his gaze, instead looking at her again. She was scrolling through her phone, her expression unreadable.

"She never knew," I said finally, more to myself than to Ethan.

"She didn't have to," Ethan replied. "The point is, you stood up for her. And from the way she talked about you, I think she would've done the same."

Ethan leaned back in his chair, a mischievous glint in his eyes. "Oh, man... I still remember it. You were *ruthless*, dude."

I froze mid-sip of my drink, my fingers tightening around the glass. "What are you talking about now?"

"Don't play dumb." He leaned forward, his elbows on the table as if he were about to share some grand secret, raising his voice slightly. "You walked right up to those girls and started insulting the *hell* out of them. It was legendary!"

"Ethan," I warned, my voice low.

But he didn't stop. If anything, my reaction egged him on.

"Man, you just let them have it! You called them uneducated, said they were wasting their time and had no future. And then—" He smirked, pointing a finger at me. "You started *numbering* all her achievements. Like, 'Oh, she won this piano competition,' and 'Oh, she topped the national rank with her academic results.' You were relentless!"

My jaw clenched. "You're exaggerating."

"Not even a little." Ethan leaned back, spreading his arms as if presenting a masterpiece. "And you know me—I'm not one to hit a girl or anything, but damn, that one? She was asking for it. She didn't even try to listen, just kept cutting you off about some *bullshit* she'd heard 'down the street.' How ridiculous was that?"

The memory flashed in my mind, sharper than I wanted it to be. I'd been on edge that whole week, furious at everything and everyone.

It had been the week after she quit school. I'd barely been able to process it when those girls started talking, spreading their filth. At first, it was ridiculous stuff—prostitution, cheating, sexually bribing teachers to get ahead. I hadn't even realized I was listening until they crossed a line.

When they insinuated that the rival I'd thought of as my equal—someone who had bested me at everything—was nothing but a fraud, something inside me snapped.

Ethan wasn't lying; I *had* lost my shit. And in that moment, it hadn't felt noble or brave—it had felt raw, unfiltered. Maybe there was pride tangled up in it, but mostly it was shame. Shame for losing control, for caring too much, and for not being able to admit it until now.

"I can't believe you don't remember this," Ethan continued, clearly enjoying himself. "Hey, do you remember what you shouted at them to finally shut them up? Because I do. I remember it *perfectly*."

"Ethan," I said through gritted teeth, but he was already launching into it, mimicking my voice in an exaggerated tone.

"Enough! You can spit whatever filth you want, but none of it changes who she is. She's earned everything she's ever achieved—on her own merit. The competitions, the grades, the respect—she worked for that. And you? You sit here dragging her name through the mud like it makes you more than what you are: bitter, irrelevant, and too afraid to face your own mediocrity. You'll never understand the kind of drive she has. You'll never touch what she's accomplished, and deep down, you know it. That's why you talk like this. Because it's the only way you feel bigger. You're all pathetic."

I closed my eyes, the words ringing in my head as clearly as if I'd said them yesterday. I didn't know why I remembered them so perfectly. Maybe it was because they'd been so... raw. So *true*.

When I opened my eyes, Ethan was grinning like a lunatic, clearly proud of himself for the performance.

"That was *badass*, man," he said, sitting back in his chair. "If it weren't for that meddling teacher, you probably would've thrown hands. And honestly? They deserved it."

I opened my mouth to shut him up, but a faint cough stopped me cold.

She was staring at us. Or rather, at *me*.

Her cheeks were flushed, her expression caught somewhere between disbelief and... something else. Her eyes shimmered slightly under the bar's dim lights, and for a moment, I swore she was holding her breath. Something softer, quieter.

She'd heard him. Every word. Her glass was still in her hand, but her grip had tightened slightly, and her brows drew together in a subtle furrow. The silence between us pulsed, heavy and unspoken.

My stomach twisted into a knot, heat rising to my face.

"Uh... hey," Ethan said, his smile faltering slightly. "We were just talking about—"

"I heard," she said, her voice calm but laced with something I couldn't place. Her gaze flicked to me, lingering, searching.

I couldn't look at her. "It's not what you think," I muttered, the words tumbling out before I could stop them.

Her lips curved into a small, almost imperceptible smile. "Sure," she said, her tone impossible to read.

That knot in my stomach tightened. This was bad. This was a *misunderstanding*.

I hadn't said those things to defend her. It wasn't about her at all.

It was about me. About the idea of someone being better. About the unbearable thought of her achievements being anything less than real. Because if her accomplishments were false, then it'd somehow invalidate my own.

But looking at her now, her faint blush still lingering, I knew she wouldn't see it that way. *Fuck.*

Ethan chuckled, shaking his head. "At that moment, man, I knew—I knew—you were head-over-heels for her. You couldn't have been more obvious if you'd put up a billboard." He leaned back, gesturing toward her casually. "And it was so tragic because you probably never even told her. So, yeah, when I ran into her at my part-time job, I figured, why not try to arrange something for the two of you?"

I blinked at him, trying to process his words. The alcohol wasn't helping.

"So... that's why you invited me here tonight?" I asked, my voice slower than I intended.

Ethan smirked. "Why else? You're my friend, right? You've been looking so down lately, man, I thought this might cheer you up."

I stared at him, my fifth beer sweating in my hand. The edges of my vision were hazy, my mind swimming somewhere between agitation and outright anger. My "wasted" features—the slack jaw, the heavy eyelids—did a pretty good job of hiding it, though.

"You didn't have to," I muttered.

Seriously, you didn't have to. I exhaled through my nose, gripping the glass tighter. *You fucking idiot.*

I avoided looking at her. She hadn't said a word through all of this. I could feel her eyes on me, though—heavy, searching, expectant. Why wasn't she saying anything? Why wasn't she stopping him from saying all this?

Ethan glanced at his phone and groaned. "Oh! That's my girlfriend. She's texting me." He stood up, wobbling slightly. "Sorry, guys, gotta go!"

"What?" I stared at him, dumbfounded. "You have a girlfriend? What are you even doing here, then?"

He grinned, leaning in slightly. His breath reeked of warm beer, and I had to fight the urge to push him away. "Tonight was for you, man," he whispered, his voice conspiratorial. "Enjoy yourself, will ya?" He stood up to his full height. "Have fun you two," he teased, twiddling his fingers at us in a goodbye.

And with that, he was gone.

I watched him weave through the crowd, leaving me alone with her. The noise of the bar faded to a dull murmur, and my heart thudded in my chest, heavy with resentment and something dangerously close to dread. Alone with the silence and the weight of his words still hanging in the air.

Asshole.

~ 9 ~

CHAPTER NINE

Familiar Eyes

The room felt too loud, too bright. Laughter stabbed through the din like shattered glass, and the neon signs outside bled through the windows in a dizzying pulse of color. The alcohol had me swaying slightly in my seat, but my mind was hyper focused. Life and time seemed to move too fast around me, slipping through my fingers like sand.

I still couldn't look at her. My gaze remained fixed on the table, on the condensation pooling around my glass. The silence stretched between us, taut and uncomfortable, and I wondered what she was thinking.

Would she say something? Would she laugh it off, call Ethan an idiot, and put this whole thing to rest? The silence stretched on longer than I could stand. Every second felt like an eternity, the air thick with tension, neither of us willing to break it.

Then, out of nowhere, she spoke. Her voice was softer than I expected, but still sharp in its clarity.

"So," she started, her tone measured but... almost... *genuine.* "How have you been? Since you moved out, I mean. Things gotten any better?"

It hit me, her question. Coming from her, it felt disarming—this wasn't the biting sarcasm I was used to, the verbal sparring from years ago. It felt real. And that made it harder to ignore. It was so simple, so... unexpected. Like she actually cared, like she wasn't just here because of some weird setup, some stupid plot from Ethan. Like the last time we spoke didn't startwith me yelling at her.

I hesitated, the words catching in my throat. I wasn't sure what to say. Was I supposed to tell her everything? That nothing had really changed? That life was still a mess? I wasn't even sure I wanted to talk to her about it, but—

She raised an eyebrow, and her lips quirked into a small, teasing smile. "Or are you still getting by with your 'mysterious brooding' routine?" she added with a hint of sarcasm, but there was something warm in it, something almost... nostalgic.

It was like we were back in high school again, sitting next to each other at some table in the library, a textbook between us. Nothing ever felt quite as *real* back then, not with the way we bantered, half-studying and half-ribbing each other. I remembered those moments—her teasing, always gentle and amused, never cruel, and me, just as defensive and standoffish as ever. I wanted to snap back, to throw some clever remark at her.

But... this time was different. My mouth was dry, and I could feel the weight of the years between us—the distance, the silence, the space that had stretched between us since high school. It didn't matter. It felt like those old patterns were slipping right back into place.

"Still doing alright," I muttered, finally looking up at her, though my gaze immediately flickered back down. "Just... trying to make it, you know?"

Her eyes widened just slightly, a shift I didn't miss. She wasn't expecting that answer. For a second, she didn't say anything—just looked at me, maybe trying to figure out if I was just saying it to shut her up or if there was something else behind it.

"Really?" Her voice softened. "You don't sound so sure about that. Is everything okay?"

I shrugged, trying to play it cool. I could feel her eyes on me, waiting for me to say something more, and for some reason, I felt like I owed her an answer.

"Yeah," I said, the word feeling like a lie on my tongue, but it was all I had. "I mean, I'm getting by. School's fine. Just... trying to keep up, you know?"

She nodded slowly, like she wasn't buying it, but she let it slide for now. She shifted in her seat, her eyes darting to the side as if gathering her thoughts. Then, almost hesitantly, she asked, "And your mom? How's she doing?"

The question hit me harder than I expected. My chest tightened. I hadn't talked about her in... years. The image of my mom, distant and quiet, flashed in my mind, and I could feel the old weight of it settling on my shoulders.

"Mom's... she's the same." I kept my voice steady, but I couldn't hide the edge in it. "Quiet. Doesn't really... doesn't really say much."

She studied me for a moment, her gaze softening. "And your dad? Still...?"

I swallowed hard. I could already feel the tension building, but I didn't want to shut her out again. I wasn't sure I wanted to share this, but there was something in her eyes, some mix of concern and curiosity, that made it harder to lie.

"Yeah," I said, my voice quieter now. "Still... the same. He's... not around much. Just passed out or whatever." I looked down at the table, my hands gripping the beer bottle a little tighter than necessary.

She didn't say anything right away, just gave a small nod. I could feel her looking at me, waiting for me to say more. The silence stretched, and I could feel myself starting to withdraw again, but I didn't want to. I wanted to say something—anything that would let her in a little more.

"So..." She broke the silence, her tone casual but probing. "How's school been? You're still taking classes, right? I remember you were always a good student."

For a second, I felt something flicker—some memory of those early days when I actually cared about getting grades, about learning. It felt like a different life. Back when I still had her around. Before she left.

"Yeah... I'm still in it," I said, surprising myself by speaking a little more freely than I intended. "Not exactly thriving, but I'm getting by. Some days are better than others."

I wanted to say more. I wanted to explain that sometimes it felt like I was just going through the motions. My fingers tightened slightly around the bottle, grounding myself in the coolness of the glass. I wanted to tell her that I wasn't really living, but I didn't know how. And I didn't think I wanted her to know all of it. How her absence affected me.

"You don't have to do this alone, you know," she said, her voice soft but firm, as if she actually meant it. "I mean, you can always ask for help. People at school, your friends... They're not just there for the good times. You don't have to keep everything inside."

I didn't know how to respond to that. I wasn't used to hearing someone—especially her—talk to me like that. I didn't know what to do with it.

"Yeah, well..." I looked away, clearing my throat. "I'm not really great at asking for help. Besides, I don't really have friends."

She smiled, but it was a little sad. "You never did. What about Ethan?"

I shook my head, a bitter laugh escaping me. "Dunno how I feel about him."

Her gaze softened. "You know, it's okay to let people in. People care about you, even if you don't always see it."

I couldn't meet her eyes then. I couldn't handle it, the way she was looking at me—like she could see right through the walls I'd built. *How was it that she was still behind them?* I had to pull away again, couldn't keep talking about this.

"So," I said, the words coming out a little sharper than I meant, "what about you? What'd you get up to after"—I couldn't stop myself from emphasizing it, the words coming out with a trace of bitterness—"dropping out?"

She paused, her expression momentarily guarded before a small, almost wistful smile flickered at the corner of her lips.

"Well, after that," she started, her voice quiet, "I guess I just... moved around a bit. Nothing too exciting. Some time away, some new places. My dad thought it might be good for me. Help clear my head or something." She paused, eyes flicking away. "I didn't really have a plan."

The way she spoke made me think she wasn't telling me everything, but I wasn't about to meet her gaze again to confirm it. It was weird, hearing her talk like this. Like we were more than just... the past.

“Did it help?” I asked, not even trying to sound like I cared, but it came out a little softer than I’d planned.

Her smile turned into a laugh, but it wasn’t light or happy. “I don’t know. I guess... sort of. I mean, I came back, right?” She shrugged like it wasn’t that important. But I could see the subtle tension in her shoulders, the way she moved like she wasn’t sure whether to stay or leave.

I was still trying to process what she said, still grappling with the way she’d just slid into this conversation like it was... normal. "That’s what you’ve been up to?" I said, feeling the words slip from my mouth before I could stop them. "I mean, didn’t you have, like, big plans?"

Her eyes narrowed a little, like she wasn’t sure if I was mocking her. “Plans?” she repeated softly, her gaze steady now, like she was really looking at me for the first time tonight. "You could say that. But sometimes... life finds a way to make any plans obsolete." She exhaled sharply, glancing at the drink in her hand but not really looking at it.

The quiet hung between us for a moment. It was like I could almost hear everything unspoken.

Finally, I broke it. “Yeah, I get that,” I muttered, though I wasn’t sure I did. The whole thing with her seemed different than what I was used to, and I couldn’t really tell if I wanted to understand it, or just get away from it.

But she leaned forward, just a little, like she was trying to bridge the gap. “You don’t have to act like you’re fine all the time, you know,” she said softly, her voice gentler than I was used to. “It’s... okay to not have everything figured out. I get it. Trust me. I do.”

I couldn't stop the laugh that came out—dry and bitter. "Yeah, sure. You don't have to pretend, either. I know things don't just 'fix themselves,' you know?"

Her eyes softened a little, but the teasing glint was back, just a little. "You're really not good at taking advice, huh?" She chuckled, but there was something almost apologetic about it. It was that same old vibe we used to have—arguing and teasing, but with that undertone of... familiarity.

And for a second, just a second, it felt like maybe things weren't so bad. But I had to shut that down fast.

I turned away slightly, taking another drink, feeling the warm buzz seep into my brain again. "Maybe I just don't want to hear it from you."

Her smile didn't drop. Instead, it lingered, but she didn't say anything.

I didn't want to speak to her anymore—not because I disliked her presence, but because I found myself growing too comfortable in it. That was what unsettled me. It was easier to stay guarded, to keep the distance. But here she was, disarming me with every word, every glance. Still, I couldn't walk away—not yet. Social etiquette, I told myself. Just making sure she got home safe.

I glanced down at the half-empty bottle in front of me, my thoughts muddled. The alcohol was doing its job, dulling the sharp edges of everything, but it wasn't enough to make this situation go away. It wasn't enough to stop the constant weight in my chest, like I was still carrying everything I'd left behind.

"So," I muttered, shifting in my seat, feeling restless now, "I should probably get going."

She didn't seem surprised. In fact, she looked almost like she'd been expecting it, like she could see the way my gaze kept flickering toward the door.

"You sure you're alright to leave?" she asked, her voice unsteady, a little slurred. It was then I realized she'd been drinking a lot more than I had. She hadn't exactly kept pace, but there was that slight looseness in her words that made me uneasy.

"I'll be fine," I said, trying to push myself up from the table, but my body wasn't quite listening. The beer was catching up with me, blurring my senses just enough to make my movements feel slow and uncertain. "But you're a bit... I don't know. Maybe you should sober up before you go anywhere."

Her eyes flickered over to me, narrowing slightly, the teasing edge in her voice back. "Are you saying I can't handle my liquor?"

I shot her a look, but something about her expression made me hesitate. Something in the way she looked at me made me feel like she didn't need me to be here. Didn't need me to care. I didn't know what I was trying to prove anymore.

"I'm not saying that," I muttered. "But I'm also not saying you're gonna make it home in one piece if you keep this up."

She laughed softly, but it didn't sound real. It was like she was trying to brush it off, but I could see that uncertainty in her eyes now. She was starting to wobble just a bit as she leaned back in her chair.

"Yeah, well," she said slowly, her voice quieter, "I'm not really sure if I care about getting home in one piece anymore."

I froze at her words, her tone almost too casual, too distant. Something about it sent a chill down my spine.

I stood up straighter, the words catching in my throat. "What does that mean?" The question slipped out before I could stop it. I didn't want to hear the answer, but I needed to.

Her eyes flickered to me, then quickly away, her hand gripping her drink a little too tightly. "It means... it's just one of those nights, I guess."

I felt my stomach tighten, that familiar feeling of unease creeping back in. "Yeah, well. That's not really something I can just leave you to, you know?" I paused, looking down at her, but she wasn't even meeting my gaze now. "I'm not just gonna walk away. Not like this."

She finally looked up at me, her expression unreadable. "So what? You're gonna babysit me now?"

I bit back a frustrated sigh. "Maybe not babysit," I muttered. "But I'm not leaving until I know you're not gonna do something stupid."

Her lips pressed together, and for a moment, I thought she might laugh it off. But instead, she just gave a slight, almost imperceptible nod.

"Fine," she said quietly. "I guess I can live with that."

"Then let's get out of here," I said, my voice softer now. She accepted without hesitation. She didn't show any fear of being alone with me... even though, in many ways, we were still strangers. "How about I just walk you home?" I offered, then added, "Or maybe call a cab?"

But she said, "Let's walk for a bit, all right?"

I exhaled softly, not quite a sigh, not quite a huff. She didn't seem to notice, or if she did, she didn't let on. That faint smile had stayed on her face since we left the bar, calm and unbothered. It was... disarming. Not in a bad way, but in a way that made me hyper-aware of her presence—of how effortlessly she carried herself now. She didn't look like the girl I remembered. She was sharper around the edges, more composed. And beautiful in a way that felt harder to ignore the longer we walked.

We didn't talk at all. We were completely silent. And it was fine... until she stumbled and brushed up against my shoulder accidentally. It was barely a touch, but it made my pulse skip, and my thoughts slid into a place I wasn't comfortable with.

I wondered if she knew how much she destroyed me. Stole away everything I strove for, my motivation, my desire. If she hadn't quit school that day, I'm sure our expressions would be different. I'd be the one with the smile. We continued walking silently, but we were somehow closer now that she bumped me.

What would it be like, to make her feel how I did? To finally win. I mean, it would be so easy. She's so vulnerable right now.

I caught myself, breath catching in my throat. No. Fuck that. I wasn't like that. I wasn't someone who needed to win, not like this. I was just... I didn't know what I was thinking. My mind was racing, every thought turning darker.

But the thoughts wouldn't stop. Maybe she was a virgin? Wouldn't that be wonderful. I pictured it again—her falling, finally ripping away that pride. That smile. It'd be such a shame for her to be ruined by someone like me. To be completely stained.

A look would've given away where my thoughts were heading. The thoughts of control, the thoughts of *possessing* her. The idea was repulsive. I wanted to make her cry, realizing she will lose something she will never get back. At that time, I will lick every last tear from her face until she's completely drained out.

If I can simply get my hand around her, to 'help her keep her balance' as an excuse, I could easily control our destination. That moment will seal her fate. And maybe, in some twisted moment of justice, I'd finally wipe away that smile—that infuriating, perfect smile that haunted me. Maybe then, I could let go. Maybe then, I could forgive her. Or myself.

Maybe at the end of the day, I will finally become whole again.

Fuck. I'm disgusting.

My fists clenched at my sides, my teeth grinding. I couldn't let this go any further. I tried to shake it off. Tried to focus on the ground ahead, but then she spoke. Her words snapped me out of the immoral trance I found myself in.

"I knew you hated me," she said quietly, breaking the silence like it was nothing. She was looking at me. She must have seen it. That, I'm sure of it. My disgusting expression... already tarnishing her with my eyes. She saw everything.

I froze.

"You... what?" My voice came out rougher than I wanted, sharper.

"I knew," she repeated, looking at the sidewalk beneath us. "I always knew. And I'm sorry. I should've tried harder."

Her words hit me like a punch to the chest. For a second, I couldn't even breathe. What the fuck was she talking about? Why was she apologizing? This wasn't her fault. Didn't she see the look on my face?

I couldn't process it, couldn't make sense of the words. My thoughts spiraled.

Tension built in my chest, an anger that had nowhere to go. Why the hell did she think I hated her? Why the hell would she think she needed to apologize?

"Don't fucking apologize," I snapped, spinning on my heel to face her. My eyes burned with frustration, a mix of confusion and anger I didn't know what to do with. "You didn't do anything wrong, okay? I'm the one who—" I cut myself off, struggling to vocalize the feelings welling up inside me.

She didn't answer, and the silence stretched out, the night air thick with the weight of it. I could feel my hands shaking, like I was losing control of something I couldn't even explain.

"Forget it," I muttered, turning away from her, my mind still spinning. "I'll call you a cab."

I didn't wait for her response. I pulled out my phone, hands trembling as I dialed. The whole situation felt wrong, like I was too far into this now to turn back. Like I couldn't understand why any of this mattered. All I wanted was for the night to end, for the whole thing to be over.

"What are you doing?" I didn't reply to her. I didn't even look her way. Instead, I....

"Yes... yes... At the intersection of 5th and 12th," I put away my phone, numb.

"I thought... I thought it would've been nice to talk for a bit. D-Don't you wanna?" She seems so let down, her shoulders drooping slightly and her gaze falling to the pavement. What does this woman want from me? Didn't she see my face just a moment ago? Is she that desperate to be assaulted by some loser like me? I took my wallet out, took two 20 dollar bills, and shoved them roughly into her hand, the notes crumpled.

"The taxi will be there in five minutes. This should cover the bill." I turned around without waiting or saying goodbye for all that matter. She doesn't say anything either. She simply looked at me with those eyes.

Those eyes that are even colder than mine.

~ 10 ~

CHAPTER TEN

A Cog in the Machine

The apartment was dead quiet except for the steady rhythm of my fingers against the keyboard. The dim glow from my desk lamp stretched shadows across the stacks of paper—résumés, references, and the rejections I hadn't bothered to throw away. A framed photo of my graduation sat on the edge of the desk, mostly buried beneath the clutter. I wasn't smiling in it—just standing stiff in my gown, the tassel on my cap crooked, my eyes avoiding the camera. My parents weren't there. It was a quick, impersonal snapshot taken by someone I didn't know, surrounded by classmates I could hardly name. It didn't feel like a celebration. Just another box checked off. Outside, the rain tapped against the window in uneven bursts, but I didn't look up.

Each word on the screen blurred into the next, my brain on autopilot as I crafted another cover letter. Research, rephrase, send, repeat. I'd learned the game by now—fill every line with just the right keywords, nothing too personal, nothing that made me sound like a person instead of another cog in their machine.

The email ping made me pause. My chest tightened—reflexively, stupidly—as I clicked it open. Another rejection. They all sounded the same: polite, professional, and completely indifferent.

I leaned back in the chair, letting out a slow breath. The ache in my temples spread as I stared at the ceiling, the faint cracks in the paint more interesting than the empty inbox. This was fine. Expected. I just had to keep going.

The phone buzzed on the desk, breaking the silence again. I grabbed it before the sound could dig under my skin.

"Hello?" I didn't bother hiding the flatness in my tone.

"Hi, is this..." The voice on the other end fumbled with my name. I didn't correct her. "I'm calling from Asteris Corp! We reviewed your application, and we'd like to offer you a position."

Her words hung in the air, so casual and cheery they didn't feel real.

"Oh." I blinked. "Thank you."

She rattled off details about the job—onboarding dates, schedules, benefits—but I barely absorbed half of it. I kept up with the occasional "mm-hmm" or "sure," enough to keep her from asking if I was still there.

When the call ended, I set the phone down carefully, staring at the screen until it dimmed. This was it. The next step.

The office was just as bland as I expected—glass walls, sterile furniture, and the faint hum of fluorescent lights that made my jaw clench. It smelled like nothing, which somehow made it worse.

"Welcome aboard!" My new manager greeted me with a handshake that was too firm and a smile that was too practiced. "We're glad to have you on the team."

Her tone suggested she wouldn't remember my name by the end of the day. I didn't mind. It made things easier.

She walked me through a maze of identical desks and quiet conversations. The hum of voices faded into background noise as I followed her, nodding at the polite smiles of my new coworkers. They glanced at me like I was part of the scenery.

"This will be your space," she said, gesturing to a corner cubicle. "Take some time to settle in, and let us know if you need anything."

"Thanks," I replied.

The chair creaked under me as I sat down, my fingers brushing over the smooth surface of the desk. It wasn't much, but it was mine. My inbox was already flooded with onboarding forms and emails marked urgent. I focused on the first task, the rest of the office fading away.

I was halfway through my second assignment when someone broke the rhythm.

"You're really diving in, huh?"

I looked up to see a woman leaning against the edge of my cubicle. Her arms were crossed, her grin easy, like she already knew me. She had light brown hair tied back, a loose strand framing her face, and eyes that were sharp but not unkind—curious, maybe, or quietly assessing, like she was trying to figure out what made people tick.

"Emily," she said before I could ask.

"Hi." My tone was clipped, but she didn't flinch.

"You've got that overachiever vibe already," she said, smirking. "Careful—they'll start piling more work on you if you're not careful."

"That's fine." I turned back to my screen, hoping she'd get the message.

"Alright, Mr. Lone Wolf," she said, undeterred. "If you ever come up for air, some of us are grabbing lunch at noon. No pressure."

"Thanks."

She walked away with a casual wave, her voice trailing off as she joined another conversation. I didn't watch her go. Office politics didn't interest me unless they served a purpose.

The first month passed in a blur of deadlines and late nights. I fell into the rhythm easily—arrive early, stay late, keep my head down. Supervisors nodded approvingly when I passed, and my coworkers offered polite smiles. None of it mattered.

Except for Emily.

She made a point of stopping by my desk whenever she could, cracking jokes and tossing out comments like we'd been friends for years. I didn't go out of my way to respond, but she didn't seem to care.

"You're like a machine," she said one afternoon, leaning on my desk with a coffee cup in hand.

I didn't look up. "Is that supposed to be a compliment?"

"Depends." She tilted her head, grinning. "Do you even drink coffee? Or is caffeine too inefficient for you?"

"I don't drink coffee."

Her eyebrows shot up. "What kind of monster doesn't drink coffee?"

"The kind that doesn't need it," I said, typing another line.

She laughed, unoffended, and walked away with a playful, "Suit yourself."

For someone who seemed so eager to talk, Emily never pushed too hard. Her visits were quick, her tone light, as though she didn't care whether I responded or not. I filed it away as harmless—another coworker trying to build rapport or climb the social ladder.

But sometimes, late at night, I caught myself wondering what she was playing at. Not that it really mattered. It never did.

The days bled together. I kept my head down, carving a path through the workload that seemed to multiply the more I finished. Promotions weren't handed out—they were earned, extracted from the monotony by sheer force of effort. That was fine. I understood the rules of the game.

Emily was a persistent outlier. No matter how often I brushed off her comments or shrugged at her suggestions, she circled back. Some days, she'd plop into the chair across from my desk uninvited, spinning her cup of coffee like it was a conversation starter. Other days, she'd toss a paperclip onto my desk to get my attention, grinning like it was some inside joke I wasn't in on.

"You should come to happy hour," she said one Thursday afternoon, her voice cutting through the hum of office chatter.

"Why?" I didn't look up.

"Because working yourself into the ground isn't as impressive as you think," she said. "You might even have fun."

I glanced at her, more out of irritation than interest. "I'm fine."

"Right," she said, leaning back. "The lone wolf thing. Very mysterious." She tapped her fingers on the desk, her grin still firmly in place. "Just so you know, people are starting to place bets on how long it'll take for you to snap."

"Let me guess," I said dryly. "You started the pool?"

"Guilty as charged." She stood, brushing imaginary dust from her sleeve. "My money's on three weeks, but don't feel pressured to break down on my account."

Her laughter trailed behind her as she walked away, leaving me to wonder—again—why she bothered.

Two months in, the promotion came as a surprise. I'd expected recognition eventually, but the timing felt abrupt. My supervisor handed me the news with a stiff handshake and a few obligatory words of praise.

"Your work ethic hasn't gone unnoticed," she said.

"Thank you," I replied, my voice even.

"Keep it up."

That was it. No pomp, no ceremony. Just another step forward.

Emily caught wind of it before I even made it back to my desk.

"Look at you, moving up in the world!" she said, her grin wider than usual. "Big shot already."

"It's just a title," I said, turning back to my screen.

"Don't downplay it," she said, leaning against my cubicle wall. "You should celebrate."

"I'm fine."

"Of course you are," she said, rolling her eyes. "But come on—one drink won't kill you. I'll even buy it, just to make sure you don't overthink it."

I hesitated, more out of reflex than consideration.

"Don't make me call it an order from management," she added, smirking.

That earned a faint scoff from me. "Fine."

The bar was louder than I expected, the dim lighting casting a faint haze over the crowd. Emily led the way, weaving through the tables with ease, her voice cutting through the noise as she flagged down a server.

"To promotions and not losing your mind," she said, raising her glass when our drinks arrived.

I clinked mine against hers out of politeness, taking a sip before setting it down.

"So, how does it feel?" she asked, leaning forward.

"How does what feel?"

"Moving up," she said, as though it were obvious. "Being noticed."

I shrugged. "It's just work."

She tilted her head, studying me like I was a puzzle she couldn't quite solve. "You're impossible, you know that?"

"Good to know," I said, taking another sip.

She laughed, shaking her head. "You're lucky I like impossible people."

The words slipped out casually, her tone light, but they lingered longer than they should have. I didn't respond, and she didn't press.

By the end of the night, I'd chalked it up to her usual banter—harmless, forgettable. Another step in the game, nothing more.

The first time Emily kissed me, it caught me off guard.

We'd stayed late to finish a project, the office nearly empty by the time we wrapped up. I was gathering my things when she stepped closer, her voice softer than usual.

"Hey," she said. "You did good today."

"Thanks."

She hesitated, her eyes searching mine for something I didn't have. Then, before I could process what was happening, she leaned in, her lips brushing against mine.

It wasn't unpleasant, but it felt hollow, like going through the motions of something that should've mattered but didn't. I didn't feel warmth or excitement—just the numb sense that I was checking off a box I hadn't meant to open. I didn't pull away, but I didn't lean in, either. When she stepped back, her expression was a mixture of nerves and satisfaction, like she'd accomplished something important.

"See you tomorrow," she said, walking away without waiting for a response.

I stood there for a moment, my bag hanging loosely from my hand. It didn't feel like much of a milestone, but I filed it away as another move in the game.

From then on, Emily became a constant. She texted me during off hours, dragged me to the occasional dinner, and slipped into my routines like she belonged there. I didn't object. It was easier to let her fill the space than to question why she wanted to.

She seemed happy enough, though sometimes her eyes lingered on me too long, like she was searching for something she'd never find.

And I couldn't shake the feeling that something was off.

A week after the kiss, Emily invited herself into my routine again, this time at a small café near the office. She'd picked the table near the window, the sunlight catching her hair in a way that made her look almost ethereal. I couldn't tell if it was intentional, but it fit her style—effortlessly calculated.

We'd barely started eating when she put her fork down and leaned forward, her expression oddly serious.

"Are we dating?" she asked, cutting through the silence like a blade.

I blinked, caught off guard. "What?"

"You heard me," she said, her voice calm but firm. "Are we dating? Or are you just letting me think we are?"

I shrugged, not sure how to answer. "I don't know. Maybe?"

Her jaw tightened, frustration flickering in her eyes. "That's not an answer."

"I guess we are?" I tried, though the words came out more as a question than a statement.

She sighed, pressing her fingers to her temples. "Do you even like me?"

I hesitated, the weight of her question crashing against the numb wall I'd built inside. There was a time when that kind of vulnerability might've scared me, but now it just felt... foreign. Like she was speaking a language I hadn't learned.. The silence stretched between us, thick and uncomfortable.

"I..." The words felt clumsy, heavy. "I don't dislike you."

Her eyes widened slightly, a flicker of hurt crossing her face before she quickly masked it. "That's it?"

I looked away, focusing on a chip in the edge of the table. "Sorry."

She leaned back in her chair, exhaling sharply. "No, it's okay," she said, though her tone suggested otherwise. "I guess I shouldn't have expected more."

We sat in silence for a moment, the café's ambient noise filling the void. Something about her expression—disappointed but not entirely surprised—stirred something uncomfortable in me.

"I'm not good at this," I admitted finally, the words feeling foreign.

"At what?" she asked, her tone softer now.

"People. Relationships. Whatever this is." I gestured vaguely between us. "I don't... I've never really thought about it the way you probably do."

Her frustration eased slightly, her shoulders relaxing as she leaned forward again. "Then what do you think about?"

I stared at the table for a moment, debating whether to say anything at all. But she didn't rush me, and that small patience made it easier to speak.

"Work. Getting things done. Moving forward. I'm... not used to thinking beyond that."

She tilted her head, studying me with a mix of curiosity and something gentler. "Why not?"

I hesitated again, the words tangling in my throat. "Because it's easier," I said finally. "If I keep moving, I don't have to think about what's behind me or... what I'm missing."

Her brow furrowed slightly, her fingers curling slightly on the table, but she didn't press further. It was the kind of silence that didn't feel passive—it felt like a pause, like she was weighing whether to ask what I wasn't saying.. "You know, that's not really living."

"Maybe not," I said, meeting her gaze. "But it's working so far."

She didn't argue. Instead, she reached across the table, her fingers brushing against mine. "You don't have to keep moving all the time, you know. Sometimes it's okay to just... stop."

The gesture was small, but it felt heavier than it should have. I didn't pull my hand away, though I didn't quite return the touch either.

"Maybe," I said after a moment.

For the first time, Emily didn't smile or tease. She just nodded, her hand lingering for a moment longer before she pulled it back. As Emily pulled her hand back, her fingers curling into her lap, I felt a sudden, uninvited flicker of something else—something distant but sharp, like the echo of a memory you can't quite place. Her eyes had reminded me, for just a second, of another pair.

Hers.

I saw her as clearly as if she'd been sitting across from me instead of Emily—her sharp gaze, the way it cut through every excuse I told myself, and the rare softness in her expression when she thought I wasn't looking.

For a moment, I felt that same uncomfortable tightness in my chest, the one I never quite understood. It wasn't anger, though I'd mistaken it for that often enough. It wasn't regret, either—at least, not entirely.

I shifted in my seat, the café suddenly feeling too warm, too loud.

"You okay?" Emily's voice broke through the haze, her brow furrowed slightly.

"Yeah," I said quickly, forcing myself to focus on her. "I'm fine."

She didn't seem convinced, but she let it go, her attention drifting back to her plate.

As she started talking again—something about a new project at work—I found myself nodding along without really hearing her. The memory of those eyes lingered, along with the faint, unsettling ache in my chest.

I didn't know what it meant. Or maybe I did, but it was easier to bury it, to focus on the here and now.

~ 11 ~

CHAPTER ELEVEN

Unraveled

Our first official date wasn't anything special—it was intentionally ordinary, and that was exactly how I wanted it. Just dinner—nothing fancy, nothing extravagant. The kind of place where the lights were soft, the air warm, and the conversations around us quiet enough that I could almost pretend I wasn't completely self-aware of every word that left my mouth.

Emily had this way of looking at me, like she was genuinely interested, even when I wasn't saying anything particularly important. She wore a deep wine-colored dress—simple, yet it gave her an air of quiet elegance that caught me off guard. More than just the girl who had somehow managed to keep up with me at work, more than the one who smiled at me in that way that made everything feel a little less heavy. I wasn't used to that.

The first half of the night was easy. Small talk—about our day, the food, the weather. Things people say when they don't want to jump into anything too deep too soon. But I could feel her studying me, her eyes lingering on me like she was trying to figure me out, like I wasn't some closed-off mystery but a puzzle with pieces just waiting to be put together.

I wasn't sure if I liked it or hated it. Maybe a little bit of both. But somehow, I couldn't bring myself to look away.

There was something about the way she laughed when I cracked a joke—like I wasn't just trying to be funny, but I was actually funny to her. I think that's what got me. It wasn't forced. She wasn't humoring me. She was really listening. And when I got too quiet, when I started slipping back into my old habits, she didn't press. She just sat there, waiting. Watching me, like she had all the time in the world.

At some point, we started talking about our childhoods. She asked me about my family, and for a second, my stomach knotted. It was the kind of question that asked for vulnerability, and I wasn't sure if I could give it. I shifted in my seat, buying time, before offering a carefully chosen slice of the truth. It's not like I wanted to lie—I didn't. But the truth? It always felt too raw, too heavy. So, I picked the parts that seemed safer. I told her about my dad, about how he was never really there for me. I didn't mention the pills, or the booze, or the way his presence in the house was more like a shadow than a father. She didn't ask for more, but I knew she could tell. There was no pity in her eyes—just quiet understanding.

I could have said more. But the more I talked, the more I realized something was shifting. She wasn't judging me. And I wasn't sure how to handle that.

The months that followed felt like a slow burn. It wasn't fireworks or some grand romantic gesture, but something about it felt real. We spent more time together—not just on dates, but in the kind of moments I never thought I'd share with anyone. Sitting on my couch, watching movies that neither of us were really paying attention to. Eating takeout from places I only went to when I didn't feel like cooking.

It was easy, maybe too easy. But that's what made me nervous.

I wasn't used to this—us. The idea of having someone in my life like this, in a way that felt serious, made my chest tighten every time I thought about it. I told myself it was normal to feel this way. To not be comfortable with the idea of actually being in a relationship. I'd always been fine on my own, had learned to take care of myself—needed to. And now, here I was, spending time with Emily, wondering if she expected something more. If she wanted something more.

I kept it all hidden. The doubts. The fear. I didn't want her to see it, to know how much I was struggling with the thought of this—of what this was becoming.

But Emily—she wasn't rushing me. She didn't demand anything from me I wasn't ready to give. She was patient in a way I didn't know how to appreciate at first, but now... now it made sense. She didn't need me to open up all at once. She was okay with the silence between us, the spaces where I didn't say anything at all.

Still, as the weeks went by, I couldn't help but feel like I was supposed to be someone more emotionally present for her—someone who could reciprocate her patience and openness with a kind of vulnerability I hadn't yet figured out how to give. I should have been more affectionate. I should've wanted to take the next step, whatever that even was. But every time she leaned in a little closer, every time her hand brushed mine in a way that felt like she was asking for something more, I froze. My mind would race with a thousand reasons why it wasn't the right time, why I couldn't do this. Why I wasn't ready.

But then, there were those moments—moments when I would catch her watching me, her eyes soft with no agenda, no expectation. And I'd feel something inside me shift, like maybe I could be that person for her. Maybe I could be someone she could depend on, someone who was more than just the guy who kept his walls up. But the thought scared the hell out of me.

One night, we were sitting together at my apartment. The air was thick with the silence we often shared, but it didn't feel uncomfortable. She was reading a book, and I was doing my best to focus on a report from work, though my mind kept drifting back to her. I'd been quiet for a while when she looked up at me.

"Hey," she said, her voice a little soft. "What's going on in that head of yours?"

I stared at the report in my hands, knowing I should say something. But what? What could I tell her? That I was terrified of what this was becoming? That the idea of actually being in a relationship made my stomach twist with unease?

Instead, I gave her a half-smile and shrugged. "Just work stuff," I said. But I knew that wasn't enough.

She closed her book and set it aside, her gaze never leaving me. "You know, it's okay to not have everything figured out. You don't have to be perfect."

I almost laughed at that. Perfect. I wasn't even close.

But I didn't say that. I just nodded, because maybe, for the first time, I wanted to believe her.

The weeks after that night, the doubts kept building. The fear, the uncertainty—it wasn't something I could shake off. Every time I looked at Emily, I wondered if she could see it. The cracks, the broken parts of me I kept trying to hide, the parts I didn't even fully understand myself.

It was like there was this pressure inside me, a weight that kept growing with each passing day, and I couldn't hold it in anymore. One night, it all came spilling out.

We were sitting on my couch again, like we always did after work, the TV muted in the background, neither of us paying attention to it. I could feel her next to me, but I couldn't focus on her anymore. My chest felt tight, and I could feel my breath getting shallow.

Emily turned her head toward me, sensing something was off. "Hey," she said softly, "What's wrong?"

I didn't answer right away. My fingers drummed against the side of the couch, the air between us thick with the unspoken. But I couldn't keep it in anymore.

"Why do you even bother with me?" I blurted out, the words tumbling out before I could stop them. My voice cracked—not just with frustration, but something deeper, something more vulnerable. I hadn't meant to sound so sharp, but the pressure inside me had finally pushed its way out. It was like I couldn't stop myself. "What the hell do you see in me? I don't deserve this, Emily. I don't deserve you. I'm not—" I cut myself off with a bitter laugh. "I'm not worth anything. I'm just—just a broken mess of a person. I don't even know why you put up with me."

Her eyes widened slightly, her hand instinctively reaching out for mine, but I pulled it back, like I couldn't bear her touch right then.

"I can't even do anything right," I continued, my voice growing louder, the frustration in my chest spilling out, unchecked. "I've been living like this for years, and I'm still the same guy. The guy who can't keep his shit together. I've got a shitty past, a shitty family, I'm a mess. I don't know how you could ever look at me and think—think I'm worth anything. I'm not good for you, I'm not good for anyone."

I didn't stop. The words just kept coming, like a dam breaking. "I've got nothing going for me. I can't even—" I stopped, because I was starting to sound pathetic. But I couldn't hold it back anymore. "I can't even let anyone close. I'm always pushing people away. And you—" I turned to her now, and my eyes burned with unshed tears. "You deserve someone better. Someone who isn't as broken as I am. Someone who isn't—" I trailed off, the words too raw to finish.

I felt like I was suffocating in my own emotions, like they were drowning me, and there was no escape. No way to fix it. I stood up abruptly, pacing the small space of my living room, my hands shaking with the release of all the things I had been carrying for so long.

But then, before I could even gather my thoughts, Emily was there, her hands on my arms, gently pulling me to face her. I couldn't look at her—couldn't bear to see pity or disappointment in her eyes—but she wasn't looking at me like that. She was looking at me like she understood.

"You don't get it, do you?" she said softly, her voice calm but firm. I met her gaze, finally. She wasn't angry. She wasn't disappointed. There was something else in her eyes, something that made me freeze in place.

"Listen to me," she said, her hand reaching up to touch my face. "I'm not blind. I see your flaws. But I also see what you don't. I see how hard you work. How much you push yourself to do better, to be better. Yeah, you have a past that you can't change, but that doesn't define you. What matters is who you're becoming."

She took a deep breath, like she was choosing her words carefully. "I see the way you've been improving, even if you don't see it yourself. You stopped smoking, for one. I know you didn't even realize it, but you've done that. You've been taking care of yourself in ways you never have before."

I didn't know what to say. I didn't even know I had stopped smoking. The habit had been so ingrained in me that I hadn't even noticed the change.

Emily continued, her hands still on me, her gaze unwavering. "And I see how you treat me, even when you don't think you're treating me well enough. You listen to me. You make time for me. You try. And that—" She let out a soft laugh, shaking her head. "That's what matters. I don't need you to be perfect. I just need you to be you."

Her words hit me harder than I expected. I didn't know what to say. I wanted to argue, to push her away, because everything inside me was telling me I didn't deserve her. But the warmth in her eyes, the sincerity in her voice—it made me falter.

"I'm proud of you," she said quietly. "You've come so far. And I see you, even the parts you hide from the world. I see the good in you."

That was all it took. The walls I had been holding up for so long crumbled. I felt everything I had been holding back—every ounce of pain, fear, and self-doubt—spill over. It was like a crack had opened in me, and everything came flooding out.

I dropped to my knees in front of her, overwhelmed by the weight of her words, by the weight of everything I had been keeping inside. "I'm sorry," I whispered, my voice breaking. "I'm sorry for being such a mess. For not being what you deserve."

Before I knew it, Emily was kneeling down in front of me, pulling me into her arms. And for the first time, I didn't try to push her away. I let her hold me. I let her comfort me, and in that moment, everything felt raw and real. I didn't know how to handle it, but I didn't want to let go.

"Shh," she whispered softly, her voice gentle against my ear. "You don't have to apologize. You're not a mess. You're human. And I'm here. I'm not going anywhere."

And for the first time in as long as I could remember, I allowed myself to hope.

~ 12 ~

CHAPTER TWELVE

Fading Illusions

The fog I'd been moving through felt... thinner, like waking from a long, vague dream. The day after that night with Emily, I woke up with an unexpected clarity, like something inside me had let go. Even the air felt easier to breathe. The little routines—getting dressed, making coffee, walking to the office—felt almost normal. Like living, not just getting by.

But then there was that question that kept creeping up on me.

Did I love her?

It was a question that felt as large as it was unwelcome. What did love even mean to someone like me—someone who had spent most of his life keeping people at arm's length, hiding behind efficiency and restraint? And yet, the thought of Emily lingered like a light in a dim hallway. I wasn't sure what the answer was, but the very fact that I was asking... that had to mean something. I didn't know what to make of it. The idea felt too big, too overwhelming to fully process, but whenever I thought about Emily, my chest tightened. Maybe that was it. Maybe that tightness in my chest was something real, something deeper than I had allowed myself to recognize until now. Could it be love?

The thought was terrifying. But then again, if I was being honest with myself, I couldn't imagine going back to the way things were before Emily. She had cracked something open in me that had been closed off for so long. Even if I wasn't ready to admit it, maybe she had changed me.

I pushed those thoughts away as I stepped out of the office. Nevada heat hit me like a wall, the dry air clinging to my skin as I made my way to the car. The drive to my next meeting felt strange. It was a route I'd taken before, but today it felt like something was off, like I was seeing everything through a new lens. Maybe it was because of Emily, maybe it was because of everything that had happened between us lately. Either way, it felt... uncomfortable.

I pulled into the parking lot of the establishment, already feeling the familiar knot forming in my stomach. I had been here before, twice already, for business meetings with a client who preferred doing things in unconventional places. It wasn't unusual, but today, the idea of stepping inside felt different.

This wasn't a strip club—not in the traditional sense. The place leaned into sex appeal, but with polish: sleek decor, expensive drinks, and an atmosphere curated for seduction. The women didn't dance or undress; they poured drinks, smiled, and made their clients feel seen. It was an act, but one the patrons were willing to buy into.

I understood the game. These women were paid for more than company—they offered the suggestion of connection. Not real intimacy, but a convincing illusion. It was a business, and people paid well to pretend it wasn't.

I had told myself that this was just business, that there was no reason to think about it any more than that. But today? Today it felt wrong.

I stood there for a moment, staring at the building. I had been here twice before, but something about it now made my skin crawl. Maybe it was because of the shift in me since Emily. Maybe I was starting to see things differently.

I wasn't sure I liked the person I had allowed myself to become when I frequented places like this—a version of myself shaped by detachment, transactional habits, and a refusal to confront what I truly felt. The discomfort in my stomach wasn't just nerves or anxiety about the deal—it was something deeper, a growing recognition that this wasn't the kind of man I wanted to be. Maybe that was a sign of change, or maybe I was just being sentimental. Either way, I didn't want to go in.

I hesitated for a moment, my hand resting on the door handle, but I knew I didn't have a choice. This was business. But even as I walked inside, I couldn't shake the feeling that I was stepping into something I was no longer comfortable with. And maybe that was a good thing.

The meeting went like it always did. Small talk, meaningless chatter. My client was a middle-aged man, obsessed with the latest tech trends, his voice always a bit too loud, a bit too enthusiastic for me to truly care. The air around us was thick with fake pleasantries and thinly veiled sales pitches, both of us trying to get something out of the other without admitting what we really wanted.

He went on about his latest venture, a new project that was somehow more important than everything else in his life. I nodded, pretending to listen, silently wishing I was anywhere but here. Patience, I told myself. Just a little more patience, and I'd have the deal wrapped up. The numbers were good, the potential was even better. It was the kind of opportunity I couldn't afford to pass up, no matter how much I despised the setting.

Then she walked over.

I didn't even hear the initial part of her sentence. I just saw her, standing there. She was asking if we wanted another drink, but paused halfway through, her voice cutting off sharply, like someone had just flipped a switch inside her.

I turned toward her, confused, my mind trying to catch up to what my eyes were seeing. And then I understood.

It was her.

The girl.

The breath caught in my throat, and for a long second, I couldn't do anything but stare. Her eyes—those same eyes I thought I'd buried deep inside my memory—met mine with a coolness that made my stomach twist. I wasn't sure what it was in her gaze. Recognition? Something deeper? I couldn't figure it out.

Her smile was the same, but now it wasn't playful or mocking, like it had been years ago. No, this was different. It was calculated. It was practiced. And yet, there was still something familiar about it—something that made my heart pound in my chest.

She stood there, her outfit impossibly seductive, impossibly perfect. A black dress that clung to every curve, the fabric tight against her skin, showcasing everything she had in a way that made my mind race. Everything about her screamed sex, from the way she moved to the way she carried herself. It was impossible not to think of her like that—she was made for it. Made for men like me, who thought they could see beyond the surface, but couldn't stop looking.

She paused again, and I couldn't look away.

God, she was beautiful.

Everything about her—from the way her dark hair cascaded over her shoulders to the sharpness of her features—was so striking that it almost felt like a punch to the gut. It was the same feeling I had when I saw her in high school—the uncontrollable desire to possess her, to make her acknowledge me, to somehow matter to her. But now... it was more than that. It wasn't just that I couldn't stop thinking of her; I was seeing her as something else, something I didn't want to see.

Everything came rushing back—confusion, anger, and the ugly thoughts that had twisted my mind into knots years ago. I remembered that night. The way I'd looked at her, convinced she was just a cruel joke. Not the girl who'd caught my eye, but a mockery of everything I believed her to be.

I had wanted her. Desperately. But I'd resisted—like a fool.

And now... here she was.

Working here. In this place.

How long had she been here? Was she mocking me then, pretending to be the sweet, innocent girl I'd dreamed of? Was she playing me, just like she might be now? How had I not seen it?

Anger swelled inside me, bitter and sharp. She wasn't who I'd imagined. Not the girl I'd clung to in my mind. She was something else—something darker. Not evil, but shadowed by pain and secrets buried deep. She was a contradiction: vulnerability wrapped in bravado, honesty cloaked in performance.

I saw now how little I'd truly known her. How much of what I remembered was shaped by my own projections. And I hated myself for it. For clinging to a fantasy I had created, just to fill the space she left behind.

My jaw clenched. Maybe I shouldn't have resisted those urges back then. Maybe I should've taken what I wanted. Maybe she wasn't the pure, delicate woman I had believed her to be—maybe that image had only ever been a product of my own immaturity and longing, not a true reflection of her character. I'd convinced myself she was something untouched and perfect because it was easier than facing the truth: that she, like everyone else, had her own complexities. Maybe she'd always had layers I couldn't—or wouldn't—see. And maybe, just maybe, she hadn't been pretending at all. Maybe she'd just been herself, and I was the one who had projected a fantasy onto her.

The thought gnawed at me. The anger surged again, stronger this time, as I fought to keep my cool. I didn't want to feel this way. I didn't want to think about her this way. But damn it, she was here, standing in front of me like nothing had changed, like she hadn't shattered everything I thought I knew about her.

I dragged my gaze away from her, trying to force myself back to the present, to the business at hand. But the frustration wouldn't leave. It tangled around my mind, choking out the ability to focus on anything else.

And all I could think was: Why?

Why was she here? Why was she doing this?

As I sat there, trying to focus on the numbers and the potential deal in front of me, the buzzing sensation from the back of my mind crept in. That feeling I used to get around her in high school and middle school, the one that made everything feel dizzy, like my head was full of static, refusing to let me concentrate. It was back, stronger than ever, thrumming beneath my skin. I tried to ignore it, but it clawed at my insides, making it harder and harder to keep my cool.

I glanced at my client, nodded in all the right places, said all the right words. But my attention kept drifting to her—the hostess, the girl—who still stood there, waiting for the right moment to leave. Her eyes flickered toward me a couple of times, and each time, my heart seemed to skip, my chest tightening in ways I couldn't control.

She wasn't the same girl I remembered. She was more. More seductive. More dangerous. More everything.

I took a breath, tried to calm myself, but my nerves were shot. I didn't want to feel like this again. I didn't want to be a slave to whatever pull she had over me. Not anymore.

I reached for my drink and took a heavier sip than I should have, hoping the whiskey's burn might dull the edges of the storm inside me. It didn't. If anything, it made things worse—blurring reality while sharpening all the wrong details. Her smile. The way she looked at me, like she was daring me to respond. Thoughts of her—the girl she'd been years ago—distorted into something darker. Confusion. Rage. Lust. Each returned with brutal clarity. My chest clenched, my mind fogged, and it felt like I was slipping.

I forced myself to focus, rattling off numbers, discussing percentages, trying to keep the deal moving forward. My hands were shaking, but I hid it. He didn't notice, or if he did, he didn't care. He was too busy leaning in, all smiles and fake enthusiasm, pulling me further into the farce of it all. I couldn't believe I was still sitting here, negotiating with a man like him, in a place like this.

But somehow, I closed the deal. The papers were signed, the handshake was made. I didn't even feel the relief I expected.

I stood up, ready to leave, desperate to escape, but then my client's voice stopped me.

"Come on, don't run off so soon," he said, his voice slurred, a little too eager. "Why don't you stay a while? Enjoy the place. There's no rush."

I hesitated, my mind still reeling, trying to make sense of the mess inside my head. And then it happened—the words that I couldn't ignore.

"Come on, treat yourself," he said with a smirk, voice thick with indulgence. "You've got the cash—might as well make it worth your while."

He slid a few bills across the table, the gesture so casual, so matter-of-fact, like it was the most normal thing in the world. But all I could see was her, standing there, waiting.

A crack formed in my resolve. I hadn't come here to fall back into old habits. I hadn't come here to repeat mistakes I'd made before. But the buzzing in my head, that insistent pull, it was too much to fight. The whiskey, the confusion, the years of repressed feelings... it all mixed together.

"Yeah," I breathed. "What's one more mistake?"

~ 13 ~

CHAPTER THIRTEEN

Cracked Mirror

My mind screamed at me to stop, to walk away, but my feet didn't listen. My body was already in motion, already heading toward her.

When I got to her, I had to swallow a lump in my throat. She didn't even blink, just gave me that same practiced smile. I could barely form the words. My throat felt tight, like I was suffocating.

"Let's go," I muttered, the words escaping before I could catch them. It was like they'd already been spoken somewhere inside me, and my mouth was just catching up. My mind scrambled, trying to catch up, trying to understand what I had just done. But it was already too late.

Her smile didn't waver. She led me to a private room, a separate building that doubled as a hotel, her eyes glinting with something I couldn't quite place, something I didn't want to understand. I could still hear Emily's voice in the back of my head, a soft whisper reminding me of what I had—what I was throwing away. But it was like she was miles away, the buzzing in my head too loud, the liquor too potent.

As we sat down, she poured another drink for me, and I downed it without thinking. My thoughts were hazy, swirling around. I was too far gone, too wrapped up in the moment.

“Do you remember me?” she asked, her voice smooth, her eyes locked onto mine.

I wanted to say something, to ask her what she meant, but the words caught in my throat. I remembered her—of course I did—but not like this. Not as this carefully crafted caricature of desire, this mask of seduction. That wasn’t the girl I remembered.

The alcohol made everything blur. It numbed the guilt, the fear, the confusion. All that mattered was her.

The buzzing in my head surged, and my chest still ached—but I couldn’t say why. For a split second, I thought of Emily. Her face floated into my mind, blurred and fragmented, as if my memory couldn’t hold her features anymore. Her smile slipped out of reach, her eyes replaced by shadows. I was already too deep in the fog to pull her back, too far gone to care about the doubts clawing at the edge of my mind.

"Of fucking course I remember you! How could I forget you?"

I didn’t bother keeping my voice down—there was a raw edge in it, a bite sharpened by alcohol and everything I couldn’t say. My chest tightened, and the liquor didn’t dull it—it made everything worse. Made me sharper, meaner. My mind scrambled, heart pounding like it wanted out of my chest. She tensed, her eyes dropping for just a second, and the silence that followed only made it worse. It felt like a game, like she was pulling strings I couldn’t see, like she thought she could still control me. But I was done playing.

I inhaled sharply, dragging in a breath like it might cool the fire burning in my throat.

"Strip," I said, my voice low but sharp. It wasn't a request. It wasn't even a demand. It was a command.

She froze for a second, her hands trembling slightly, then she looked at me, her lips twitching like she was going to say something. But she didn't.

"Hold on," she said, her voice soft but steady. "We just got here. Maybe we should slow down a little. Enjoy it."

My jaw tightened. My hands curled into fists in my lap, each knuckle white under the skin. The pressure in my chest twisted like a vice, building, pulsing. I didn't want slow. I didn't want soft. That wasn't something I was allowed to have. I just wanted this to end—fast, detached, brutal. I wasn't in this for connection. I was here to erase, to carve out the ache with something harder than pain. And even if it meant breaking something—maybe both of us—I couldn't stop now.

"You're kidding," I said, voice flat. "You've been at this how long, and now you're flinching because I didn't hold your hand first?"

I couldn't stop myself. I was angry—ice cold now—but the kind of anger that tightened behind my eyes and sat in my chest like lead. Somewhere, deep in the back of my mind, I knew I was being irrational. I knew none of it made sense. But I didn't care. Not about her. Not about what was right. I just wanted it done—clean, final. I wanted to punish her for everything I'd buried, everything I couldn't forget. And the worse it felt, the more it made sense.

I took a step forward, my eyes burning with anger, and she shifted, just slightly, but enough for me to notice. She was hesitant, unsure. And that just pissed me off more.

"Isn't this your job?" I spat, venom lacing every word. "You fuck strangers for money, don't you? So what's with the sudden modesty?"

Her eyes fell, frustration flickering in them, but she didn't say anything. The room was too quiet. All I could hear was the sound of my own breath—shallow, erratic, like I was suffocating from the inside out. My skin felt tight, my hands clammy, every nerve fraying at once. The silence wasn't just empty; it was crushing, and I couldn't outrun it.

I looked at her, studying her like I hadn't seen her in years. Then, with a subtle shift, she reached beneath her dress and slid her panties down. I watched every movement, my stomach churning as my brain screamed at me, but I couldn't stop myself from getting closer, from seeing her like this. But then... something hit me. The underwear was... ordinary. Plain cotton. Some childish fucking print—a simple heart. What the hell was this? Where was the lace, the silk, the illusion? Why would someone like her wear something so... normal? It didn't fit the fantasy. It was stupid, jarring—like a punchline to a joke I didn't understand. She wasn't dressed to seduce. And that defiance—whether deliberate or careless—undermined everything I'd told myself about her. It made her real. And that made me sick.

"That's your idea of sexy?" I asked, voice low and cold. "What, trying to look cute for your customers? With a dress like that? I thought you were supposed to be a professional."

Her eyes fell to the floor, and for a second, I felt something twist inside me. It wasn't guilt—no, it was something else. But I wasn't going to let that stop me. Not now. I wasn't going to let myself fall into some kind of weakness.

"How disappointing," I muttered, trying to hold onto the anger, trying to make it feel better. I wanted to humiliate her. It's what I needed. It was the only thing that could get me through this moment, through this overwhelming feeling. It was her fault, anyway, right?

But then, as I looked at her, something shifted. Something in the back of my mind. I couldn't stop thinking about how she'd been pretending all these years—pretending to be someone else, someone pure. Someone I admired. Someone I saw as an equal, a rival, someone to compete with. But it was all a lie. She wasn't that person. She never had been.

The bitterness in my chest flared, and I clenched my jaw.

"You know what?" I said, voice cold and precise, each word slicing through the tension. "You've been playing innocent for years. Acting like you're better. Like I'm the fucking monster. But this?" I gestured between us. "This is exactly what you built."

I stepped forward again, watching her kick her panties aside. She still wasn't looking at me, and that pissed me off even more.

"Look at me," I hissed, each word like a blade. My voice didn't rise—it carved through the silence. My breath came fast, heart pounding in my throat. "You're no fucking angel, don't pretend you are." I stepped in closer, tone hardening. "Look at me. Fucking. Look. At. Me."

I grabbed her chin roughly, forcing her gaze to meet mine. Her skin was warm beneath my fingers, but I wasn't looking for connection—I just needed her to see me. To *really* see me. Her eyes flicked to mine, wide and uncertain, something flickering behind them that I couldn't place. I tilted her head slowly, first to one side, then the other, as if trying to find something—confirmation, truth, guilt. Anything that made sense. But all I saw was the reflection of someone just as lost as me.

"You were always the one ahead, weren't you?" I said, cold and steady. "Now look at you. Pretending like this is a slow dance." I scoffed, shaking my head. "This isn't prom, sweetheart."

Her voice came at last, soft and uncertain, almost a whisper. "This wasn't how it was supposed to be..."

I didn't respond. I didn't want to. My hands were shaking with a strange mix of rage and something else I couldn't place—something desperate. I let go of her face, pushed her, and to my surprise, she didn't resist. She didn't fight back. She just... let me.

I froze. My mind reeled, trying to make sense of this. I wasn't used to this kind of silence. She wasn't pushing me away, she wasn't calling for help, she wasn't even crying. Her face was blank, just... waiting.

I swallowed, my breath ragged. What the hell was going on? Why wasn't she fighting me?

I pushed her again, pinning her to the bed, the weight of my body on hers. I felt the heat of her skin beneath mine, the softness of her. But my thoughts were a mess, tangled and chaotic, and I clung to the only story that let me move forward—this was her fault. She brought this on herself.

She made me this way. She always had the upper hand—laughing, mocking, looking down on me like I was beneath her. Like I didn't matter. If she hadn't treated me like a joke, none of this would've happened. That's what I told myself. That this was her fault. She needed to see what she'd done. She needed to own it. Apologize. Maybe even beg. That was the only way this could make any kind of sense.

A small voice inside me screamed, encouraging me to keep going, pushing me further into this madness. There was something almost satisfying about seeing her like this, about having her in front of me like this. I was finally in control. Finally. I took a deep breath, feeling like my chest was about to burst with how much I wanted this.

But as I looked at her, as she lay beneath me, I realized something that stopped me dead in my tracks.

Her arms were no longer in the way. I could finally see her body. One of her dress straps had slipped off her shoulder, exposing more than she probably intended, and the fabric bunched awkwardly at her waist. It didn't fit the fantasy. It made her look vulnerable. Human. The buzzing in my head didn't stop, but now... I was aware of her breathing. Her tears. They weren't from anger or frustration. No, they were different. Her eyes—those eyes—were wet, but there was something in them, something so much darker than my own rage. It was disappointment, yes. But it wasn't about me. It wasn't even about her.

I hesitated.

Wasn't this what I wanted? This was my fantasy, right? To take everything from her? To break her down the way she had broken me for all those years? This was my opportunity to finally win. To finally prove myself. I could *feel* it—this was my chance to take away that damn smile. I was supposed to hate her, wasn't I? But I didn't know anymore.

I could feel her eyes on me, and it was too much. Those big brown eyes—so full of something I couldn't name—were staring right into mine, and it was like I was seeing something I had never seen before. Something in her... and then I realized it.

Her smile, that smile I had always remembered, had never been real.

It hit me like a slow, cold flood. I had built so much around that smile—memories, longing, resentment. And now, staring into the truth of it, everything began to unravel. That smile wasn't joy or confidence. It was armor. A mask.

And for the first time, I saw her without it. It wasn't a happy smile. It wasn't a smile of someone who loved life, or loved me, or even loved herself. It was the same smile I saw every day in the mirror. The same smile I had worn for so long. The same smile that hid everything underneath.

I pulled back.

I saw the darkness in her eyes—the same darkness I had been running from in myself. I saw the truth. She was just as broken as I was. No. Worse. She had always been worse. I wasn't the monster in the room.

She was.

Her voice, barely audible, trembled through the silence, sending a jolt through me. The echo of my own thoughts hadn't even settled when she spoke—too soon, too fragile against the weight of everything I'd just admitted.

"I... I loved you. I always loved you..."

My stomach twisted. I almost couldn't process it. What did she say? Had I heard her right?

I stared at her, the words drifting through the fog of my thoughts, but they didn't land. They hung there, hollow. It wasn't relief. It wasn't comfort. It was a silence I didn't know how to fill, a truth I didn't know how to carry.

I pulled away further, but I didn't leave. I couldn't.

She spoke again, her voice still soft, but now more urgent, as if trying to make sense of this chaos between us. As if this was her only opportunity. Her last chance. "I... I always wanted to say it. I always wanted to tell you. But I couldn't. I just couldn't find the right words." Her eyes didn't leave mine, though her voice faltered. "I've always known. I've known how much you hated me. How much you despised everything I did. Everything I said. And I needed to get it off my chest. I couldn't keep pretending anymore. Not after everything we've been through. Not after all the years of—"

She swallowed hard, her chest rising and falling quickly as though the weight of her words was too much to carry.

"I'm ready now," she said, a raw desperation creeping into her tone. "I'm ready to stop pretending. Please... please don't look so sad. Don't act like that anymore."

Her voice cracked, and for the first time, I saw something else in her eyes. Something softer. Something I hadn't expected. She wasn't afraid. She wasn't afraid of me. But I was.

I was the one who was scared.

I shuddered, a dry, manic chuckle scraping out of my throat before I could stop it. It wasn't laughter—it was something broken, a sound with no humor left in it. My chest cinched tight, some jagged fusion of panic and disbelief. How the fuck could she say all that? How could she just... say it like it was nothing?

My laughter choked off, caught mid-breath as my lungs struggled to pull in air. I gasped, the sound sharp and shallow. She saw through me. She always did. The things I thought I hid from her, the things I thought were buried—she saw through them with ease, as if I was the transparent one.

She knew. She always knew. I was never a match for her.

Climbing off of her, I sat at the edge of the bed, my back to her. My mind was spinning, the echo of laughter still crawling around in my head. I was dizzy. Weak. Everything felt like it was unraveling at once. Behind me, she remained still. Not calm, not collected—just frozen. Like even she didn't know what to say. Like she was caught in the same storm, holding her breath, waiting to see which way I'd shatter.

My hand clenched at my side, a tremor running through it. I couldn't be here anymore. I couldn't look at her.

"Get out," I said, my voice cracked, defeated. "Just get out."

It wasn't just the anger anymore. Nor the betrayal I thought I'd carried for years. It was more than that. The hopelessness that had defined my entire existence, the constant ache that gnawed at my soul—none of it mattered now.

There was nothing left to take from her.

I had nothing left to give.

She didn't leave.

I felt her sit up, the bed shifting beneath me. "No," she said—soft, but firm, like something inside her had finally clicked into place.

My heart skipped a beat. Why wasn't she listening?

"I told you to leave," I said, voice cracking, the rage hollow now, replaced with something far quieter—something closer to defeat. I still didn't look at her.

She didn't get up. Instead, she moved closer, and before I could react, her arms wrapped around me from behind.

It was awkward—the kind of hug only an inexperienced teenager could give. Her arms wrapped around me with all the finesse of someone unsure of their own strength, too tight in places, too hesitant in others. It wasn't smooth or graceful, but it clung with a kind of desperate urgency. A need to be close, to hold on, even if she didn't know how.

She wasn't holding me gently. It wasn't tender. It wasn't affection. She was holding me like she was trying to anchor me down, like she was trying to keep me from floating away. I could feel her body pressed against my back, her warmth seeping through the thin fabric of my shirt.

I felt it then—her grip tightening around me, firm and unyielding. It wasn't just a hug; it was a declaration. A silent refusal to let go. Her strength radiated from every trembling muscle, and beneath it, a raw determination that made my skin crawl.

I hated it.

I hated it because it was everything I wasn't. She was still standing. She was still here, still fighting, still holding on to something that didn't make any fucking sense to me. It irritated me more than I could put into words.

I wanted to pull away. I wanted to get out of her grasp. But my body froze, paralyzed by the realization that I couldn't escape. I couldn't escape her.

Not now, not ever.

"I'm not going anywhere."

I spun around, breaking out of her hold, and grabbed her by the shoulders. My grip was tight, grounding, and my eyes locked onto hers, sharp and demanding. For a second, I didn't know if I wanted to consume her or destroy her. The air between us felt thick, almost suffocating. It was so close now—so close that it burned in a way that had nothing to do with desire. It was heat. It was anger. It was a mess of every emotion I couldn't control anymore.

I could have devoured her in an instant, taken everything from her, ripped her apart in ways I don't even want to admit to myself.

"Don't you understand?" My voice cracks, raw and hoarse, a mix of frustration and something darker, something I can't name. "If you stay here, I'll break you!"

But she doesn't move.

She doesn't flinch.

Her eyes don't dart away—they stay fixed, unwavering. Not defiant, not resigned. Just... steady. The silence between us stretches out, weighted, pressing in from all sides. And then it hits me—not loud or sudden, but slow and cold, like ice cracking down my spine.

There's no sign of retreat, no pleading, no fight. She sits there, unshaken, as if she's already accepted everything I'm about to do. As if she knows how this ends, knows exactly what I'm capable of. And that realization cuts through me deeper than anything else. She's showing me her true self now. Not the girl who mocked me, not the girl who pushed me away.

This is who she really is.

I feel my heart hammering in my chest, but it's not the rush of excitement I thought it would be. It's anticipation. It's fear.

I hate how much of me is already lost in this moment, how much she has already taken from me just by being here.

Then she speaks, her voice low, almost too soft to hear, and it sends a shiver down my spine:

"That's *exactly* what I want you to do."

Her words hang in the air, heavy, suffocating. And for the briefest moment, everything inside me stops. I freeze.

The weight of her words hit me hard, like a wave crashing over me, pulling me under. I've wanted this. I've wanted her. In ways I can't explain. But hearing her say it—hearing her ask for it—shatters everything I thought I knew. She's not afraid of me. She wants me to do this. She wants me to break her.

I feel hot—too hot. It's like a switch was flipped inside me. The door I'd kept sealed for so long blasted open, and every restraint was gone. My chest burned as I surged forward, pushing her back onto the bed. Her arms came up instinctively, but I caught them, dragging them above her head and pinning them there with one hand. The other settled along the side of her neck, not quite gentle, not quite threatening—just there. My breath came fast, my vision blurred at the edges, and all I could hear was the blood rushing in my ears. Her eyes locked on mine, lips barely parting as she tilted her head toward me, breath hot against my skin.

"Make it hurt," she whispers.

I'm not sure I even register the words. They don't feel like a request; they feel like a command. Like an invitation into something darker, something I don't know how to handle. My hand trails down from her neck to her chest, grazing the fabric of her dress, then further to her hips, anchoring her.

I can't remember what I expected this to feel like, but it's nothing like I thought. The first kiss is rough, too much teeth, too little air, but it's needed. It's like a release, like all the tension that's been building between us finally snaps. I don't know who moves first—her or me—but it doesn't matter. Her body is against mine, and my hands are everywhere, desperate for something I don't fully understand.

I released her wrists, my fingers brushing down her arms as I sat up just enough to strip off my shirt, the fabric clinging to my skin for a moment before falling away. She didn't move. Her hands remained where I'd left them—above her head, resting obediently against the mattress. Her chest rose and fell, shallow breaths marking the tension in the room. Her skin was warm beneath my touch, trembling with something I couldn't quite place. Her eyes searched mine, flickering with a frantic need—but something else lingered there too. Something darker. Something I didn't want to name.

She wanted this. She wanted it all.

I pushed forward, her body melting against mine as my fingers dug into her skin. Somewhere between the tangle of limbs and gasped breaths, her dress ended up bunched around her waist, then gone altogether. My pants followed, discarded in haste. There was no gentleness in the way I moved, but it wasn't about that. Not right now. Right now, it was all about feeling her—every inch of her—as if it were the only thing that existed in the world. The pressure of her hips against mine, the soft gasp that escaped her lips, the way she tugged at me like she was trying to pull me deeper.

It was rougher than I expected, but it felt too good to stop. Her arms wrapped around me, nails digging into my back, dragging along my skin with every thrust. She clung to me, matching my rhythm, pushing against me with just as much urgency. There was no gentleness. Just a frantic need to consume, to lose myself in her, to feel her react, to hear her voice break.

But underneath it, underneath all of this, there was something more—a need I couldn't name. A hunger that felt like it would never be sated. I couldn't stop. I didn't want to.

Her breath quickened, matching mine, and her legs tightened around my waist as she pulled me deeper, harder. I couldn't think. There was only the heat, the sweat, the frantic pace of our bodies as we crashed against each other, both of us too desperate for something we didn't fully understand.

When it ended, it was with a crash, a release that left me gasping for air, her name slipping from my mouth like a prayer, but it wasn't enough. It was never enough.

We lay there, tangled together, but I couldn't look at her. My chest felt too tight. I wanted to say something, but there was nothing left to say. The room was too small, too hot. It felt like everything was closing in.

And yet, I didn't move away. I didn't want to.

I didn't want to remember the rest of the night. I didn't want to think about it, but it was there—flashes of her beneath me, the pressure of her skin against mine, the taste of liquor still bitter on my tongue, the mix of rage and lust pushing me forward, again and again.

I had never been so lost in anything in my life.

It wasn't about love. It wasn't about anything but wanting to make her feel the same darkness that had been eating at me for years. To have her experience the chaos I'd lived with. To rip apart whatever she thought she knew about herself.

It was all a blur, a haze, but it felt like drowning. Like I was suffocating, and she was the one pulling me under.

When I finally stumbled out of bed—somewhere around five in the morning, I think—she stopped me. Her voice was calm, too calm. It shouldn't have been that calm.

"You'll be back to see me next week. Alright?"

I turned to look at her. She was still in that same position, blankets pooling around her body, pale and covered in sweat, her hair messy and sticky against her forehead, yet that same unwavering calm about her, a regalness that couldn't be hidden. The way she said it made my stomach twist. Like she already knew. Like she had been waiting for me to break. Waiting for me to come back.

"Not a chance," I snapped, but my words felt hollow. There was no strength in them.

She didn't flinch. Didn't seem hurt. Instead, she smiled—one of those smiles that was almost too sweet, like it held some secret I would never understand. A smile that was too fucking familiar. And I felt a knot form in my chest.

I should have walked away. I should have left. But there was something in her eyes, something that made my feet feel like they were stuck in wet cement.

I wasn't the one in control here.

As I closed the door behind me and headed for the elevator, the cigarette burning between my fingers, the feeling didn't go away. It lingered, gnawing at me.

She had won.

I didn't know how or when, but she had. Somehow, she always had me.

And the worst part was, I didn't even know what to do about it.

I wondered if she knew. I wondered if she already had me in the palm of her hand, even before that night.

I wasn't the one who had the power there. I realized that I never was.

~ 14 ~

CHAPTER FOURTEEN

Guilty Thorns

The apartment greeted me with silence, a vacuum that swallowed even the smallest sound. The door clicked shut behind me, the latch settling with a finality that felt heavier than it should have. I paused there, hand lingering on the knob, as if the weight on my chest might ease if I stood still long enough. It didn't.

I let the door go and walked further in, my keys clinking faintly as I dropped them on the counter. They felt like they should've made more noise, something sharp and accusatory, but the room stayed quiet. My jacket slipped from my shoulders, landing in a heap on the back of the couch. I didn't bother fixing it.

Her name came to me in a whisper. Emily. She always came first, her face soft and warm in the corners of my mind. I thought of her as she was that first night, sitting across the table with that small, patient smile, one hand lightly tracing the rim of her glass. Her eyes had sparkled when I said something clever—what had it even been? I couldn't remember. All I remembered was how she looked at me, like I was someone worth her time.

The thought twisted uncomfortably in my chest, the guilt coiling tighter. What did she see in me? I'd asked myself that before, but the question never felt fully answered. Not by her laugh, or the way she rested her head on my shoulder when we watched TV, or even the quiet, steady way she said my name. She was better than I deserved, but instead of gratitude, all I could feel now was this creeping ache, sharp and dull in turns.

I dropped onto the couch, hands on my knees, fingers twitching like they wanted something to do but didn't know what. Her face faded, and another one replaced it. Sharper. Louder. The girl didn't haunt me the way Emily did. She invaded, her image cutting into my thoughts with a precision that left no room for anything else. Her voice echoed, teasing and sharp, but in a way that felt deliberate, calculated even. She always knew exactly where to aim.

I let out a shaky breath and reached into my pocket, my fingers curling around the crumpled pack of cigarettes I'd picked up earlier. I'd told myself I was done with this habit, but that felt like a lie now, as easy to break as every other promise I'd made to myself. The pack felt rough in my hands as I pulled one out, the lighter flaring to life in my other hand.

The first drag burned, a reminder of the vice I thought I'd left behind. Smoke curled upward, twisting into shapes I didn't bother to follow. Emily hated when I smoked. She'd wrinkle her nose and say something about my lungs, her voice light but with an edge of genuine concern. I could already picture the look she'd give me when she smelled it on me again.

She would forgive me. She always forgave me. For this? I wasn't so sure.

I stared at the cigarette, the ember glowing brighter with each inhale. What was I doing? Why had I done it? Why had I gone to the girl, let her voice pull me back in like she always did? The question itched at the back of my mind, one I didn't have the nerve to answer.

She hadn't offered me anything real. I was sure her words were rehearsed, a way to entice me to come back. I knew it was wrong. Yet I stayed.

Why?

The cigarette dangled between my fingers as I leaned back, staring at the ceiling. The weight in my chest pressed harder, making it difficult to breathe. I thought of Emily again, her voice soft and steady in my head. She didn't deserve this. She deserved someone who would've gone home, someone who didn't feel like they were being pulled in two directions at once.

But even as I thought of her, the girl's voice intruded again, louder this time, demanding attention. I hated it. Hated that I could still hear her, that her words lingered long after she was gone. But maybe I hated myself more—for not regretting the time I'd spent with her.

I sighed, the sound heavy in the quiet room. The cigarette had burned down to the filter, the only one resting in the ashtray—a lone, neglected reminder that I hadn't touched the habit in a while. I crushed it, the faint sizzle breaking the silence. The smoke still hung in the air, a ghost of the moment I couldn't undo.

Emily's face came back to me, her eyes bright with that warmth she never failed to show. What did she see in me? I couldn't make sense of it. And if I couldn't, how could I expect her to?

The girl's face flashed next, her expression colder, more guarded. Why had I entertained her? Why had I let her take up space in my mind and my time, knowing she would leave nothing but splinters behind? And why—why hadn't I walked away when I could have?

My jaw tightened, the questions circling without answers. I leaned forward, elbows on my knees, my head in my hands. My pulse felt uneven, matching the erratic rhythm of my thoughts. Emily was everything I should want, everything I should hold onto. The girl? She was a mistake I couldn't stop making.

But deep down, in a part of me I couldn't admit to, I knew the truth.

I didn't regret going to her. Not the way I should.

I knew it was a mistake I'd make again.

The next day passed in a blur, the hours stretching longer than they should have. I didn't go to work, and I didn't have the energy to pretend that I cared about anything other than the chaos in my head. I sat on the couch, my mind running through everything—Emily, the girl, the mess I had made. The guilt gnawed at me like a rat in a cage, clawing and scratching at my insides.

I'd been down this path before, after making mistakes, after doing something I shouldn't. The guilt always felt the same—cold, heavy, suffocating. But this time, it was different. This time, I could taste the consequences even before they hit me. I could feel the weight of them, the pressure of having everything on the verge of crumbling.

I watched my phone buzz with Emily's calls, and for a moment, I almost reached for it. Almost. But I didn't. The idea of hearing her voice—hearing her ask me why I was avoiding her, why I was so distant—felt like it would unravel me completely. So, I let the calls go unanswered. I let the silence pile up between us, each missed call another brick in a wall I was building between us, even if I didn't want to.

When the doorbell rang the next day, I almost didn't answer. The apartment was a mess, my thoughts more so. But Emily wasn't someone who took a hint. And I knew, deep down, that she would show up anyway, even if I ignored her.

Her knock came soft at first, a hesitant tap on the door, followed by a louder, firmer rap, as though she was trying to force her way through my defenses.

I sighed, rubbing my face with my hand. I couldn't hide from her forever.

When I opened the door, she didn't hesitate. Her eyes were tired, shadowed with concern, but she stepped inside without waiting for an invitation.

"You weren't answering," she said, her voice soft but insistent. "I've been calling."

I could already feel the weight of her gaze, tracking every little detail of me—the way I was standing, the way I wouldn't meet her eyes. She always noticed these things, always read me like an open book, even when I tried to close the cover.

"I was busy," I muttered, avoiding her stare, my eyes dropping to the floor.

Her eyes darted to the table, and I knew what she was seeing before she even said anything. The ashtray, the half-burned cigarette still sitting there, the lingering smell of smoke in the air.

She wrinkled her nose, a soft wrinkle of disapproval. "You're smoking again?"

I didn't feel like defending myself, didn't feel like justifying it. So, I shrugged, letting my shoulders slump. "Just a little. It's nothing."

The words felt hollow, even to me.

Her gaze softened, but the disappointment still lingered in her eyes. "It's not nothing," she said quietly. She didn't press, though.

Instead, she moved past me, her presence a quiet reassurance as she settled on the couch next to me.

Her warmth, the way she filled the space around me with something gentle, was the only thing keeping me from spiraling into my own head. But even that felt like a reminder of how far away I was from her, how much I was hiding.

She sat quietly for a moment, her hand resting at her side. I could feel the tension in the air, thick like the smoke still lingering. She was waiting for me to speak, but I didn't know what to say.

Finally, she broke the silence, her voice softer than before. "Are you okay?"

I felt it then, the way her voice seemed to slip into me, like she was reaching in, trying to find something, something real. It made my chest tighten, and for a moment, I thought I might actually crack under the weight of it.

"I'm fine," I said, the words dragging out slowly, heavy on my tongue. It sounded like a lie because it was, tired and limp, but I couldn't bring myself to offer anything else. It was easier than admitting the truth.

She didn't believe it, of course. Why would she? She tilted her head, watching me closely, her eyes soft with concern but sharp in their search.

"You don't seem fine," she said, the quiet accusation hanging between us.

I snapped, the words coming out harsher than I intended. "I said I'm fine."

Her eyes widened, and I saw the hurt flicker in them for just a moment. But instead of pulling away or getting angry, she just watched me, her gaze searching, as if she were trying to find the pieces of me that I had buried.

The way she looked at me made something stir in my chest, but it was a feeling I couldn't quite place, not entirely. It was guilt, yes, but also frustration—frustration at how much she could see of me without me ever showing her. The fact she could get past my barriers as easily as *she* did.

She sighed, her shoulders sagging slightly, and dropped the subject without a fight. But I could feel the tension still hanging there, thick like smoke.

The silence between us grew, but it wasn't comfortable. It wasn't peaceful. I couldn't breathe right, couldn't shake the feeling that I was suffocating, that I was falling apart in front of her and she wasn't even sure if she could save me.

She shifted next to me, her legs crossing beneath her. "Okay," she said, her voice softer now. "If you don't want to talk, I'll drop it for now."

It didn't matter that she'd let it go. The weight of her eyes was still on me, still reading the cracks in my armor.

After a beat, she looked at me again, but this time her expression shifted, like she was trying to focus on something else. "So... the deal with that man. Is it working out?"

The mention of the deal brought everything back, sharp and clear. The girl's voice, her eyes, the way I couldn't stop thinking about her even now, even after everything. I glanced away, my throat tightening.

"It's... almost worked out," I said, my voice low. The lie felt like a stone in my stomach. "I'm meeting with him again next week."

The words hung between us, and I could feel the heaviness of them pressing down on me. I wondered why I lied, why I kept telling these half-truths. Why was I even contemplating going back, when it made me feel like this?

But still, I lied.

Emily was quiet for a moment, her eyes studying me closely, as though she could see through the mask I wore. She didn't question it. Instead, she just nodded, but I could see the way her lips pressed together, the way her jaw clenched just slightly. She wasn't buying it, but she wasn't going to push either.

The silence that followed was deafening. I wanted to say something, anything, but the words didn't come. I sat there, the guilt still gnawing at me, and wondered how long I could keep this up before it all fell apart.

But I didn't say a word.

It was strange, the way everything seemed clearer now, when it was already too late. Only after I'd made the mistake did I see how much Emily had come to mean to me. Before, I took it all for granted—her presence, her patience, her quiet way of holding me together when I was falling apart. She was like the steady rhythm of a song that I barely even noticed until the melody stopped. I hadn't realized how much I needed her—how much I relied on her—until I'd already started tearing everything down. The realization was like a jolt to the chest, a shockwave rippling through my mind, but it was all too late to fix. I'd already destroyed it.

It was almost cruel, the timing of it. The clarity that came after the fall. The idea that you can only truly see what you had once it's gone—it was something I had always read about, heard people talk about in half-hearted clichés, but I never truly understood it until now. How was it that I couldn't appreciate her until I'd already ruined what we had? How could I have been so blind?

It wasn't the act itself that haunted me—it was what came after. Only when she began to slip from my life did I finally see how much she'd meant to me, how deeply she'd embedded herself into the spaces I didn't even know were empty. The irony was cruel: I didn't realize what I had until I'd already broken it. Now, all that remained was the fallout, and the hollow ache of knowing I couldn't take it back.

~ 15 ~

CHAPTER FIFTEEN

Frayed Edges

The air hung thick, heavy with everything I couldn't say. She'd left only minutes ago, yet the echo of her words lingered like smoke, clinging to my thoughts no matter how hard I tried to push it away. I stood at the window, watching her silhouette disappear into the night.

Emily's call came an hour later, her name lighting up my phone screen. The sight of it sent a jolt through me—a tug of obligation mixed with something darker. My thumb hovered over the green button, but instead, I pressed decline.

She was probably waiting for an explanation. She always waited, like it was her job to pick up my pieces. And me? I let her wait. Let her hope. It wasn't fair to her. Or to me.

The thought made me reach for a cigarette. The lighter sputtered on the first flick before catching, and I inhaled deeply, trying to ground myself. It didn't help. The quiet hum of the city outside only amplified the storm in my chest.

I replayed the night in fragments—her voice, her gaze, the way she didn't look back when she walked out. *Did she know?*

No. She couldn't.

Emily didn't know about her. About last night. About anything.

Or did she?

I swallowed hard, my throat tight against the possibility. Emily was too perceptive for her own good. The thought of her piecing together the lies, noticing the cracks in my excuses—it made my skin crawl.

The phone buzzed again. This time, a text:

"You sure you're okay?"

The words felt like a test. I stared at them, willing them to mean something less, something simpler. But they didn't.

I texted back: **"Yeah. I'll call you tomorrow."**

Her response was immediate: **"Don't forget. I miss you."**

I miss you.

I exhaled sharply, the cigarette burning low between my fingers. Her words hit harder than they should have. Not because I believed them, but because I wasn't sure I deserved them anymore.

The place was dimly lit, all red lights and velvet curtains that gave it the illusion of exclusivity. Music played softly in the background, a beat slow enough to match the languid, practice movements of the women weaving between tables.

She spotted me the second I stepped through the door, clad in the same alluring black dress as last time. For a second I wondered if that was the only one she had. Her smile flickered, hesitant at first upon spotting me, but it settled into something that felt too polished, too rehearsed.

"You're back," she said, striding toward me with the kind of confidence that only barely concealed uncertainty. "Good. For a bit I thought you wouldn't come back."

"Neither did I."

She stopped just short of touching me, her head tilting slightly as she studied me. Her lips quirked up into a teasing grin, the same one I remembered form high school, though now it carried an edge—like a knife sharpened to a point. "Sit tight. I'll grab us something to drink," she said before disappearing into the crowd.

I watched her go, my jaw tight. She moved differently now—there was still that bounce in her step, but it was slower, as if weighed down by something I couldn't name.

I slid into a booth near the back, away from the main floor. The seat creaked under my weight, the faux leather sticky against my palms as I shuffled further in. The room hummed with low conversations, punctuated by the occasional burst of laughter, but it all felt muted—like the sound couldn't quite reach me.

My gaze tracked her as she crossed the room, weaving effortlessly between the other hostesses and their clients. She didn't look back, not once, but I knew she was aware of my eyes on her. She always was.

When she returned, she was carrying two glasses of something dark and amber, the ice cubes clinking softly with every step. She set them down on the table and slid into the seat across from me, her movements fluid but deliberate.

"You're lucky it's a slow night," she said, pushing one of the glasses toward me. "If it wasn't, my boss wouldn't be so happy about me spending all this time with you."

"It's your job to spend time with me," I said, the bite in my voice surprising even me.

She smirked, taking a sip of her drink. "That may be so, but maybe I also want to."

I didn't respond. My eyes dropped to the rim of my glass, the faint trace of her lipstick lingering there.

"Why did you come back?" she asked, breaking the silence. Her tone was light, almost casual, but her eyes told a different story—sharp, probing, like she was trying to read something I wasn't saying.

"I don't know," I admitted after a moment. The answer felt inadequate, even to me, but it was the truth.

"Hmm." She leaned back, swirling the drink in her glass. "Well, whatever the reason, I'm glad you did."

Her voice was warm, her smile almost genuine, but there was an undercurrent to her words—a subtle weight that I couldn't quite place.

The conversation drifted into safer territory after that. She teased me about the way I was holding my drink—"You look like you've never had whiskey before," she said with a laugh—and I shot back a half-hearted retort. But even as the banter continued, I couldn't shake the tension coiling in my chest.

I studied her as she talked, letting her words wash over me without really hearing them. Her smile still had that same spark, that playful edge I remembered from years ago, but now it felt like a mask—something she wore for the benefit of everyone else.

Would she be happier if things had gone differently? If I hadn't... if we hadn't...

The thought burrowed into my mind, unwelcome and relentless.

"Earth to you," she said, snapping her fingers in front of my face. "Where'd you go just now?"

"Nowhere," I said quickly, shaking my head.

"Liar," she said, her smile softening. "But that's okay. You don't have to tell me."

Her understanding felt too generous, too forgiving.

By the time the bar was closing, the tension between us had shifted—less sharp, but no less present. She stood, gathering her things with practiced ease, and glanced over her shoulder at me.

"You coming, or are you just going to sit there all night?" she asked.

I hesitated for a moment before following her out into the cool night air.

We walked in silence, the sound of our footsteps echoing against the empty street. I shoved my hands into my pockets, my head down, while she walked a few paces ahead, her shoulders relaxed like she didn't have a care in the world.

When we reached the hotel, she stopped just outside the door, turning to face me.

"You really didn't have to come back, you know," she said quietly.

I looked at her, really looked at her, and for the first time that night, I thought I saw something real—a flicker of relief, of vulnerability, quickly buried beneath her usual smirk.

"Like I said, I almost didn't," I said, my voice barely above a whisper.

She tilted her head, watching me, and for a moment, I thought I saw the edges of a smile, but it wasn't the teasing grin I remembered. It was something else—a quiet, knowing sort of smile, the kind you give someone when you understand their struggle more than they think.

"Well, like I said, I'm glad you did," she said after a beat, her voice low but steady, like she was trying to convince herself as much as me. She stepped closer, her presence almost overwhelming, her scent clinging to the air between us. The tension between us tightened, like a wire being pulled just a little too taut.

"Yeah?" I asked, unable to keep the skepticism out of my voice.

She didn't answer at first. Instead, she reached out and touched my arm, the motion casual but deliberate. It wasn't the touch of someone who had no claim on me—it was a reminder of what we were, of what we'd been. Her fingers lingered, just enough to leave an imprint, then slid away, as if she'd tested the waters, unsure whether she wanted to pull back or dive in deeper.

"I needed you to come back," she said quietly, looking up at me with those eyes of hers, deep and unreadable. There was something in her gaze, something I couldn't quite place—a quiet plea, masked by a confidence she wore like armor.

I swallowed, feeling that same familiar knot tighten in my chest. It wasn't just her words; it was the way she said them, like they meant something more than what was on the surface. "I didn't think you needed anyone," I muttered, almost to myself.

Her lips twitched, like she was suppressing a laugh, but there was no humor in her eyes. Instead, there was something sharper, darker, a glint that reminded me of a knife's edge.

"Maybe I don't," she said, stepping forward until there was barely any space between us. "But I need something. And you—well, you're good at giving me what I need, whether you want to or not."

There it was. That feeling, that subtle shift in the air—the familiar taste of her darkness, thinly veiled beneath her soft tone. She was trying to lure me in, as always. But this time, I wasn't sure if I wanted to fight it.

The silence stretched between us, heavy and thick. I felt the pull—the desire to let go, to forget everything and just be here, in this moment. But I couldn't. Not this time.

"Let's go inside," she said, her voice softening just enough to sound almost inviting. She turned, gliding toward the door like she knew I would follow, and without thinking, I did.

The air between us was thick, heavy with the remnants of what had just happened. My body still buzzed with the intensity of it all—the way her skin felt against mine, the press of her lips, the urgency of it all. It was messy, tangled in a way that left me breathless.

I pulled away first, retreating just enough to catch my breath. My chest heaved, and I could feel the sweat on my skin, the sticky reminder of what had transpired. She sat back against the bed, her chest rising and falling in sync with mine, her gaze distant for just a moment before she looked at me. It wasn't the same playful gaze as before, or the teasing one from earlier. There was something else in her eyes—something softer, more uncertain.

I needed a cigarette.

I reached into my pocket for the pack, pulling one out with shaking fingers. The lighter flicked to life, the flame burning too brightly in the dim room. I inhaled deeply, the smoke filling my lungs, grounding me in something more real than the haze of our interaction. The taste of nicotine settled in my mouth, a bitter contrast to the sweetness of the moment we'd just shared.

"Do you ever just... need to feel something?" Her voice broke the silence, soft and almost fragile.

I took another drag, exhaling slowly. "I think I've been feeling like that for years."

She shifted beside me, pulling her knees to her chest, her eyes never leaving me. "You're different than I thought," she said, her tone laced with a quiet curiosity. "Last time, you... you were angry. But now, it's like there's something else."

I didn't know how to respond to that. I wasn't sure what had changed. I had come here thinking it would be the same, thinking I could just walk away again, forget about it. But now, with her sitting beside me, the scent of sex still clinging to the air, I realized I didn't know what I wanted.

I took another long drag of the cigarette, my fingers trembling slightly as I held it between them. "Maybe I'm not the same as I was," I muttered. It wasn't something I was proud of. It wasn't something I wanted to admit. But it felt true. The last time I'd been here, I was filled with a mix of rage and confusion, but now? I didn't know what this was. I didn't know what she was.

She studied me for a long moment, her expression unreadable. I could feel her pulling at me, trying to peel back layers I wasn't ready to expose. She always had a way of getting under my skin, of making me feel like I was an open book even when I thought I was hiding it all.

"You know," she said, leaning back against the pillows, her fingers absently tracing the edge of the sheets, "I never thought I'd see you again. Not like this."

I met her gaze, my own words caught in my throat. I couldn't say anything that would make sense. "What do you want me to say?" I asked, the bitterness seeping into my voice without meaning to.

She didn't flinch. Instead, she smiled softly, like she understood something I couldn't quite grasp. "Nothing. I don't want anything from you."

Her words hung in the air, and I wasn't sure what to do with them. I had expected something different. Maybe I was still trying to figure out what I wanted from her, what this was. But that wasn't what she was giving me.

I took another drag, letting the smoke swirl in the air before I exhaled slowly. "You've been doing this for a while, haven't you?"

Her eyes flickered to me, but she didn't say anything at first. She seemed to weigh the question, like it was something she didn't want to answer. When she finally spoke, her voice was quiet, almost detached. "Yeah. A long time. But it's not about that anymore. It never was."

I could feel the weight of her words, even if I didn't fully understand them. "What is it about then?"

She looked away for a moment, almost like she was searching for something in the shadows of the room. "I don't know," she murmured, her voice barely audible. "Maybe it's about finding someone who... understands. Someone who doesn't ask questions."

I didn't know what to say to that. I wasn't sure if she meant it, or if it was just another layer of armor, something she used to keep people at a distance. I wasn't sure where I fit into any of it.

I took another drag of my cigarette, my eyes lingering on her as she shifted on the bed, her body still warm from our time together. There was something about her, something I couldn't quite put into words. Maybe I was just as lost as she was. Maybe we were both just looking for a way to fill the space between us, the emptiness that we couldn't ignore.

"I didn't think I'd come back," I said after a long pause, my voice rough. "But here I am."

Her lips curled up in a soft, almost wistful smile. "Yeah. Here you are."

I couldn't explain it. I couldn't explain why I'd come back, why I kept coming back. It wasn't about the sex. It wasn't about the anger or the guilt or anything else. It was something else entirely. Something that made my skin itch with confusion.

She shifted again, this time moving closer, her fingers lightly brushing against my hand. It was a small thing, but it felt like everything. Like she was letting me in, just a little. And maybe that was the scariest part of all.

~ 16 ~

CHAPTER SIXTEEN

Fiction

I stumbled through the front door, my body heavy with the weight of the night. The smell of whiskey, cigarettes, and sex was still thick on my skin, and it hit me the moment I stepped inside. I didn't want to feel it. I didn't want to think about what had happened, but the stench—familiar and suffocating—lingered, like it was written into the very fibers of my clothes.

And then I saw her.

Emily sat on the couch, waiting, her arms folded tightly across her chest. The way her eyes narrowed as soon as she saw me made it clear she'd been expecting me, though I hadn't said when I'd be back. She wasn't even looking at me like I was just the guy who came home late. No, this was something else. She was studying me. *Waiting for me to crack.*

I froze for a beat, then cleared my throat. "What are you doing here?" I asked, my voice rougher than I intended. "How did you get in?"

She didn't flinch. She didn't move. "You gave me a spare key, remember?" Her voice was steady, but there was an edge beneath it. One that cut deeper than I wanted to admit.

When did I give her a key? The thought hit me like a hammer, and for a moment, I couldn't answer. I couldn't remember. But I nodded, trying to sound casual. "Right, of course."

She looked at me like she knew I was lying, and something in me twisted. She was too sharp. *She always was.*

"Your smell," she said, wrinkling her nose. "It's... strong. You've been drinking, haven't you? And you smell like—" She hesitated, looking at me like she was waiting for the rest of the story to spill out, but I couldn't let it. Not this time.

I shrugged it off, trying to focus on keeping my composure. "I was out with a client," I said, the words coming quickly, slipping out before I could second-guess them. "You know how it is, one of those late-night meetings. I didn't want to wake you up, so I just went straight from there to here."

She stared at me for a moment, clearly not satisfied. Her gaze moved over me—over the disheveled state I was in—and her lips tightened. She opened her mouth like she was about to say something, but then she just shook her head, like the words weren't worth it.

"Where?" Her voice was cold now, quiet, controlled. "Where did you go? Why didn't you call me?"

I could feel the weight of her questions pressing down on me, heavy and suffocating. I didn't want to lie to her. But I also didn't want to tell her the truth. I couldn't. Not now.

"I told you, I was with that client," I repeated, more firmly this time. "You know he likes to meet at a hostess bar. He insisted on it this time, said it was the only place he could *really* talk. And I still feel guilty about even being in a place like that, you know?"

The words hung in the air, hanging on the lie I was telling her, but it was the only thing I could say that wouldn't make her ask questions I didn't want to answer. It was *technically* true. It wasn't a complete lie. Not really.

She narrowed her eyes at me, but there was a hesitation there. She wanted to believe me. I could see it. The doubt was there, but she was clinging to the hope that I was still the guy she trusted. The guy who came home at the end of the day.

But then her face softened. And that softness—the way she let herself *feel* in front of me—was the thing that made me want to pull away. She *wanted* something from me, and I wasn't sure what it was. I wasn't sure if I could give it.

Her voice wavered slightly when she spoke again, quieter now. "Why are you so cold with me? I can't keep doing this if you keep shutting me out."

I felt something stir inside me at her words. Guilt. But also something darker, a flicker of something I wasn't ready to acknowledge.

"Emily..." I trailed off, unsure of what to say. She was right. She had every right to question me, to feel hurt. But there was so much I wasn't telling her, so much I couldn't. And the guilt only made it worse.

Before I could think better of it, I stepped forward and pulled her into my arms. It wasn't a natural gesture, but it felt like the only thing I could do in that moment. She stiffened at first, but then her body softened against mine, and I felt her tremble as she exhaled, like she'd been holding it all in.

She sniffled, and I felt a stab of something sharp inside me, something like regret. "Why do you always lie?" she asked, her voice muffled against my chest. "Why do you always keep me in the dark?"

I swallowed hard. "I don't want to hurt you," I muttered, though I wasn't sure I believed it. "I just... I just didn't want you to worry. You wouldn't understand."

She pulled back slightly, her eyes filled with unshed tears. "What do you mean, 'I wouldn't understand'? I'm trying, okay? But you won't let me."

Her words were like knives, each one finding its mark. I wanted to tell her everything. To confess—to say that I'd just spent the night with another woman, that I'd been chasing something I couldn't have, that I was falling apart inside. But I couldn't. I couldn't say it, not like this.

"I'm sorry," I said, the words heavy on my tongue. "I didn't mean to hurt you. I swear I didn't."

She looked at me for a long moment, and then, finally, she sighed. "I just want you to be honest with me," she whispered. "I can't keep doing this if you keep lying."

I nodded slowly, guilt swirling through me. "I will. I'll talk to you. I'm sorry."

The silence between us felt suffocating, and I could feel the distance between us widening. But I didn't know how to close it. Not yet. Not when the truth was something I couldn't bring myself to say. I swallowed back the guilt, and simply pulled Emily to the couch next to me. She didn't resist, though there was something in her eyes—something that still wasn't satisfied, still wasn't sure of me. But she let me lead her, let me sit her beside me, and for a moment, the weight of everything felt a little lighter.

"Here," I said, the words feeling strange as I said them. "We can go out and do something, just the two of us. I'll even call out of work tomorrow for it. A whole day, just you and I."

I watched her closely, trying to gauge her reaction. Was she buying it? Or was she still waiting for something more from me? Something *real*. The idea of taking her out, making a day of it—something so normal, so clean—felt so far from the mess I was wrapped in. But maybe that's exactly what she needed. And maybe I needed it, too, though I couldn't quite admit that to myself.

She blinked, her expression softening just a fraction, but there was still a subtle hesitation in her eyes. "You're sure?" she asked quietly, her voice sounding unsure. "After everything tonight... you really want to spend all day with me?"

I nodded quickly, too quickly, trying to mask the nervousness crawling through me. "Yeah. Of course. It'll be good for us, you know? We don't need to worry about anything else for a while. Just... forget about everything else."

The words slipped out before I could stop them, and a part of me flinched at the irony. Forget about everything else. If only it were that simple.

She didn't say anything for a moment. Instead, she leaned against me, her head resting on my shoulder, and I could feel the weight of her sigh against my skin. It wasn't a relieved sigh, though. It was something else. Something heavier, something she was still holding inside.

"I want to believe you," she murmured, her voice barely above a whisper. "But sometimes, I don't know if you're even here with me. Not really."

I could feel my chest tighten, and my hand instinctively reached up to rest on her arm, as though I could pull her closer, as though

I could fix whatever was broken between us with the mere gesture. But I knew it wouldn't be that simple.

"I'm here, Emily," I said, trying to make the words sound convincing, trying to make her believe it. "I am. I'll prove it to you. I'll show you that I'm still here. Just trust me."

She turned her face up toward mine, her eyes searching, looking for something. I couldn't give her everything she wanted. Not yet. Maybe never. But I could give her this: a promise to spend the day with her, to give her a part of me she could hold onto, even if it was just for a few hours.

"I'll try," she said softly, but I could hear the uncertainty in her voice, like she wasn't entirely sure she should believe me. She wasn't entirely sure she could. But she wanted to. And that made something twist inside me, deep and aching, like I was holding onto something I wasn't ready to let go of.

"That's all I can ask for," I whispered, my voice rough, though I didn't know why. "Let's just... try to be us for a little while. Just us."

And in that moment, as she leaned back against me, her warmth spreading through my chest, I couldn't shake the feeling that whatever came next, I might be losing her before I even knew what I had with her.

I excused myself, muttering something about needing a shower. Emily gave me a nod, still distracted by whatever thoughts were swirling around in her mind, and I took the opportunity to slip away.

The water was hot, almost scalding, but I let it pour over me, letting the steam fill the small bathroom. It gave me a brief, almost temporary feeling of relief, but it didn't last long. My thoughts began to spiral, the edges of my mind racing, gnawing at me relentlessly.

I let my hands brace against the tiles, leaning into the water as I let my mind roam. Emily. The girl. The mess I had made of everything. How could I even look at Emily the way I did after everything? The girl had come back into my life—into *our* lives—and I could feel her presence everywhere. It was suffocating, and I hated it. I cursed her name in my mind. She had no right to come back, to ruin the fragile balance I'd built with Emily, to make me question everything.

Why did I even keep going back to her? What was it about her that drew me in so much? My body responded to her every time, but my mind—my mind *revolted* against the idea of needing her, of keeping her in my life. I didn't have to do this. I didn't have to keep seeing her. I could just stop. I could cut her out. I could *focus* entirely on Emily, on what I was supposed to have with her. The lie I told her tonight could become the truth if I just kept my distance from the girl. If I just stopped playing this game, stopped being caught up in the twisted mess of everything.

I breathed in deeply, my chest tightening at the thought. The weight of it all. The clean, simple lie that could turn into a life. Emily was real. She was normal. She deserved better than this confusion, this chaos that I'd dragged her into without even meaning to. I could have something with her. I *should* have something with her. I could make this work. If I tried.

I reached out, running my hand over my face, the droplets sliding off my skin like my thoughts sliding through my mind—so fast, so frantic. But then—*her.*

I stopped, suddenly feeling the sharp edges of reality cut into me again. The girl. My chest tightened at the thought, and I felt a heavy weight settle over me. I couldn't.

I won't.

No matter what, I knew I couldn't let go of her, not completely. Not now. Maybe never. She was still a part of me, a part I couldn't erase.

The shower felt too hot. My skin was flushed, and it wasn't just from the steam. I shut off the water, stepping out with a heavy sigh. As I dressed, I caught my reflection in the mirror—familiar, but...different. The mess in my mind hadn't changed. And now, neither had my feelings.

When I walked back into the living room, Emily had gotten up, pacing a little with her arms crossed over her chest. She looked up when I came into view, her lips curving into a small, soft smile.

"Better?" she smirked. I nodded, though I didn't feel better. I let her drag me to bed. The next morning, after we had gotten dressed and had breakfast, I turned to her.

"Ready to get out of here?"

She grinned, and for a moment, I actually felt a flicker of something close to normality. Something clean. Just the two of us. A whole day to ourselves.

We spent the next few hours doing exactly that—shopping, laughing, passing through stores without really caring about anything. The weight of the past few days, the mess I'd made, started to lift. I kept telling myself that this could work. That maybe, just maybe, I could forget about everything else. Focus on Emily.

It was nice. She was nice. I could almost believe I could live in this lie, build something real with her, something uncomplicated.

But then we went to dinner.

We had been seated at a cozy corner table, the low lighting of the restaurant flickering in the soft glow around us. We were talking, the easy conversation flowing, when she appeared.

Her.

She walked in with another man—tall, broad-shouldered, laughing at something she said. They were too close, too intimate, their energy unmistakable. She had her hand on his arm, casually flirting with him, and my stomach dropped.

But then her gaze met mine, and time froze.

The world around me blurred for a moment. My mind screamed, jealousy flooding my veins, hot and sharp. Seeing her with him... *Him.* I clenched my jaw, my fingers curling into fists beneath the table, but I couldn't look away. What the hell was she doing? What was *he* to her?

She stopped mid-laugh, her eyes narrowing just slightly as they locked onto mine. The air between us changed, and I could feel the shift.

Emily noticed my sudden change in demeanor, her voice breaking through the tension. "Do you know her?" she asked, her tone curious.

I swallowed, a dry, bitter taste in my mouth. "No," I said, the word coming out with a lie I barely recognized. "I don't.'

The rest of dinner passed in a haze. I could feel the girl's eyes on me, burning, like she was daring me to admit something, anything. The jealousy I'd been fighting only grew stronger, gnawing at me.

When the meal ended, I excused myself, muttering something about needing to go to the bathroom. I needed a moment, a breath. A space to think, to breathe, to forget what I'd just seen.

I walked toward the small hallway leading to the restrooms, my head spinning. But before I could reach the door, I felt a presence behind me.

It was her.

She stepped in, her movements slow, deliberate, and locked the door behind her.

My heart skipped a beat as I turned to face her. “What the hell are you doing? And who the hell was he?” I hissed, but she only smiled, a knowing, mischievous grin curling her lips.

She took a step toward me, and before I could say anything else, she pressed herself against me, her arms circling around me in a hug.

My mind screamed at me to pull away, but I couldn’t move. I just stood there, frozen, the weight of it all pressing down on me.

“Aw, you’re jealous,” she whispered, her breath hot against my ear. “Don’t worry, he’s just a client.” I felt disgust ripple through me, as much as I didn’t want to admit it. “Who’s that girl you’re with?”

I stepped back slightly, my chest tightening. “She’s just... someone I’m seeing,” I muttered, the words feeling like ash in my mouth. “It’s nothing.”

Her smile faltered, her brow furrowing slightly. “You’re cheating?”

“I am,” I said, my voice flat, numb.

“With me?”

I nodded, though I felt the weight of the words—heavy, suffocating. “I am.”

Her grin returned, wider now, teasing. “I feel so special,” she cooed, her voice dripping with mock sweetness, and I couldn’t stand it.

I shoved past her, pushing the door open. The cool air hit my skin, and I exhaled sharply, trying to shake off the taste of her words.

Before I could walk away, I heard her voice again, quiet but insistent.

“I’ll see you later, right?”

I stopped in my tracks, my stomach turning. I paused, before turning back with a cold, sharp glance.

"Of course not."

And with that, I walked away, feeling the weight of everything I was losing pressing down on me harder than ever.

I walked back to the table, my mind spinning, trying to get my bearings. I couldn't stay in that bathroom. I couldn't be near her anymore. I had to get back to Emily. I had to act normal.

I returned to the table, forcing a smile that felt more like a grimace. Emily was still waiting, her expression soft but expectant. She smiled, and when I sat down, she leaned in, kissing me gently on the lips. But as soon as she pulled away, her brow furrowed, a flash of confusion in her eyes.

"Why do you smell like perfume?" she asked, her voice a mix of curiosity and suspicion.

I froze, my stomach lurching. The smell. The girl's perfume, faint but unmistakable, still lingered on me like a taint. I didn't want to think about it. I didn't want her to think about it. I didn't want to explain.

I took a breath, my mouth dry. "It's... nothing," I said, but even to me, it sounded too quick. Too defensive.

Emily pulled back, eyes narrowing just slightly, like she was trying to piece something together. The concern in her gaze deepened, a knot of hesitation growing between us. She was starting to pick up on something.

I tried to force a reassuring smile, but it felt like a mask. "It's probably yours. Must've rubbed off on me."

But Emily didn't buy it. She stared at me, her eyes piercing into mine. "I didn't wear any perfume tonight, though," she said, her voice quieter now, softer, but there was an edge of worry creeping in. "And it smells... the same as the one under all the whiskey, from last night."

Her words hit me like a cold slap. I felt exposed, cornered. She was too sharp, too perceptive. My throat tightened but I could feel the lie crawling up, ready to spill out. Before I could speak, *she* walked past us, waving with the tips of her fingers, a coy smile on her lips. Emily's voice cracked just slightly when she asked again. "Do you know her? That girl?"

My hesitation was too obvious. I could feel it.—my heart pounding, blood rushing in my ears. I wasn't ready for this. Not for her to see through the carefully constructed front. Not for her to call me out on the things I'd tried to hide.

But the truth... well, it was a twisted version of it, a truth wrapped in a lie. And I couldn't lie to her, not entirely. Not anymore.

I nodded. Slowly. "Yes," I said, my voice barely above a whisper. "She's a hostess at the bar."

I watched Emily's expression, how the tension in her face tightened as I spoke, her lips pressing together as she waited for the rest.

"She likes flirting with me when I'm with the client," I continued, the words coming easier now, but heavy with the weight of them. "There's nothing between us, though. Nothing. She cornered me in the bathroom, but I shoved her away and came back to you. Nothing happened."

I knew it sounded hollow. Empty, even though it was the truth—at least, the truth I could give her without breaking everything. The truth I could still live with.

Emily hesitated, looking at me for a moment, her expression torn. Then, she exhaled sharply, the tension in her shoulders dropping ever so slightly. She nodded slowly, though I saw the glimmer of hurt in her eyes.

"Okay..." she said quietly, the word hanging in the air. Then, her gaze flickered away, and her voice took on a different note, one that was soft but edged with something else. "I don't like it though."

It stung, even though I knew it wasn't a condemnation. It wasn't *yet* a full betrayal of trust. But it felt like one. Something shifted between us, a subtle crack starting to form in the veneer of what we were building. And I knew, deep down, it was only a matter of time before the whole thing shattered.

But in that moment, I stayed silent, the weight of her words pressing down on me, and the smell of the girl still clinging to my skin, refusing to let go.

Again, I silently cursed her. Why was she there? Why had she come back into my life, upending everything I had built with Emily? The girl, with her goddamn smile and that unsettling presence, had ruined the fragile calm I'd started to carve out for myself. I should have been able to move on. I should've been able to walk away and leave all of this behind. But no, she had to reappear, dragging me back into that mess I never fully understood.

I felt a bitter knot twist in my gut as I thought of her—of the way her eyes burned with that frightening intensity, the way she seemed to possess something I couldn't quite define. She was like an itch I couldn't scratch, always there, lurking under the surface, demanding attention. It didn't matter that I hated everything she represented. Every time I went back to her, it was like I was unraveling a little more.

And now Emily was starting to see through the cracks. The perfume. The hesitation. She knew something wasn't right. She wasn't blind, even if I wanted her to be.

I shook my head, willing the thoughts away, but they clung to me. *I'm just a client,* I told myself. *That's all it is.* I didn't want to think about how she might be more than that. I didn't want to think about how I kept going back to her. I certainly didn't want to acknowledge the simmering tension, the guilt, the desire that I couldn't explain.

I dragged my hands down my face, trying to reset. Trying to get back to Emily. Trying to forget the girl.

I plastered on a smile, imitating the one *she* had used all our lives, one practiced and fake, and I leaned into Emily. "I love you," I whispered, forcing the words through my clenched teeth. "Let's get out of here, shall we?"

Her eyes softened for a moment, like she wanted to believe me. It was all I could give her. The warmth in her smile—real, naive—was the last piece of the puzzle I had to hold onto. And I hated myself for it.

"I love you too."

I pulled away, trying to mask the guilt gnawing at my insides, hoping that maybe, just maybe, I could get through this. I wanted to keep her. I needed to make her believe it was still just us, that I could be the man she wanted me to be.

But as we left the restaurant and the door swung shut behind us, the weight of the girl's smile lingered in the back of my mind. And no matter how much I tried to push it away, I couldn't forget that look—that look that told me I would never truly be free of her.

I felt like throwing up. Why did I tell Emily I loved her? Why then? That was the first time I said those words, and I used them like a poison. The words tasted bitter on my tongue, like a lie so deeply ingrained I couldn't escape it even if I wanted to. I hadn't meant it. Not really. Not in the way she needed me to.

It had been a reflex, a way to smooth over the cracks, to keep her from asking too many questions. It felt wrong—so wrong—saying it while my thoughts were tangled in the mess with the girl. The girl who haunted my mind, who still had a hold on me despite everything. I didn't deserve Emily's love. I didn't deserve any of this.

But I'd said it anyway. I'd fed her the lie, hoping it would be enough to make her stay, to make her forget the scent of someone else on me.

I felt something rise up in my throat, not quite guilt, not quite disgust. A feeling of unease, of self-loathing. I tried to swallow it down, blinked away the pricks of moistness in the corners of my eyes. At no other point in my life did I hate myself more than in that moment. The weight of my own hypocrisy sat heavy on my chest, suffocating me. I could taste the bitter remnants of my actions, all the lies I had told myself, all the compromises I had made.

Emily deserved better. She deserves someone who could look her in the eye and say those words with conviction, without the knots of doubt strangling every syllable. But I wasn't that person. I never could be. And the worst part was that I was still willing to drag her deeper into the lie, as if somehow, if I repeated it enough, I could convince myself it was real.

When we got home, we crashed into each other. Emily and I intertwined, our bodies finding themselves covered in blankets. I don't know what feelings were intertwined between us. I knew I felt guilt, that the act of making love to her was closer to covering up my lies than actual desire. Each touch, each kiss, felt like a desperate attempt to erase the truth, to bury the pieces of myself I couldn't face. Her warmth against me was comforting, but it only made the coldness in me more unbearable.

I told myself it was love. I told myself it had to be. But the knot in my stomach, the lingering taste of something I couldn't quite name, kept me from fully believing it. My mind kept slipping back to her—the girl. Her eyes, her touch, the way she had made me feel things I couldn't even articulate. And then back to Emily, lying beside me, soft and trusting. I hated myself for it.

I pulled Emily closer, but it wasn't for her. It was for me. To remind myself that this was where I was supposed to be. That this was who I was supposed to be with. But the nagging doubt, the thought of her, refused to let me forget.

I'm disgusting.

~ 17 ~

CHAPTER SEVENTEEN

Hidden Truths

The hotel room was familiar now. A dull, worn place we returned to out of habit more than comfort. Dim lights, faded wallpaper, and that faint chemical scent that never quite masked the undertone of mildew. It was cheap, but it served it's purpose. She sat at the edge of the bed, legs crossed, sipping cheap whiskey she'd brought from work.

I leaned against the doorframe leading to the bathroom, watching her. She always had this way of making herself comfortable no matter where she was, even when we were kids. Hell, even when my parents were being... well, my parents, she never really seemed extremely uncomfortable. Just nonchalant. Even now, she looked as if she owned the place, even when the bed itself looked like it was barely holding up. She was barefoot, her heels kicked into the corner, and her black dress clung to her like a second skin. The dress was slightly different this time—shorter, tighter, like she was daring me to rip it off her.

"I don't know what kind of coincidence brought you to the restaurant," I said, finally stepping into the bedroom. I tossed my jacket onto the chair by the cheap desk all these rooms seemed to have, the lingering smell of her perfume already triggering a headache. "It stirred up more trouble than I needed. Especially that stunt you pulled in the bathroom."

She looked up at me, her expression playful and innocent—too innocent. "Oh relax," she said, swirling the whiskey in her glass. "You looked so serious. I thought I'd lighten the mood a little. Besides, it's not like I *knew* you were going to bring your little girlfriend there. I was working, remember?"

"Lighten the mood?" I scoffed, running a hand through my hair, completely ignoring the slight rebuttal she had given me. "Emily smelled your perfume. She thought—" I stopped myself, biting back the words. "It doesn't matter. It caused tension between us. You would have ruined everything."

Her lips twitched into a smirk, but there was something sharper underneath it. "Isn't it already ruined?" she asked, her tone light but cutting. "Or are you telling me she believed whatever lie you fed her?"

I stared at her, my jaw tightening. "She did, actually," I said curtly. "I told her I was meeting with the client again and I'd try to get home at a more reasonable time in the future. It worked, but just barely. Don't pull something like that again."

She leaned back on her elbows, her eyes locking onto mine, challenging me. "Oh please, like you're not already thinking about tearing this dress off me. You're welcome, by the way. For making you realize how much you hate lying to her."

I didn't reply, instead moving to sit on the bed with her. She wasn't entirely wrong, I was imagining—well, I did hate lying to

Emily. Telling her I loved her when I did felt... dirty. The mattress creaked under the shift in weight, and for a moment, the room was quiet except for the faint hum of the heater. I reached for the bottle of whiskey, pouring myself a glass. I hated how natural this had become—sitting here with her like this was normal, like it didn't tear at the edges of my life every time I left.

"You're thinking too much," she said, her voice softer now. She shifted closer, her bare knee brushing against mine. "I can see it all over your face."

"Yeah? What am I thinking, then?" I asked, my voice laced with sarcasm.

She tilted her head, studying me with those sharp, unreadable eyes. "You're thinking about her. About whether or not you should even be here."

I didn't respond, taking a long sip from the glass instead.

She let the silence linger for a moment before speaking again, her voice lower now, more serious. "Do you love her?"

Her question hung in the air, heavy and suffocating. I set the glass down, my fingers tightening around it before letting go. I didn't look at her when I answered. "I think I could've," I said, the words coming out slower than I intended. "Now? No. I don't think I love anyone."

Her lips parted slightly, her teasing grin softening into something more vulnerable. "Not even me?"

"In your dreams," I said, my voice sharper than I intended.

She let out a soft laugh, shaking her head. "You're cruel, you know that?" she said, leaning forward and resting her chin on her palm. "But you're honest. I like that."

"Don't read too much into it," I said, grabbing my drink again and taking another sip.

Her smile returned, small but genuine this time. "I never do."

Not for the first time, I wondered if that was another lie.

Two weeks passed in a blur of careful lies and forced smiles. The tension between Emily and me had dulled, but it hadn't disappeared. It lingered, thin and fragile, like a thread ready to snap. The perfume incident haunted me more than it did her—I could see it in the way she still smiled at me, still clung to me. She was trying. God, she was trying so hard. And I was rewarding her efforts with nothing but better-hidden betrayals.

I had become an expert at masking the guilt. At brushing off her questions, at slipping into the role of the devoted boyfriend. I kissed her forehead before leaving for work. I texted her throughout the day, just enough to keep her at ease. I told her I loved her more often now, because it was what she needed to hear. And maybe, just maybe, because I wanted to believe it myself.

But every time I told her those words, I heard her laugh. Not Emily's. *Hers.* The girl's. That sharp, knowing laugh that cut through my defenses like glass. The sound of her teasing echoing in my mind as I found myself in that same damn hotel room, again and again.

The cigarette between my fingers burned lazily, thin tendrils of smoke curling toward the ceiling. She was sprawled across the bed, as comfortable and carefree as ever, her hair a mess of curls and tangles spilling over her shoulders. She was holding a magazine in one hand, flipping through it with a kind of detached curiosity.

"Look at this," she said, holding it up and pointing to an advertisement for some new movie. "They're saying it's the movie of the decade. We should go see it together!"

I didn't look up from the cigarette as I took a long drag. "Shut up."

She ignored me, her grin widening as she shifted on the bed to face me fully. "I wonder if you'd pay for my entry fee," she teased, her voice dripping with mock innocence. "I bet you would! You're that type of man, after all."

She giggled, a sound both irritating and addictive, and I finally glanced over at her. She was practically glowing, her smile wide and bright, her eyes gleaming with mischief. She always looked so alive in these moments, like the weight of the world didn't touch her. Like she was untouchable.

"You're insane," I muttered, exhaling a cloud of smoke.

"And you're boring," she shot back, tossing the magazine onto the floor and leaning forward, propping her chin on her palm. "Come on. It'd be fun. A real date for once. Can you even imagine it? You, sitting in a theater, pretending not to hate the world for two hours. I'd love to see it."

"Don't hold your breath," I said, stubbing out the cigarette in the ashtray beside me.

She laughed again, soft and amused, and for a moment, I hated her. Not because she was here, not because of the things she said, but because she made it all seem so damn easy. Like none of this mattered. Like she didn't see the wreckage she left behind every time I walked out that door.

I watched her for a moment, the way her fingers fidgeted with the magazine she'd tossed aside, the way her smile never faltered. How could someone as empty as her smile so thoroughly? It wasn't fake—not entirely. There was a sincerity in the way her grin curved, in the way her eyes shimmered with light. It wasn't like mine, the one I wore with Emily, a mask to keep everything hidden. No, hers felt like a weapon, deliberate and cutting, but real. And still, I couldn't understand it.

I wanted to know. Badly. Why did I even care? Why was I still here, still involving myself with her? It wasn't like my feelings toward her had changed. I still hated her. Hated the thing she represented. The hollow, unfeeling specter of all the things I despised about myself.

"Why are you even like this?" I asked, breaking the silence. My voice came out rougher than I intended. "How did you even end up this way, anyway? I should've asked sooner."

Her gaze snapped to me, and for a moment, she looked startled. Then her expression softened, and something strange flickered in her eyes. Her lips parted into a smile, but not her usual one—not the sharp, teasing grin I'd come to expect. This smile was different. Softer. Genuine. It looked almost like...hope. Like she'd been waiting for me to ask.

"You really want to know?" she asked, her voice low, almost unsure.

I nodded, and she leaned back against the headboard, crossing her legs beneath her.

"Well, it's not a glamorous story," she began, her voice taking on a casual tone, like she was telling some fairytale she'd read a hundred times before. "My dad was one of those rich assholes, you know? Some kind of big-shot investor or businessman or whatever. Enough money to 'get by,' as he'd say."

I lit another cigarette, inhaling deeply, only half listening as she continued.

"In fifth grade, I suddenly decided I wanted to be the best at everything. Out of nowhere. It was like a switch flipped. Started paying attention in class, acing every test. Top of my class, every year after that. My dad? He ate it up. Saw me as his golden ticket or something. Started throwing money at me like I was some startup business. Paid for my future education—some fancy, prestigious university. I didn't even know you could do that so early, but apparently, you can if you've got the cash."

She paused, her eyes narrowing slightly as if she were remembering something bitter. *Oh, yeah. She just suddenly decided. Out of nowhere. Had nothing to do with me.* Right.

"Then comes the plot twist," she said, her smile returning, though this one carried a bitter edge. "He lost everything. Some real estate market crash. Wrong time, wrong place, bad investments—whatever excuse people like him make. Doesn't matter. What matters is that he went from being the guy with all the answers to the guy with nothing. And suddenly, all those 'investments' he made in me? They weren't paying off fast enough. I wasn't graduating fast enough. Wasn't bringing home the big bucks like he expected."

I clenched my teeth, feeling a flicker of anger rising in my chest.

"He started blaming me. Said I was a waste of money, a waste of space. Like it was my fault he lost everything. And then, when he ran out of things to sell, he turned to gambling. Gambled away what little we had left. By the end of it, he was just...gone. I don't know where he is now. Don't care either."

She laughed softly, but it was humorless.

"And me? Well, I had to quit school, obviously. Started working. Tried to make ends meet. And, lucky me, some 'good men' my dad owed money to were kind enough to show me a high-paying job I couldn't refuse."

Her voice turned icy at the last part, her eyes hardening, but her smile stayed. I couldn't tell if she was mocking herself or the world, or maybe both.

I felt a surge of anger, sharp and uncontrollable. At her father, at the men who'd cornered her into this life, at the entire damn world. And then, at myself.

Because somewhere in the back of my mind, a question lingered, unshakable: *Would it have been different if I hadn't forced that stupid rivalry on her?*

I remembered all the times I pushed her down, tried to beat her, tried to be better than her. It had been everything to me, and for what? To prove I was superior? To fill whatever void was inside me?

Would she have ended up like this if I hadn't been such a selfish bastard? Or, even if she had, could I have done something for her? Could I have saved her?

My anger turned inward, spiraling into self-loathing.

Is it my fault? Does it even matter?

She tilted her head, watching me carefully, as though she could see the turmoil brewing inside me. But she didn't say anything. Just smiled that same soft, genuine smile.

"You know what the last thing he said to me was?" she asked, her voice light, almost playful, though the bitterness in her eyes betrayed her tone.

I didn't answer, didn't even blink. She didn't need me to.

"'You're the golden egg that never hatched. The definition of useless.'"

The words hung in the air, heavy and cruel, and I felt my stomach churn.

I stood abruptly, the motion sharp and jarring. "I need to go," I muttered, grabbing my coat from the back of the chair.

She blinked, startled by my sudden movement, and then pouted, puffing her cheeks like a child. "Already? It's so early," she whined, sulking as she crossed her arms. "You're no fun."

If I didn't despise her, I might've found it cute. The way she puffed up like a scolded kid, her bottom lip jutting out just enough to make her look absurdly vulnerable. But I did despise her—everything she was, everything she represented—and the sight only made my skin crawl.

"You're disgusting," I said coldly, not even looking at her.

Her mouth opened, as though she wanted to say something, but I didn't give her the chance. I walked toward the door and yanked it open.

"Will you be back next Thu—" she started, but the door slammed shut behind me, cutting her off mid-sentence.

I stood there in the hallway, motionless, the silence pressing down on me. My fists clenched tightly at my sides, my nails digging into my palms as I stared at the peeling paint on the opposite wall.

I was frustrated. No, that wasn't the right word—I was furious. At her, at myself, at the entire goddamned situation. My breathing was uneven, my chest rising and falling in harsh bursts, and I felt the anger clawing at me, relentless and unyielding.

If I'd stayed a moment longer, I might've taken it out on her.

The thought made my stomach twist, a sickening mixture of guilt and shame creeping in. I loosened my fists, flexing my fingers as if that could rid me of the lingering tension.

After a moment, I forced myself to move, to step away from the door and walk down the dimly lit hallway. Each step felt heavy, my mind a mess of tangled emotions, but I didn't stop. I couldn't.

Not if I wanted to keep the thin thread of control I still had.

"God damn it." I grumbled, walking away.

~ 18 ~

CHAPTER EIGHTEEN

A Delicate Balance

I was with Emily again. The steady rhythm of her breath beside me, the warmth of her hand in mine, it almost felt like things were back to how they used to be. Almost.

But no matter how tightly I held onto her, how carefully I played my part, the gnawing feeling of guilt kept creeping in, slipping through the cracks of my carefully constructed calm. The lies, the manipulations, the girl I couldn't escape... it all lurked just out of sight, threatening to undo everything.

She smiled at me, her eyes soft, and I found myself smiling back. But it wasn't real. None of it was.

"Are you okay?" she asked, her voice filled with the kind of concern that only made it worse.

I nodded, forcing the words out before I could stop them. "Yeah. I'm okay."

I didn't say I was fine—because when you say that, people know it's a lie. I left it vague, just enough to dodge concern. And she let it slide. I knew she would.

The crisp air cut through the late afternoon, the streets emptying as the world around us settled into a quiet lull. Emily walked beside me, her laughter light and easy as she pointed out some random thing that caught her attention—a couple of birds perched on a nearby lamppost, a child riding a bike too big for him. The kind of simple moments that used to bring a sense of peace, a feeling I thought I might've lost forever.

I glanced at her, her features glowing in the soft light, and for a second, I almost forgot. Almost.

I took a deep breath, trying to push away the heavy weight pressing on my chest, but it lingered. The girl. The lies. The growing distance between me and Emily, even though she didn't see it.

"You're awfully quiet today," Emily said, her voice snapping me back to the present. She was looking at me now, concern creasing her brow.

I smiled, as naturally as I could. "Just thinking."

"About me?" she teased, nudging me lightly with her elbow.

I didn't answer right away. The truth was, I wasn't thinking about her—not entirely. But I couldn't say that.

"About everything," I finally said, my words wrapped in half-truths.

Emily smiled again, clearly content with my answer, and kept walking, oblivious. I followed her, taking one step after another, each movement feeling like I was walking on thin ice.

Emily's laughter floated past me, soft and real, but it didn't stick. Instead, I kept hearing *her* voice—edges sharp, questions unanswered—like a splinter lodged too deep to pull free. Even now, with everything perfect, she wouldn't leave me alone.

Her father. The investments. The way her life unraveled after high school.

It wasn't like I hadn't heard stories like it before—people losing everything, falling through the cracks. Life isn't fair, and it doesn't pretend to be. But somehow, knowing *her* story felt... different. It bothered me in a way I didn't expect, a way I hated to admit.

What was it about her that had this hold on me? Was it guilt? Pity? Or something uglier—an unwillingness to face the part I might've played in how she ended up?

My jaw tightened. I didn't want to think about her. Not now. Not while I was here with Emily.

Emily deserved better than this half-attention, the shadow of someone else hanging over me.

"Damn it," I muttered under my breath, earning a curious glance from Emily.

"Hmm? What's wrong?" she asked, slowing her pace to walk closer to me.

"Nothing, just stubbed my toe," I said quickly, forcing a small smile to ease her concern.

But it wasn't *nothing*. I could still see that look on her face—*her* face—when I asked how she ended up this way. That strange, unexpected smile, like she had been waiting for someone to care, waiting for someone to ask.

The memory felt like a slap, and I silently cursed myself. Why the hell was I even thinking about her?

I forced myself to focus on Emily. On the soft sound of her laugh, the way the wind played with her hair, the faint warmth of her hand brushing against mine as we walked. She had this way of grounding me when I let her. A way of reminding me of what mattered—or at least, what *should* matter.

She stopped to point out some flowers growing wild along the edge of the path, her voice full of that quiet excitement she always had for small, beautiful things. I nodded along, smiling when she turned to me for a reaction, and for a moment, it was almost easy to forget everything else.

Almost.

The tension between us had eased somewhat over the last few weeks, between Emily and me. Emily wasn't watching me as closely anymore, her suspicious glances growing less frequent. She had started to trust me again, though I couldn't decide if it was because I had gotten better at hiding my betrayals or because she wanted so desperately to believe in me.

I hated that I noticed the shift, that I could recognize the exact moments her walls began to lower. The way her smile softened when I came home on time. The way she leaned into me a little more when we sat on the couch together.

But instead of feeling closer to her, I felt more distant. It was as if every bit of trust she offered me pushed me further away, like the weight of her faith was suffocating.

And all the while, *she* was still there.

I hadn't stopped meeting the girl. At first, I told myself it was habit or some need for closure. But as the weeks dragged on, I stopped making excuses. I showed up, and so did she, and that was all there was to it.

By the seventh week, we had abandoned the pretense of her workplace entirely. We didn't even meet at the bar anymore. Now, we went straight to the hotel room, the routine as natural as if it had always been this way.

If Emily ever noticed the faint smell of cigarettes clinging to me when I came home, she never said a word.

I entered the hotel room with the practiced nonchalance I always did, letting the door click shut behind me. She was already there, sprawled lazily across the couch at the far end of the room like she owned the place.

"Oh! You brought us food!" she exclaimed, sitting up with a grin that lit up her face. "You're so diligent... I hope you didn't forget a fork this time around."

Before I could respond, she launched herself toward the bags in my hands, moving with the kind of reckless energy that was somehow typical of her.

"Hey!" I snapped, pulling one of the bags just out of her reach. "This is *my* lunch!"

"You say this," she teased, her eyes sparkling with amusement as she tugged at the other bag, "yet there are two bags! You're so not honest with yourself...!"

Her laugh was irritatingly infectious, and I hated how easily she disarmed me. I sighed and let her take the second bag, watching as she rummaged through it with the enthusiasm of a kid unwrapping a present.

"Unbelievable," I muttered, setting my own bag on the small table and taking a seat. "You're like a raccoon digging through trash."

"Aww, don't be mean!" she chirped, pulling out a container of fries and holding it up triumphantly. "See? Sharing is caring!"

She flopped back onto the couch, legs tucked underneath her as she popped a fry into her mouth. I watched her for a moment, unable to help myself. She was so... carefree. Or maybe careless was the better word.

"Why do I even bother?" I said under my breath, picking at my own meal.

"Because you like me," she shot back without missing a beat, smirking at me over the rim of her drink. "Don't worry, though—I like you too. Enough to forgive you for not bringing ketchup."

"You're insufferable," I said, but my voice lacked any real bite. "Your fork is in the—" I stopped mid-sentence, something catching my attention.

Wait a minute.

She was too engrossed in the bags to notice my shift in demeanor, rummaging through the contents with the giddy excitement of a child. My stomach twisted as I dropped everything I was doing and stepped toward her, grabbing her arm with enough force to make her wince.

"Hey, what—?" she began, but I didn't let her finish.

With my free hand, I gripped her chin and tilted her head toward me, forcing her to meet my gaze. My fingers brushed along the delicate curve of her face, tilting her head this way and that, searching for something I hadn't noticed before.

"What is it...?" she asked, her tone playful despite the situation. "We're not even in bed yet... You're so naughty today."

"Shut up!" I snapped, my voice cutting through her teasing like a blade.

Her mouth closed instantly, the lightness in her expression replaced with something warier. My thumb brushed around her left eye, and her eyelid fluttered shut instinctively at my touch. But the dark bruise beneath her makeup was impossible to miss, even if she'd tried to hide it.

"I don't remember doing this to you," I said, my voice low and hard. "Who did this?"

She blinked at me, caught off guard, her lips parting as though she was scrambling for an answer.

"A-Ah? This...?" She let out a nervous laugh, brushing her free hand through her hair. "It's really nothing... It doesn't hurt, see?"

She pressed two fingers against the corner of the blackened skin, forcing a smile even as her features betrayed her pain.

I grabbed her wrist to stop her. "Don't. Don't lie to me."

Her smile faltered completely. "It's not a big deal," she mumbled, looking away. "You don't need to get worked up over something like this. I can handle it."

Something about her tone made my chest tighten. I released her wrist, though my grip on her arm remained firm.

"Who did it?" I asked again, softer this time.

She hesitated, her eyes darting to the side as if looking for an escape. "I told you, it's nothing. Just some idiot getting too handsy, but I sorted it out. It's over."

"That's not an answer."

"Why do you even care?" she shot back suddenly, her voice rising. "It's not like you're my boyfriend or anything. What, are you going to play knight in shining armor now?"

Her words stung, but they didn't deter me. "You didn't answer my question."

She sighed, shaking her head. "You're so stubborn."

"And you're deflecting," I countered, tightening my grip just slightly. "If this happens again—"

"It won't!" she interrupted, her voice sharp. She pulled her arm from my grasp, rubbing where my fingers had left faint marks. "Seriously, you don't need to babysit me. I can take care of myself."

I wanted to push further, but the look in her eyes stopped me. She wasn't going to give me anything more, not right now.

"Fine," I said after a long pause, my tone clipped. "But if I find out you're lying..."

She gave me a weak smile, her usual playfulness returning, though it didn't reach her eyes. "You're such a worry wart," she said, flopping back onto the couch. "C'mon, let's eat before it gets cold. You're way more tolerable when you're fed."

I didn't respond, my eyes lingering on her a moment longer before I turned back to my own meal. But even as I unwrapped the food, the image of that bruise stayed with me, gnawing at the back of my mind.

I didn't answer her, nor did I meet her gaze. My mind was spiraling, caught in a tangle of thoughts and emotions I couldn't unravel. I didn't understand why I was so frustrated, so angry. It was uncontrollable.

And the worst part? I knew it was irrational. I knew I was acting on emotion instead of logic. But knowing something doesn't mean you can stop yourself from succumbing to it.

Fuck.

"I-Is this because you don't like it?" Her voice was hesitant, uncertain. "I can try to apply more makeup if you want... I'm sure you won't even notice it when we're—"

"Shut up," I snapped, cutting her off before she could finish.

She flinched, her words dying in her throat. My grip on her arm tightened, and a flicker of pain crossed her face. I knew I should let go. If I kept adding pressure, her arm would bruise, maybe even swell.

Yet I couldn't.

"Come, we're leaving," I said abruptly, my voice firm.

"What...?" She blinked up at me, confusion evident in her eyes. "Already? And what about the food?"

"You can eat it in the car," I replied, already pulling her toward the door. "Now come on."

"But it'll get cold!" she protested, digging her heels in slightly. "And where are we even going?"

"Far from all this," I muttered, not looking back. My voice dropped to a near whisper. "Really far from all this."

I didn't wait for her to respond. I couldn't.

Because if I stopped to think, if I gave her a chance to argue, I might lose the last thread of control I was barely holding onto.

The ride to my house was silent, except for the crinkling of paper as she picked at her food. Normally, she'd be teasing, trying to pull me into her rhythm. But now, there was nothing but an uneasy quiet, like she could sense something was wrong.

When I pulled into the driveway, I cut the engine and stared out the windshield for a moment, my hands gripping the wheel tightly.

"Stay here," I said, my voice flat.

"What? Why? Where are we going?" Her tone was cautious, uncertain.

"I just need to grab some things," I replied. "Just... stay."

I didn't wait for a response, stepping out of the car before I could second-guess myself.

Inside, the house felt oppressive. Every step I took seemed heavier, my movements mechanical as I headed to the bedroom. A bag. Clothes. Cash. Essentials. It was all a blur until her voice cut through the fog.

"Who's in the car?"

Emily's voice was quiet, but the weight of her words hit me like a freight train.

I stopped mid-motion, my back still to her.

"Who's in the car?" she repeated, louder this time.

I zipped the bag slowly, deliberately, and slung it over my shoulder before turning toward the door.

"It's not what you think," I muttered, brushing past her.

"Don't lie to me." Her tone was sharper now, more desperate. "You come home like this, acting... strange, and there's a girl in the car? Tell me the truth."

I paused in the doorway, my chest tight, my throat dry.

"You want the truth?" I turned to her, finally meeting her eyes. They were filled with hurt, confusion, and something I couldn't bear to see. "I'm horrible. I'm... I'm not who you think I am. I don't deserve you." My voice cracked as the words spilled out, faster and louder than I intended.

"What are you talking about?" she asked, her voice trembling.

"I've been cheating on you," I snapped, the weight of it all crashing down on me. "This whole time. With her. And now I'm... I'm running away with her."

Emily stood there, frozen, her expression shifting between disbelief and devastation.

I took a step back toward the door, unable to bear the silence.

"I'm sorry," I added, though the words felt hollow, meaningless.

She didn't move for a moment. Then, with a sudden burst of motion, she stepped forward and slapped me hard across the face.

The sting was immediate, but I didn't react, couldn't react.

Her hand lingered in the air for a moment before she let it drop, her breathing shaky.

"I knew," she said quietly, her voice breaking. "A part of me knew. I just... I didn't want to believe it. I wanted to pretend that I was just imagining things."

Her eyes, glassy with unshed tears, locked onto mine, piercing through whatever wall I had tried to build around myself.

"I-" she started to speak, then stopped, shaking her head as if trying to physically push away her own thoughts. "I-" her voice broke. "Get out."

I swallowed hard, my throat dry, and opened my mouth to say something—anything—but she cut me off.

"Get out!" she screamed, her voice raw and trembling with anger and pain.

The force of her words hit me harder than the slap. My body felt heavy, rooted to the spot, but her glare—filled with betrayal and anguish—was enough to make me move.

I didn't try to explain, didn't try to justify myself. There was nothing I could say that wouldn't make it worse.

Wordlessly, I turned and walked out the door, my steps slow and deliberate.

The moment the door shut behind me, it felt like all the air had been sucked out of my lungs.

I walked back to the car in a daze, opened the door, and slid inside.

She looked up at me from the passenger seat, her expression curious but wary.

"Everything okay?" she asked, tilting her head slightly.

I gripped the steering wheel tightly, my knuckles turning white. "Yeah," I lied, the word barely audible.

"Then... let's go," she said softly, her usual teasing tone absent.

Without another word, I started the engine, the sound of the car drowning out the silence that had settled over us.

As I drove away, I glanced at the house one last time in the rearview mirror. It felt like I was leaving behind more than just a place—I was leaving behind a part of myself.

I wasn't sure if I'd ever be able to find it again.

~ 19 ~

CHAPTER NINETEEN

The Point of No Return

It was on impulse.

Two hours had passed since we left the hotel. The road stretched endlessly before us, swallowed by the night. The soft hum of the engine filled the silence, broken only by the occasional crunch of gravel beneath the tires when the car strayed too close to the shoulder. I didn't know where I was going, and I didn't care. I just kept driving, my hands gripping the wheel tighter than they needed to.

She hadn't touched the food, the bag still sitting untouched on her lap. Her usual energy was gone. Instead, she stared out the window, her face blank, half-lit by the headlights of oncoming cars that passed like fleeting phantoms in the dark.

I glanced at her for a moment but quickly looked away. What was I expecting? Gratitude? Anger? Relief? I didn't even know why I was doing this anymore.

No, that's a lie. I knew.

It wasn't responsibility—not really. It wasn't love, either. I wasn't even sure if I could call it guilt. It was something messier than all of that, something I couldn't put a name to. A desperate need to feel like I was doing something right for once, like I wasn't the worthless bastard I'd been proving myself to be over and over again.

Maybe I was running away. Running from Emily, from the wreckage of our life together, from everything I'd ruined with my own two hands. And in running, I'd clung to the one thing that felt like it was just as broken as me.

Her.

But what was I hoping to accomplish? Fix her? Save her? I couldn't even save myself.

The thought twisted in my gut, and I tightened my grip on the wheel. I didn't know what I was doing. All I knew was that I couldn't stop. Not now. Not after everything.

"You're really doing this, aren't you?" Her voice cut through the silence, sharp and cold. She didn't turn to look at me, her eyes still fixed on the passing scenery. "Do you even know the impact of this choice you're making?"

"I don't care..." I muttered, my voice low and strained.

"Then why are you doing this?" she pressed, her tone rising. "If you don't care—"

"I'm doing this because I can't stand seeing you like this anymore, that's why!" I snapped, the words spilling out before I could stop them. "Don't you understand that this life of yours is not worth living? If this continues on like this, they're going to—"

"To what? Kill me? Break me? Is that it?" she interrupted, her voice thick with bitter sarcasm. "Why should you care? Shouldn't you be rejoicing? After all, you hate m—"

"Shut up..."

"But it's the truth, isn't it—?"

"Shut up!" I shouted, my voice reverberating through the car. My hands trembled on the wheel, my knuckles white. I didn't want to have this conversation. I didn't even know the answers to the questions she was asking. I just wanted her to stop. To stop talking. To stop forcing me to confront things I wasn't ready to face.

She fell silent for a moment, and the quiet in the car was deafening.

"...Is this because you feel responsible? Is that it?" she asked, softer this time.

I said nothing, my eyes fixed on the road ahead.

"Then I'm going to clear things up for you once and for all," she continued, her voice trembling. "This has nothing to do with you! It never had! This has always been my father's fault to begin with... This is not your responsibility! You understand?"

Her words hung in the air, heavy and suffocating.

I swallowed hard, my jaw clenched tight. "I'll be the one judging that," I said, my voice low and firm, though the conviction in it felt hollow.

She didn't respond, and the car fell silent again, the tension between us growing thicker with each passing moment. I glanced at her once more, her profile barely illuminated in the dark.

What was I even doing? Where was I taking her? Where was I taking myself?

"I owe them a lot of money, y'know. If I disappear like this, they're going to pursue me and find me. And if you're with me when that happens, they're not going to let you off easily! They're going to..."

Her voice wavers and she trails off, her breath shaking. From the corner of my eye, I can see her tears rolling down her cheek, uncontrollably, as if the very thought of my death was enough to bring her to this point.

"What of it?" The words leave my mouth without thinking, cold and cutting.

The silence between us thickens. Her gaze, once gentle and understanding, hardens. It's different this time.

"Don't you understand how dangerous this is?" she snaps, her voice rising, laced with something I've never heard from her before: pure anger. "They're going to ruin you! And didn't you have a girlfriend? A job you worked hard to obtain? If you go down this road, you're going to throw everything you've been building your whole life away! You can't sacrifice all this for something as stupid as—"

I slam my foot down on the brake pedal with all my strength. The tires screech, the sound tearing through the air for what feels like an eternity, until the car lurches to a stop. Without a word, I lean across the seat, unlocking her door and flinging it open in one swift motion.

"If you don't like this, then get out," I growl, my voice harsh. "We're still close to a bus station... You can probably get back to the city before morning. I've made my decision. I don't expect you to understand it. I'm doing this for myself."

She doesn't move. She doesn't flinch. But I hear her mutter a single word.

"Liar."

I chuckle, bitter and loud. "How stupid are you? I'm not lying! A girlfriend? A job? A life? None of that ever meant anything to me! I've always been empty—like I'm watching my own life from behind glass! This whole damn existence is a joke! And now I finally have a shot to get away from it. Tonight's the night. So either be my partner in crime—or get out and crawl back to the miserable wreck you call your life."

She stares at me, her eyes cold, unblinking, unwavering. The same way she always looks at me when we're together. Only this time, there's no smile. No softness. No warmth. The purity I once thought I saw in her is gone. All that's left is the sharp edge of her gaze, devoid of anything resembling hope or innocence.

She leans in instead, her face inches from mine, never breaking eye contact. There's no hesitation—only intensity, unwavering and unreadable.

"I've been waiting for this my whole life," she says, her voice quiet but unwavering. "And there's no way I'm going to let it slip away now."

There's no hesitation in her words, no trace of doubt. It's like she's made up her mind, and I don't know what to make of it. Part of me feels a sense of relief—maybe because she's finally choosing this too—but there's something dangerous in the way she says it, something darker than I expected.

I don't respond. I don't know how to. The words die in my throat. Instead, I nod. It's instinct, not thought. Then, I turn the key in the ignition and pull back onto the road, my gaze fixed ahead.

I can't look at her. Not now. Not when the weight of everything I just said is starting to settle in, heavy and suffocating.

We drive in silence. The world outside is dark, unfamiliar, but the road is all I know. The only thing left to do is keep moving forward. I push aside everything—my regrets, my fears—and focus on the only thing that matters now: the road ahead.

The headlights cut through the night, carving brief, flickering shapes across the road ahead. Each mile was just more distance between me and what I left behind, but it didn't feel like progress—just motion. I wasn't heading toward anything. I was just leaving.

I didn't know where I was going. Didn't care. I just needed to be away—from Emily, from the chaos, from myself.

The wheel was slick under my hands, my grip too tight. Thoughts crowded in, loud and suffocating. Was this about her? About me? Or just a way to avoid facing what I'd done?

I glanced sideways. The dash glow lit up her face in fleeting flashes. She was silent, but it screamed louder than anything else. I couldn't read her anymore. That terrified me.

Why had I thought this would be simple? That she'd just come with me, no resistance? She was never someone to be led blindly. Neither was I.

She was right—I was running. But it wasn't just about escape. I wanted everything gone. Burned. The life I'd built was fake. I never cared about it.

And what did I think I was giving her? Another mess? Another lie disguised as freedom? I couldn't fix her. I couldn't fix anything. But part of me still wanted to try.

She finally spoke. "Where are we even going?"

I didn't answer. I just drove. Too far gone now.

This wasn't freedom. This was destruction. And even with all the guilt, I felt something like relief.

I glanced at her. This time, she looked back. A challenge flickered in her eyes.

Her words echoed: "I've been waiting for this my whole life."

Was that hope—or something worse?

We drove on, no destination in sight, only distance.

"Is this what they call eloping? It's exciting!"

Her voice, light and carefree, cuts through the silence, a stark contrast to the storm brewing inside me. I glance at her, the soft moonlight catching her features, and for a moment, she seems almost angelic. The most beautiful smile I've ever seen. In a different life, I might've believed it. But in this one, it feels like a cruel joke.

After half a day of driving, we finally stop at a cheap motel. The fluorescent sign flickers, the air thick with the scent of old carpets and the promise of a broken night's sleep. We've barely scratched the surface of our journey, but even so, exhaustion is starting to catch up with me.

She's already fallen asleep next to me on the bed, a soft and even breathing filling the room. The weight of the decision I made is crushing me, but she's oblivious to it. She doesn't care. Maybe she doesn't even care how dangerous this is. Maybe she's right. Maybe I'm overthinking it all.

But I can't shake the feeling. The weight of the consequences. I thought we had time. I thought we could just drive away, disappear into the night. But reality is starting to seep in. There's no easy way out of this mess. And the more I think about it, the more I realize just how short our time really is.

I pull myself out of the bed slowly, not wanting to disturb her. I sit at the small desk, staring at the faded paper where they wrote down our room number. My mind races, but my body feels heavy. The weight of what's happening—the weight of what I'm doing—presses down on me like a vice.

I can't keep doing this on impulse. If we want to survive, if we want to make it, we need a plan. But I can't think clearly. Every idea I have seems like it will lead to disaster. The truth is, trusting anyone—hell, even trusting her—is just going to get us caught. She doesn't know it yet, but I'm dragging her into a mess she doesn't understand.

I let out a bitter laugh, but there's no humor in it. She's asleep, probably dreaming of a life she never got to have. And here I am, wide awake, trying to figure out the next step in this chaos.

I glance back at her. She's so fucking peaceful, her chest rising and falling with every breath. She doesn't know how much danger we're in. How much danger I'm in.

How much danger *she* could be in.

I could've asked her about her living situation, maybe even tried to get in touch with her so-called 'hostess' roommate. But the more I thought about it, the more I realized it would be a mistake. Too many risks. Too many loose ends that would only make our downfall more inevitable. Trusting anyone, even for a second, could destroy us. I could already feel it gnawing at me—this burning desire to control everything, to keep her in my grasp.

But it's too late for that now. It's too late to turn back.

I hate the part of me that's thinking this way. I hate how it feels, this desire to push everyone away. To ruin everything I've ever touched. To drag her down with me.

There's a darkness in my chest that I can't shake. It's always been there, a quiet whisper in the back of my mind, telling me to destroy everything. To burn it all. And tonight, it's louder than ever.

I don't know if I want to fix this, or if I just want to watch it burn.

I turn away from her again, feeling the pull of that darkness, the weight of my choices. The bed feels like a prison now, the walls closing in. I want to scream. I want to run.

But I don't.

Instead, I sit there, staring at the wall, fighting the thoughts that keep pushing me forward, pulling me deeper into this spiral.

Why the hell did I choose this? Why the hell did I drag her into it?

Was it for freedom? For a chance to feel like something more than the man I've become? Or was it because I'm too far gone, too consumed by my own destruction?

I look back at her again. The woman who's following me into this nightmare. I wonder if she knows just how much danger she's in.

I wonder if she understands what she's becoming by choosing to be here with me.

~ 20 ~

CHAPTER TWENTY

Smoke and Sunlight

The dim light of the motel room flickered above, casting uneven shadows that played across her face. I sat on the edge of the bed, unable to tear my gaze away from her. She was asleep, her chest rising and falling in a slow, steady rhythm, completely at odds with the storm raging inside me.

Her hair spilled across the pillow, long and slightly wavy, a cascade of black that seemed to drink in the weak light. It framed her face like ink bleeding into water. Strands clung to her cheeks, damp from the heat of the room, and yet, even in sleep, her expression remained guarded—like she was bracing herself for something, even in her dreams.

I traced the sharp lines of her face with my eyes: the delicate curve of her jaw, the slight hollowness beneath her high cheekbones, and the pale complexion that made her look almost ethereal. Her lips, naturally downturned, had the faintest trace of tension, even in rest.

The dark circles under her eyes stood out starkly against her skin, proof of countless sleepless nights—or perhaps the weight she carried every waking moment. Her frame was slim, almost frail-looking, as if she might shatter if the world pushed just a little harder. But I knew better.

There was steel to her, buried somewhere beneath the surface. I'd seen it in her eyes when she glared at me earlier, that cold, unwavering stare that stripped away my pretenses and left me feeling exposed. Those eyes—large, deep, and unsettling—held something dangerous in them, something that refused to be tamed.

She shifted slightly, her shoulder peeking out from the thin strap of her worn tank top. It clung to her, loose and ill-fitting, like it wasn't meant to be hers. Or maybe like it didn't matter—it was just another detail in a life she seemed indifferent to.

I leaned forward, resting my elbows on my knees, my head in my hands. What the hell was I doing? Sitting here, staring at her like some lovesick fool when I knew this was nothing close to love. Or maybe it was, but not the kind anyone writes songs about.

It was an obsession. A shared destruction.

Her fingers twitched in her sleep, curling into the fabric of the sheets as if grasping at something only she could see. I didn't know if it was a sign of fear or resolve, but either way, it felt like the most honest thing I'd ever seen her do.

I stared at her for what felt like hours, the air in the room thick and suffocating. Finally, I whispered, so quietly I almost didn't hear myself:

"Why did I run?"

The words hung there, suspended in the stillness. Why *did* I run? From the life I'd built, the one I was supposed to want? From Emily? From my job? From everything that made sense on paper?

The answer should have been simple. I ran because I couldn't take it anymore—the monotony, the hollowness, the crushing weight of living a life that never really felt like mine. But that wasn't all, was it? No. I ran because of her.

Because of *this*.

I ran because the moment she called me, I couldn't say no. Because no matter how much I told myself it was impulsive, reckless, and doomed, I knew deep down I'd already made my decision the second I saw the bruises.

And now here I was, leaving everything behind for her. For what? For *her*. The thought churned in my stomach, twisting into something unrecognizable. Where the hell were we even going? Where could we possibly go where they wouldn't find us? Where this wouldn't catch up to us eventually?

And why was I doing this with her, of all people?

I looked at her again, her face peaceful in sleep, so at odds with the chaos she always carried when awake. And I thought about everything. Everything we'd ever been.

Our shared childhood—the way we'd circled each other like planets in the same orbit, always close but never quite colliding. The afternoons we'd spent in libraries, her voice sharp and teasing as she challenged me to solve problems faster than her. The way we'd competed, driven by some unspoken need to outdo each other, to be the one who walked away triumphant.

The rivalry. The hours spent locked in battle, whether it was over academics or meaningless arguments. I hated her then, didn't I? Or thought I did.

And then there was the night at the bar.

I didn't want to remember it, but the memory came anyway, unbidden and vivid. Her eyes glinting in the dim light, her laughter cutting through the haze of alcohol. She'd looked at me that night like she was daring me to do something—anything. And I almost did, almost made a mistake I couldn't take back. That was the first time I'd realized she wasn't just some abstract figure in my life. She was real. Too real.

And now, these past few weeks. The chaos. The tension. The way she challenged everything I thought I knew about myself. The way she unraveled me without even trying.

She's always been there, hasn't she? Through all of it. She's the only thing I've ever had that felt real.

The thought struck me like a hammer, knocking the breath out of me.

Is this love?

No. It couldn't be. Love wasn't supposed to feel like this. It wasn't supposed to feel like drowning, like suffocating, like teetering on the edge of something you couldn't name.

I wanted to hate her for it. God, I *wanted* to hate her for it. But I didn't even know why. Was it fear? Fear of what she meant to me? Fear of how much power she held over me without even trying? I didn't know. I didn't know anything anymore.

The spiral twisted tighter and tighter, a vortex of thoughts that threatened to swallow me whole. I closed my eyes, pressing my palms into my temples, willing the storm to stop. But it didn't. It just kept going, pulling me deeper into the realization that everything I'd ever done had led me to this moment.

Her.

I sighed, the sound heavy and resigned, and crawled into the bed beside her. The mattress sagged beneath me, and for a moment, I hesitated, staring at the ceiling as the whirlwind in my head slowed to a dull ache.

"Las Vegas, I think," I muttered under my breath, the words barely audible, even to myself.

And then I let the exhaustion pull me under.

I woke up to an empty bed.

For one horrifying moment, I thought she'd left. That she'd finally gotten bored, taken what little we had left, and walked out of my life like she'd never been there to begin with. My chest tightened, and my breath caught, the fragile quiet of the room suddenly deafening.

Then I saw her.

She was sitting by the window, one leg pulled up to her chest, the other dangling lazily over the edge of the chair. Her face was turned toward the horizon, bathed in the soft, golden light of dawn. A cigarette hung loosely from her lips, the faint glow of the ember catching in her dark, messy hair. Smoke curled up and out into the morning air, dissipating like a ghost.

I exhaled sharply, annoyance crashing over the lingering panic. Why did I even care? Why did I even bother to panic? She wouldn't leave—not really. She was too stubborn, too irritating. She needed me too much.

And yet, I couldn't quite shake the relief pooling in my chest, no matter how much I wanted to.

The sheets rustled as I sat up, and she turned her head toward me, her eyes heavy-lidded and still hazy from sleep. A slow, lazy smile spread across her face as her gaze found mine.

"Morning, love," she murmured, her voice low and teasing, with that rasp that only came from just waking up.

I scowled. "Morning," I muttered, rubbing a hand over my face.

I dragged myself out of bed, my limbs heavy with sleep and the weight of decisions I didn't want to make. She didn't react as I shuffled over to her, just watched me through half-lidded eyes, her smirk never faltering. Without a word, I reached out and plucked the cigarette from her fingers.

"Hey—"

I ignored her protest, taking a slow drag before blowing the smoke out the window. It stung my throat, bitter and sharp, but I welcomed the burn. "I was thinking about where we should go," I said, finally breaking the silence.

Her smirk widened, the corners of her mouth curling up like she was savoring some private joke. "Did you choose where we're going, my love?" she asked, her tone dripping with mock affection.

I groaned, scowling deeper. "Stop that. It's disturbing."

"But we're eloping!" she said, feigning innocence. "I can at least call you that much, right?~"

"No, we're not," I snapped, the irritation bubbling to the surface. "Eloping would mean we're about to get married, and we're *clearly* not—"

"But I *want* to get married!" she cut in, completely unbothered by my tone. "I love you, and we're going to live together from now on, so..." She leaned her head onto my shoulder, smiling up at me like she wasn't saying the most ridiculous thing I'd ever heard.

My face burned, and I shoved her off, my chest tightening as her words echoed. "What does that even mean? You're not making any sense. Just—get off."

"Boo... you're no fun," she whined, sticking her tongue out at me like a petulant child before turning back toward the window. She slumped in her chair, her arms crossed as she sulked.

I sighed, rubbing at my temple. "You're such a handful," I muttered.

"...So?" she shot back, not even bothering to look at me.

I didn't answer. Instead, I leaned against the wall, my arms crossed as I stared out the window. The horizon was painted in soft oranges and pinks, the kind of quiet beauty I hadn't had the luxury of appreciating in years. But my mind wasn't on the dawn.

It was on her.

After a long moment, I spoke again. "I've decided our destination."

That got her attention. She turned to me, her eyes narrowing slightly as she studied my face. "Yeah? And?"

I hesitated, my jaw tightening as I forced the words out. "What do you think of Las Vegas?"

Her face lit up instantly, her earlier teasing replaced with genuine excitement. "So does that mean we're *really* going to get married after all? I've always wanted to go to Las Vegas!"

"Back off," I muttered, rolling my eyes. "I chose it for convenience, not for your little fantasy."

"Convenience, huh?" she said, tilting her head, her voice thick with disbelief. "Suuure..."

Her grin widened, and I could see the faint spark of victory in her eyes. She wasn't wrong. I'd chosen it partly because I knew how much she wanted to go. She'd talked about it more than once, her voice full of a kind of wistful longing I couldn't quite understand.

But I wasn't about to admit that.

"Don't get your hopes up," I said, my voice low and firm.

She only giggled, turning back to the window with a soft hum. Her excitement was almost contagious, the energy radiating off her in waves, and for a moment, I let myself bask in it.

But the feeling didn't last.

She always seemed so carefree, so maddeningly unaffected by everything. And me? I could feel the weight of it all pulling at me, dragging me deeper into this mess we'd created.

And, as always, she was at the center of it, her presence both a comfort and a curse.

I sighed, running a hand through my hair. "Las Vegas," I muttered under my breath.

It was going to be a long journey.

~ 21 ~

CHAPTER TWENTY-ONE

Mirage on the Horizon

The hum of the air conditioning blended with the rhythmic buzzing of the radio, a faint tune struggling to rise above static. I wasn't paying attention to the music anyway, the faint melody nothing more than background noise to my thoughts. Outside, the Nevada road stretched endlessly, a monotonous ribbon of asphalt cutting through barren desert, with the occasional tumbleweed rolling by as if to mock the sheer emptiness of the landscape.

The car vibrated faintly beneath my hands as I gripped the steering wheel, my eyes fixed on the road ahead. There wasn't much to see—just sand, scattered shrubs, and the hazy shimmer of heat rising in the distance. The endless sameness felt like a physical weight pressing down on me. It gave me too much time to think, too much space for the doubt to creep in.

The silence in the car was heavy, broken only by the faint whirring of the AC and her occasional shifting in her seat. She had her legs tucked up, leaning against the window, her face turned toward the blinding horizon. I couldn't tell if she was asleep or just lost in her own thoughts. I let myself glance at her, only for a second, before snapping my eyes back to the road.

Then, she spoke, her voice breaking the stillness like a pebble dropped in water.

"Why Vegas... seriously?" She turned her head to look at me, her expression unreadable. "I know I've talked about it a lot, but doesn't it seem counter intuitive to go to the city of sin to avoid... well, y'know."

"Not necessarily," I replied without looking at her.

"Explain."

"The best place to hide a tree is inside a forest, right?" I glanced at her briefly before returning my focus to the road. "If you were them, you'd assume we'd try to disappear into some distant, isolated place. That's exactly how they'll think. So naturally, they'll search every remote corner first—every small town, every backwater village. You get where I'm going with this?"

She shifted in her seat, sitting up straighter. "Yeah, I get it. But while it sounds good on paper, it doesn't mean it'll go that smoothly. That place is known to be run by criminals, right? So it wouldn't be too far-fetched to think they've got ties to our pursuers."

"If we went somewhere small, we'd attract more attention. Everyone knows each other in those places, and look at us." I gestured vaguely between us. "We're not exactly the 'small-town local' type, are we?"

She stared at me for a moment, her expression skeptical but thoughtful. "If you say so..."

Her voice trailed off, and I could sense the unease behind her words. Was she scared? She shouldn't be. Not now.

"One more thing." I tightened my grip on the wheel, my voice firmer now. She needed to understand this. "Even if they find us, it doesn't change anything, does it? Both of us... our lives have never been worth living. I won't spend what's left of mine rotting in some boring village, or crawling in fear in a hole somewhere. My life has already been nothing but boredom. So..."

She looked at me, her eyes wide, unsure.

"Let's try to have some fun, shall we?"

It took a moment, but then it came—the smile. That same smile she always wore so naturally. Bright, beautiful, unrestrained. A smile that once infuriated me to no end, a smile I would've done anything to destroy. But now... now I was the reason it existed.

I should feel proud of that. I should feel something good, at least. But all I could feel was a sick, twisting sensation in my chest.

'How disgusting,' I thought to myself.

But even as the words echoed in my head, they felt hollow. My chest betrayed me, warming with a feeling I couldn't name.

She laughed softly, leaning back against the seat, her eyes fixed on the horizon again. "Vegas, huh?" she murmured. "Fine. Let's see what kind of fun we can have."

The road stretched endlessly ahead, a mirage flickering in the distance. Somewhere, just beyond that shimmer, the city waited.

The gas station was a quiet outpost in the middle of nowhere, its neon sign buzzing faintly in the heat. I pulled the car up to the pump and turned off the engine, the silence only broken by the soft ticking of the cooling motor.

"I'll pump the gas," I muttered, opening the door.

"Fine, but I need a drink," she replied, hopping out before I could protest.

We walked into the gas station together, the air conditioning hitting us like a blast of winter. She headed straight for the drinks cooler without a second thought, while I lingered by the candy aisle. My eyes skimmed over the rows of brightly colored packages until I spotted it—a pack of red licorice.

I picked it up without thinking, the memory hitting me like a jolt. Study sessions back in high school, her pretending to be focused on her notes while sneaking bites of this same candy. She always thought I didn't notice, but I did. I just never said anything.

By the time I reached the counter, she was already there with a neon-green soda in hand. I tossed the licorice onto the counter beside her drink. Her eyes widened in surprise, and she let out a delighted laugh. "You remembered!"

"What do you mean?" I frowned, feigning confusion.

"I used to sneak these during study sessions," she said, her voice warm with nostalgia. "You caught me once, and I swore you were going to snitch." She opened the pack right there, pulling out a piece and biting into it, chewing contentedly. "But you didn't. Guess you were a softie even back then."

I rolled my eyes. "I just didn't want to deal with you whining if you got detention for smuggling snacks."

"Sure, sure," she teased, grinning as she held the pack out toward me. "Want one?"

"No," I replied, but the corner of my mouth twitched before I could stop it.

The gas station attendant, an older man with a weathered face, handed me my change and gave us a friendly smile. "You two on a road trip?"

"Something like that," I replied curtly, grabbing the bag of snacks.

"Newlyweds, huh?" the man said, his grin widening as he looked between the two of us.

Her laugh bubbled out before I could say anything. "Why, yes, we are," she said, linking her arm with mine dramatically.

I froze, glaring at her. "We're not—"

"Not officially married yet," she cut me off, her grin teasing. "But we're thinking Vegas!"

The man chuckled, clearly entertained. "Well, you two enjoy yourselves. Congratulations."

I stormed out of the gas station with her trailing behind, still laughing. "What the hell was that?" I growled, tossing the bag onto the passenger seat.

"Oh, come on, it was funny," she said, climbing into the car. She pulled out another piece of licorice, her grin softening as she chewed. "And hey, thanks for this. Really."

I didn't respond, starting the car and pulling back onto the road. Her laughter faded into silence, but the sight of her smiling, genuinely happy for once, stuck with me longer than I wanted to admit.

A little while later, we stopped at a rest area. The desert stretched endlessly around us, the harsh sunlight glinting off the metal roof of the small bathroom building. She went in first while I leaned against the car, staring at nothing in particular. My mind wandered as it always did—what would happen when we got to Vegas? Would her presence really be enough to make this reckless plan work?

She emerged, drying her hands on her jeans. "Your turn," she said, stepping aside.

Inside, the bathroom smelled like cheap soap and cleaner. I caught a glimpse of myself in the mirror as I washed my hands. My hair was a mess, my eyes were ringed with exhaustion, and my face was hollowed out from too many sleepless nights. I barely recognized myself anymore.

When I got back to the car, she was sprawled in the passenger seat, her feet propped on the dash. A piece of licorice dangled lazily from her lips. "Took you long enough," she said around it.

"You're the one who takes forever," I muttered, climbing in. She didn't respond, just offered me the pack of licorice. I shook my head, and she shrugged.

We were back on the road, the music low in the background again. The Nevada desert blurred past us, an endless expanse of sand and sky. Despite everything—the uncertainty, the chaos we were running from—this felt strangely normal. Or maybe I just wanted it to.

For a while, she hummed along with the music. Then, she glanced at me and said, "Do you ever think about what you'll do after this?"

"No," I answered honestly.

"Why not?"

"Because I don't think there will be an 'after.' Not for me."

Her humming stopped. She didn't say anything else, but I could feel her watching me, her gaze heavy and questioning.

When she finally turned back to the window, the silence returned, stretching between us like the endless road ahead.

We've been driving for another hour or two, the road a ribbon of gray cutting through the barren Nevada desert. The hum of the engine blended with the faint buzz of the radio, the static swallowing up the last strains of a song neither of us recognized. She had her window rolled down, one arm draped lazily over the edge, her fingers tracing patterns in the wind.

"Hey," she said suddenly, breaking the silence.

I glanced at her. "What?"

She didn't answer right away. Instead, she leaned back in her seat, turning her head to look at me. Her expression wasn't teasing for once; it was softer, almost thoughtful.

"Do you ever think about... what it would've been like if we'd stayed? If we hadn't run?"

I tightened my grip on the steering wheel. "No."

"Really?" She tilted her head, watching me like she didn't believe it. "Not even a little?"

"What's the point? It doesn't change anything."

She hummed, not quite agreeing but not pressing the issue either. "You're probably right," she murmured, looking back out the window.

The silence returned, heavier now. I wanted to leave it there, to let it fade into the background like the static of the radio, but something about her quietness pulled at me.

"What about you?" I asked, my voice lower than I intended.

"What about me?"

"Do *you* think about it?"

She didn't answer right away. I could see her reflection in the window, her brow furrowed as if she was trying to decide how honest to be.

"Sometimes," she admitted. "But not in the way you'd think."

"What does that mean?"

"I don't think about what I left behind," she said, turning back to face me. "I think about what *would've* happened if I'd stayed. And every time, it's the same."

I frowned. "The same, how?"

She shrugged, a hollow smile tugging at her lips. "I wouldn't have lasted long, let's put it that way."

The words hit me harder than I expected, a sharp pang in my chest that I quickly buried. I didn't know what to say to that, so I didn't say anything.

She turned back to the window, the wind catching strands of her hair and sending them dancing around her face. "But you know what?" she said softly. "I don't regret it. Any of it."

I glanced at her again, and for a moment, she looked almost peaceful.

"Why?" I asked, my voice barely audible over the hum of the car.

She smiled, and this time, it wasn't hollow. "Because I've got you."

The words hung in the air between us, raw and unpolished, and I hated the way they made my chest tighten.

I turned my eyes back to the road, swallowing the lump in my throat. "You're insufferable," I muttered.

She laughed, light and carefree, like we hadn't just skirted the edge of something darker. "And you love it."

I didn't respond, but the corner of my mouth twitched despite myself.

The sun was beginning to set by the time we saw it—a shimmering mirage on the horizon, glowing against the deepening twilight.

"There it is," she whispered, leaning forward as if she could reach out and touch it.

Vegas.

The city of sin, of chaos, of everything we were running toward—and everything we were running from.

I tightened my grip on the wheel, my pulse quickening. "Let's see what it's got for us."

~ 22 ~

CHAPTER TWENTY-TWO

Fragile Games

The moment we entered the core of the city, she lit up like a sparkler. Every street corner, every neon sign, every flashing light was met with an enthusiastic "Ooh!" or "Look, look, look! It's so beautiful!" or, "I wanna go there! Let's go there, alright?"

I kept my eyes on the road, half-listening, half-ignoring her. When her excitement became too much, pestering me with pleas and rapid-fire questions, I'd sigh and say, "We need to find a place to crash first. Be patient, alright?"

That would quiet her for a minute or two, but then something else would catch her eye, and the cycle would start again.

I couldn't help but glance at her every now and then. She was practically bouncing in her seat, her face pressed to the window like a child seeing fireworks for the first time.

And that's what got me thinking.

She was a prostitute, right? That's what she told me, anyway. So why did she seem so... untouched by the world? So unreasonably happy over the most trivial things?

It didn't add up.

Maybe I should've left her behind. Maybe bringing her to a place like this—a place so full of temptation and chaos—was a mistake.

But it was too late for second thoughts now.

One thing we didn't have to worry about, at least, was money. I had plenty stashed away from my old part-time job, and my "current" one, though I doubted I'd still have that gig after all of this. Not that it mattered.

We made our way to the outskirts of the city, leaving the blinding neon glow behind for a quieter, dimmer area where the lights were fewer and the buildings older.

Eventually, I pulled into the cracked parking lot of a small motel. The sign flickered weakly, some of the letters barely hanging on. It was cheap, just like I'd expected—and just far enough from the heart of the city to give us some breathing room.

"This is it?" she asked as I parked the car.

"It's not much, but it'll do," I replied, cutting the engine.

We grabbed our bags from the trunk and headed inside.

The motel room wasn't much to look at—yellowed walls, a tiny TV, and a bathroom that looked like it hadn't been cleaned properly in years. But the most glaring thing was that it only had one bed.

I frowned, but before I could say anything, she plopped her bag on the floor and gave me a sly grin. "One bed? How scandalous," she teased, her tone dripping with mock innocence.

"It was cheaper," I shot back quickly, walking over to drop my bag beside the bed.

She raised an eyebrow, her grin widening. "Sure it was."

"It *was*," I insisted, my voice sharper than I intended.

She laughed, holding up her hands. "Alright, alright. Whatever you say." She flopped onto the bed with a dramatic sigh, stretching out like a cat. "At least it's comfy."

I glanced at the bed, unimpressed. "It's still trashy."

She propped herself up on one elbow, giving me a cheeky look. "Kind of like us, huh?"

I froze for a second, her words cutting through the haze of my exhaustion.

Trashy.

Was that what we were now? Running from everything, chasing some impossible dream—or maybe nothing at all?

I shook my head and sat down on the edge of the bed, rubbing my temples. "Get some rest," I muttered.

She laid back down, pulling one of the pillows over her chest and hugging it like a stuffed animal. "You're so serious all the time," she mumbled.

I didn't reply. I just stared at the wall, listening to the faint hum of the air conditioning and the muted sounds of the city far in the distance.

I sat on the edge of the bed, staring at the wall while the air conditioner hummed in the background. She stayed quiet too, lying on her back and hugging the pillow she'd claimed as her own. For a moment, it almost felt peaceful.

Too peaceful.

Suddenly, she sat up, the springs of the mattress squeaking beneath her. "Forget getting some rest!" she declared, her voice bright and full of excitement.

I blinked, turning my head toward her. "What are you talking about?"

She grinned, already swinging her legs off the bed and standing up in one fluid motion. "We're in Vegas! Let's go have some fun!"

"What?" I frowned, watching as she grabbed her jacket and slipped it on. "We just got here."

"Exactly!" She darted around the room, finding her bag and pulling out some lipstick, dabbing it on in the cracked motel mirror like it was part of some impromptu war paint ritual. "We're not wasting the first night sitting around in this dump. Let's go!"

"Hey, slow down—" I started, but she was already beside me, grabbing my arm with both hands and tugging me toward the door.

"Come on," she insisted, her voice half-commanding, half-begging. "Live a little."

I planted my feet, trying to resist, but it was like fighting against a force of nature. "You don't even know where you want to go," I muttered.

She stopped for a split second, turning to face me with that teasing grin of hers. "Does it matter?"

"Yes, it does."

"No, it doesn't," she countered, tugging on my arm again.

I sighed, letting out a defeated groan as I finally let her pull me toward the door. "This is a bad idea."

She laughed as she dragged me outside, her voice full of that carefree energy I could never quite understand. "Bad ideas are the best ones! Don't you know that by now?"

The night air hit me the moment we stepped outside. The faint smell of asphalt, car exhaust, and distant neon electricity filled my senses. She was still holding my arm, practically bouncing with excitement, as if the whole city were just waiting for her.

For us.

And despite myself, I followed her.

She insisted we go to a casino—because, of course, it's Vegas. What else was I expecting?

I figured we'd end up drinking, so I hailed a taxi instead of driving. She clambered into the backseat first, practically bouncing in her seat. The driver gave us a tired glance in the rearview mirror, but her enthusiasm filled the space, and even I had to admit it was hard to stay annoyed.

"Do you think the casinos look as crazy inside as they do out here?" she asked, her face pressed against the window as we sped down the neon-lit streets.

"They'll be loud. Crowded. Probably smell like cigarettes," I said.

Her nose crinkled at that, but she was grinning. "Sounds perfect."

The cab pulled up to one of the bigger casinos, all flashing lights and glittering glass. I paid the driver and followed her inside, where the noise hit us like a wave—clinking coins, electronic beeping, bursts of cheers from distant tables.

The casino was electric, almost alive, its chaos wrapping itself around us like a second skin the moment we stepped inside. She clung to my arm, her eyes wide as if she were a kid walking into a candy store. It was unnerving how easily she could switch from sulking silence to this kind of energy.

"Look at all of this!" she said, spinning in place to take it all in. Her voice was bright, almost too bright, like she was trying to drown out something darker beneath it. "God, it's like a movie! I've never seen anything like this."

"Don't get too excited," I muttered, steering her out of the way of a passing group of rowdy tourists. "It's not as glamorous as it looks."

But she wasn't listening. She was too busy flitting from one machine to the next, her fingers brushing over the polished surfaces as she marveled at every flashing light and colorful display. It was exhausting just watching her.

We stopped near a row of slot machines where elderly gamblers sat hunched over, pulling the levers with mechanical precision. Their faces were masks of monotony, their eyes dull and unblinking.

She froze, her excitement dimming as she stared at them. "They look... so sad," she said softly.

"It's just how it is," I replied. "They've probably been at it all day. Don't think too hard about it."

But she didn't move. She kept watching them, her gaze heavy and unsettling. "They look so pathetic it's almost pitiful," she said, her voice barely audible over the noise around us. Then she turned to me, her eyes wide and searching. "But aren't we the same? We spend our lives doing the same pointless things, over and over, until we forget why we're even here. If there's a god... don't you think he'd look at us like this? Like we're just..."

She trailed off, her fingers curling against her palm. I placed a hand on her head, not knowing what else to do. Her words unsettled me in a way I couldn't quite articulate.

"As long as we're together," she murmured, "let's not do this. Let's not lose ourselves like that. I don't care if you love me. I don't even care if you hate me. Just... don't forget why we're here. Don't forget me."

"I won't," I said, the promise heavier than I wanted it to be. "Never."

Her smile returned, but it didn't reach her eyes.

For a while, things felt lighter. She watched me play blackjack with an almost comical intensity, leaning over my shoulder and whispering suggestions in my ear. She caught on quickly, her sharp mind cutting through the rules like they were nothing.

"You know," I said, half-smirking, "you were top of our class once. Maybe you should be the one playing."

Her grin faltered, just for a second. "Yeah," she said, her tone flat. "Look where that got me."

She laughed it off before I could say anything, nudging me playfully. "Focus, genius. I'm trying to learn from the master here."

We drank too much, more than we should have. She didn't seem to have a limit, downing glass after glass like she was trying to drown something. I started to lose track of time, the night blurring into a haze of bright lights and louder laughter.

At some point, I excused myself to the bathroom. "Stay here," I told her, pointing at the empty chair I'd just vacated.

She gave me a mock salute. "Yes, sir!"

When I came back, she wasn't there. My stomach twisted as I scanned the room, the familiar anxiety clawing at my chest. Then I saw her. She was standing by the roulette tables, her back to me, but I could tell something was off.

The man she was talking to leaned in close, too close. His body language screamed confidence, his smirk practically dripping off his face. She was standing stiffly, her arms crossed, but her face was... calm. Calculated. Like she was letting him think he had the upper hand.

I walked over, my jaw tightening. She noticed me first, her eyes flicking to mine with something that almost looked like guilt. The guy turned around a second later, and his smirk widened.

"Oh, so this is the boyfriend?" he said, looking me up and down like I was some kind of joke. "Didn't realize she was taken. My bad."

"What's going on?" I asked, my voice flat.

She hesitated, her hands twisting nervously. "Nothing," she said quickly. "He was just—he was leaving."

"Leaving, huh?" I turned to the guy. "What did you say to her?"

"Relax, man," he said, raising his hands like he was some kind of saint. "She's a beautiful girl. I was just—"

"What did he say?" I asked her, cutting him off.

She looked down, her fingers gripping the hem of her dress. "...He asked how much I charge for the night."

My stomach dropped. I turned back to him, my voice cold and sharp. "You treated her like a prostitute?"

"Hey, I didn't know!" he said defensively. "Look, I'm sorry, but—"

"Leave," I said.

The man scoffed, his smirk faltering. "Whatever, man. You two deserve each other."

I ignored him and looked at her instead. "You. Leave. Wait outside."

Her eyes widened, and for a moment, I thought she was going to argue. But then she grabbed my arm, her grip surprisingly tight. "No," she whispered, her voice cracking. "Please don't. Let's just go. Let's just leave, okay?"

There was something raw in her eyes, something that twisted in my gut.

But before I could respond, the guy threw a punch. It landed squarely on my jaw, and pain exploded in my face.

The second punch knocked me to one knee.

She stepped between us, her arms outstretched as she shouted at him to stop. The guy finally backed off, muttering something under his breath before disappearing into the crowd.

I stayed on the ground, my fists clenched as I tried to calm the storm inside me. She knelt beside me, her voice trembling. "I'm sorry," she whispered. "I'm so, so sorry..."

I shoved her hand away and got to my feet. "I need a drink," I said, walking off without looking back.

She followed me to the bar, staying a step behind like she was afraid of pushing me further away. I ignored her completely as I downed shot after shot, the burn in my throat doing nothing to smother the anger still simmering in my chest.

She didn't order anything for herself, just sat on the stool beside me with her hands folded neatly in her lap. Out of the corner of my eye, I could see her watching me. Her expression was... strange. Not regretful, not sad—just quiet, like she was waiting for me to say something.

The silence between us was heavy. It felt like a chasm, one I wasn't sure either of us could cross.

When I finally stood and stumbled outside, the cool night air hit me like a slap, shocking some of the haze from my mind. She trailed after me, her footsteps light and hesitant.

I lit a cigarette and took a long drag, staring blankly at the street. The noise of the casino was muffled now, replaced by the distant hum of traffic.

"I'm cold," she murmured behind me.

"It's not cold," I muttered, the words clipped.

"Please." She moved closer, her voice soft and almost childlike. "Hold me?"

"Get lost," I snapped, not even looking at her.

But she didn't. Of course, she didn't.

She reached out, her fingers brushing against my arm. The contact was featherlight, but it sent a jolt of irritation through me. Without thinking, I shoved her away. Not hard, but enough to make her stumble and fall onto the pavement.

She didn't cry out. Didn't even flinch. She just sat there for a moment, looking down at her scraped palms like they weren't even hers. Then she got up, brushing herself off with deliberate care.

When she finally looked at me, there was a strange, sad smile on her face. "Again," she said softly.

I stared at her, dumbfounded. What the hell was her problem?

"Are you serious?" I asked, my voice rough.

She didn't answer. Instead, she took a step closer, her eyes locked on mine. There was something in them that made my stomach twist—a quiet kind of desperation that I couldn't understand.

When her hand touched my arm again, I shoved her harder this time. She hit the ground with a thud, landing awkwardly on her side.

And then... she laughed.

It wasn't a normal laugh. It was quiet, breathless, and raw, like it had been dragged out of her against her will.

"What the hell is wrong with you?" I demanded, my voice rising.

She pushed herself up, slower this time. Her legs wobbled as she stood, but she didn't stop smiling. "Do it again," she whispered.

"Are you insane?"

"Maybe," she said lightly, her tone almost playful. But her eyes... her eyes were glassy, far away, like she wasn't fully here.

She stepped toward me again, and I didn't know what to do. My anger had burned itself out, leaving only confusion and something heavier—something I didn't want to name.

When I didn't push her this time, she reached out and wrapped her arms around me. She was trembling, her face buried against my chest.

"You're such an idiot," I muttered, my voice hollow.

She laughed again, muffled against my shirt. "I know."

For a long moment, I just stood there, my arms hanging uselessly at my sides. And then, finally, I gave in. I wrapped my arms around her, holding her close as she clung to me like I was the only thing keeping her tethered to the earth.

We stayed like that for what felt like hours, the city buzzing around us as if we didn't exist.

"You're freezing," I said eventually.

She didn't respond, but her grip on me tightened.

I sighed, shaking my head. "Let's go back inside."

She nodded against my chest, and for the first time that night, I thought I saw her relax. But as we walked back into the casino, her arm locked around mine, I couldn't shake the feeling that this moment—this fragile peace—was just another piece of the game she was playing.

~ 23 ~

CHAPTER TWENTY-THREE

Beneath the Skin

We made our way through the noise of the casino, past the endless buzz of slot machines and the raucous cheers at the craps table, when she suddenly tugged on my arm.

"I wanna try this one!" she exclaimed, pointing toward the roulette table. There was a spark in her eyes, something I hadn't seen all night.

I raised an eyebrow, intrigued. "You sure? You've been pretty happy just watching."

She nodded, practically bouncing on her toes. "Yeah, c'mon. Give me twenty."

"Alright," I said, handing her the money with a chuckle. The croupier exchanged the bill for a single bright-red chip, and she held it up like it was a treasure before slapping it down on the roulette table—squarely on the number zero.

I blinked, stunned by her choice. "W-Wait. You do know how it works, right?"

She shrugged, casual as ever. "Yeah, what of it?"

"You know you've only got one chance out of thirty-seven playing like that...?"

"Sure!" she chirped, her grin widening.

I shook my head, leaning back to watch as the croupier spun the wheel. The ball danced around the spinning slots, teasing its eventual landing place. My skepticism was well-warranted—nobody wins at roulette, not like this. But as the wheel slowed, the ball bounced erratically before nestling into its final spot.

The green zero.

"Wait... what?" My jaw practically hit the floor.

She gasped, then threw her arms in the air, twirling on the spot. "Yay! I won, babe!"

The croupier pushed a neat stack of chips—over $700—toward her, and she scooped them up like she'd just robbed the place. I couldn't believe it. Sure, less than three percent is still technically a possibility, but come on.

"Unbelievable," I muttered, half laughing as she waved the chips in my face.

She leaned into me, her grin triumphant. "Guess I'm luckier than you, huh?"

"Seems that way."

She offered me the winnings, but I waved her off. "Nah, keep it. Feels like you just burned through a lifetime of good luck for that one."

She shrugged, clutching the chips to her chest. "Fine. I'll put it to good use, then."

We cashed out her winnings, and with two bottles of wine now in tow, we stepped outside into the cool night air. The adrenaline was still coursing through me, but she was calmer now, her earlier giddiness fading into something softer. She grabbed my hand, squeezing it as we flagged down a taxi.

The ride back to the hotel was quiet, the air between us thick with unspoken tension. She leaned against my shoulder, her eyes half-lidded as she traced idle patterns on my forearm with her fingertips. Every so often, she'd glance up at me, her expression unreadable, and I could feel the heat of her gaze even when I didn't look back.

When we stumbled into the hotel room, her demeanor shifted again, crackling with a new kind of energy. Before I could say anything, she turned to me, her hands gripping my collar as she dragged me into a searing kiss. It was intense, almost frantic, like she was trying to pour every bit of herself into that moment.

Her lips moved against mine with a kind of desperation, her hands tangling in my hair as she pressed her body against me. She pulled back just enough to whisper, her voice husky, "I've been waiting all night for this."

I barely had time to respond before she was tugging me toward the bed, her movements bold and unrelenting. She pushed me down onto the mattress, her knees on either side of me as she straddled my lap. Her hair tumbled around her face, her eyes blazing with something I couldn't quite place—a mix of passion, possession, and something darker.

"You're not getting away from me tonight," she murmured, her hands slipping under my shirt.

I smirked, leaning up just enough to meet her halfway. "Wasn't planning on it."

She kissed me again, slower this time, but no less intense. The weight of her, the heat of her body, the smell of her perfume—all of it was intoxicating. For a moment, everything else faded away. The bruises, the headaches, the chaos of the night—they didn't matter.

She pulled away from the kiss, her breaths heavy and her cheeks flushed, a faint sheen of sweat on her skin. Her eyes searched mine, intense and unyielding, as though she were trying to unearth something buried deep within me.

"I want to try something," she whispered, her voice trembling ever so slightly. Before I could ask, she slid off me, moving to the bedside table. She opened the drawer and pulled out a letter opener—a small, unassuming thing with a silver blade and an ornate handle. She turned it over in her hands, as though contemplating its weight, then looked back at me with a strange mix of anticipation and uncertainty.

"I want to write my name on your body with this," she said, her voice soft but steady. "Can I...?"

"Sure," I replied without hesitation, my gaze locked onto hers. There wasn't a hint of doubt in my voice, no second-guessing. I could feel the weight of the moment, the unspoken significance behind her request. This wasn't about some drunken whim or fleeting passion. It was something more—something primal, raw, and deeply personal.

She climbed back onto the bed, straddling me once more. The letter opener glinted in the dim light as she held it delicately, her fingers trembling just slightly. I watched her every movement, studying the way her brows furrowed in concentration, the way her lips parted as she exhaled. There was something mesmerizing about her, about the way she carried this quiet determination, as though this act was more than just a claim—it was a confession.

She pressed the edge of the letter opener to my chest, her touch tentative and hesitant. The pressure was so light it barely scratched the surface of my skin, leaving behind only a faint, pale line. She traced the shape of the first letter, then the next, her breath hitching with each stroke.

Her name was there, written in delicate lines that would fade within minutes, but she seemed satisfied. Her lips curved into a small, almost shy smile as she leaned back to admire her work.

I wasn't satisfied.

Her eyes flicked up to meet mine, and in that moment, something passed between us—a silent understanding, a challenge. I reached out, wrapping my hand around hers, the one still holding the letter opener. I guided her hand back to my chest, pressing the blade harder against my skin.

"What are you—!" she gasped, startled, her voice rising in alarm.

"This," I murmured, my tone low and steady, "is how you do it. If you want to mark me, to make me yours—do it properly."

Her lips parted, her expression torn between fear and something else. "Make you mine...?" she echoed, her voice trembling.

I didn't reply with words; I didn't need to. My eyes told her everything she needed to know. I was giving her permission—no, I was inviting her to leave a piece of herself on me, to take something she needed, even if it hurt.

"I-I don't want to hurt you..." she whispered, her voice breaking, but there was no conviction behind her words. She was wavering, teetering on the edge of something she couldn't quite articulate.

"If you don't want to," I said, my voice sharp, "then get off me."

Her breath hitched, and for a moment, I thought she might do just that. But then her expression changed. Tears welled in her eyes, but they weren't tears of sorrow or regret. They were something else—something I couldn't quite name. She was crying, yet her hands moved with newfound purpose, her grip on the letter opener tightening.

And then she began again. Slowly, deliberately, she carved her name into my skin, the strokes deeper this time, the pain sharp and biting. I hissed through clenched teeth, but I didn't flinch, didn't pull away. I kept my gaze on her, watching as the tears spilled down her cheeks, her lips trembling even as a faint, bittersweet smile tugged at the corners of her mouth.

Her name took shape, bold and unmistakable, etched into my flesh with an intimacy that went beyond words. She wasn't just marking me—she was leaving a part of herself behind, staking a claim in a way that was raw and unapologetic. And as she worked, I realized that this wasn't just about me. It was about her, too. About her need to feel seen, to feel connected, to feel like she mattered.

When she finished, she dropped the letter opener, her hands shaking as she pressed her fingers to the fresh marks on my skin. She traced her name with a featherlight touch, her tears falling freely now. But even as she cried, there was a glimmer of joy in her eyes, a sense of fulfillment that I couldn't quite understand.

"You're mine," she whispered, her voice cracking but resolute. "You'll always be mine."

I reached up, cupping her cheek with one hand, brushing away a tear with my thumb. "Yeah," I said softly, my voice barely above a whisper. "I'm yours."

She collapsed onto my chest, her body trembling as she buried her face in the crook of my neck. I wrapped my arms around her, holding her close as the room fell into a heavy silence. The sting of the fresh cuts was a constant reminder of her mark, of her claim, but I welcomed it. In some strange, twisted way, it felt right.

The first thing I noticed was the blood on the sheets. For a split second, my half-asleep brain thought she might've been on her period. But as I sat up, the sharp sting in my chest jolted the memory back into place.

I pulled back the covers and looked down at myself. Her name was carved into my skin, the edges of each letter inflamed, faintly oozing. It wasn't neat or precise—she'd been shaking too much for that—but it was unmistakably hers. My chest throbbed, the dull ache flaring with every movement. I should've been disturbed. Hell, I *knew* I should've been. But instead, all I felt was... I don't even know. Pride? Acceptance?

I swung my legs over the edge of the bed, groaning as every bruise and ache from the night before made itself known. My face in the mirror told the rest of the story: a swollen right eye, a nasty bruise on my cheek. She hadn't exactly come out unscathed either. Her lower back and ass were red from when I pushed her down outside, and faint blue marks on her forearms hinted at how rough I'd been in bed.

I should clean these cuts, I thought, grimacing at the inflamed letters on my chest. If I didn't, I'd be regretting it in a day or two when the infection set in. Rubbing alcohol. Bandages. Something to stop me from feeling like an idiot.

Behind me, I heard her stir. I turned just as she groggily lifted her head, squinting at the sunlight peeking through the curtains. Her hair was a mess, and her mascara had smudged around her eyes, giving her an almost haunted look. But when her gaze landed on the bloodstains and then shifted to me, her expression changed.

She sat up slowly, wincing as her hand went to her lower back. Her eyes dropped to my chest, where her name was carved in angry red letters. For a long moment, she just stared, her expression unreadable. Then, as if on cue, a soft smile curved her lips.

She reached out, her fingers grazing the inflamed letters. I hissed in pain, and she froze, blinking up at me like she'd just remembered herself. But the smile didn't fade.

"I thought I was dreaming," she said, her voice raspy with sleep.

"I guess not," I replied, my voice flat but not unkind.

She leaned closer, her fingertips ghosting over the marks again. This time, her touch was gentler, almost reverent. "You're mine," she murmured, her tone soft but firm, as if she were reaffirming the claim to herself as much as to me.

I swallowed hard, her words hanging heavy in the air. "...I guess I am."

Her smile widened at that, and she leaned back slightly, her eyes searching mine. "Do you love me?" she asked suddenly, the question catching me off guard.

I froze. The words were simple, but the weight behind them was staggering. My chest tightened as I struggled for an answer. I wanted to say yes. God, I *wanted* to. But the truth was sitting there between us, raw and undeniable.

I hesitated.

Her face fell. The light in her eyes dimmed, and her smile faded into something smaller, more brittle. "Oh," she whispered, her voice barely audible.

"I—" I started to apologize, the words fumbling on my tongue, but I stopped myself. What would I even say? That I was sorry for hesitating? That I didn't know how to explain the mess of emotions swirling inside me? The silence that followed was deafening.

For a moment, she just looked at me, her expression unreadable. Then, out of nowhere, she groaned and flopped back onto the bed, throwing an arm over her face. "Ouch, my head hurts," she whined, her voice exaggerated and full of self-pity.

The sudden shift caught me off guard, and I found myself huffing out a dry laugh. "No kidding," I said, grateful for the change in tone. "You drank half a bottle of wine after winning that roulette game, remember?"

She peeked out from under her arm, sticking her tongue out at me. "Worth it," she muttered, though her wince betrayed her hangover.

"Yeah, yeah," I said, standing up and stretching, wincing at the sting in my chest. "C'mon, let's get you something for that headache before you start whining louder."

She grumbled something under her breath but sat up, wincing as her body protested. I walked over to the minibar, rummaging through it for water and anything resembling aspirin. She followed me with her eyes, her expression softening again as she watched me work.

As I handed her a glass of water and a couple of pills, she took them with a small, sheepish smile. "Thanks," she murmured, her voice quieter now.

I didn't reply, just sat down beside her and took a sip of my own water. The silence between us was no longer as heavy as before. It was... manageable. Even as my chest throbbed and my head pounded, I couldn't help but feel a strange sense of peace.

She rested her head on my shoulder, her hair tickling my cheek. "You're still mine, you know," she said softly, her voice playful but with an edge of sincerity.

I glanced at her out of the corner of my eye, letting a faint smile tug at my lips. "Yeah," I said quietly. "I know."

~ 24 ~

CHAPTER TWENTY-FOUR

Between Heaven and Sin

"Answer me seriously, alright?" Her voice was softer than usual, but there was an edge to it, like she was holding something back.

"...I'm always serious." My brow furrowed. Something about the way she looked at me—like she was trying to memorize my face, like she was afraid of the answer—made me uneasy.

She tilted her head back slightly, just enough to meet my gaze. "Do you regret coming all the way here with me?"

I blinked, caught off guard. The question felt loaded, like a trap I couldn't see until it was too late.

I opened my mouth to answer, but nothing came out. My mind wandered instead, unbidden. I thought of Emily—her steady presence, her quiet strength. I thought about how, even in the moments I didn't deserve it, she'd believed in me. And then I thought about the girl sitting in front of me now.

Three days. That was all it had been. Three days of chaos, laughter, and strange, messy intimacy. Three days where everything felt raw, like my life had been stripped bare. The contrast was dizzying.

"Of course not," I said finally, my voice steady, masking the storm inside me. "I was the one who basically kidnapped you, remember? There's no way I'm regretting any of this."

Her lips curved into a faint smile, but it didn't feel like a victory. "Yeah, but that's because it still hasn't been a week since we ran away. In no time... I'm sure you'll change your mind. And when that time comes, you'll hold it against me."

I scoffed, trying to brush it off, but the way her shoulders tensed told me she wasn't joking. "Since when did you care what I thought of you?"

She didn't answer. Her gaze dropped, her fingers fidgeting with the hem of her sleeve. She always did that when she was uncomfortable, her movements precise, almost ritualistic. Her thumb smoothed over the same spot again and again, like she was trying to wear it thin.

She looked fragile in that moment. Too fragile. The kind of fragile that made you wonder if she might break entirely if you said the wrong thing. I sighed, the weight of it pressing down on me.

"...As long as I have your name on my chest, I won't forget the reason we've done this," I said finally, forcing a softness into my tone. "If I forget nonetheless, you'll be the one reminding me... alright?"

Her laugh was faint, almost bitter. "If only I could..."

She reached for me then, her hands cupping my face. Her touch was light but deliberate, like she was afraid I might disappear if she didn't hold on tight enough. She traced every line and curve, her fingers brushing over my skin with the kind of care that felt obsessive. Possessive.

Then she kissed me. It wasn't like her usual kisses—playful or teasing. This one was slow, deliberate. Her lips lingered, like she was trying to pour something into me that words couldn't express. When she pulled back, her eyes glistened, the smallest crack in her perfect, polished façade.

"You're so gentle," she whispered, her voice trembling. "You're the most gentle man I have ever known. I've noticed this kindness since the first moment I laid my eyes on you."

I froze, her words slicing through me like glass. Gentle? Me? She had to be delusional. There was no other explanation.

No. She wasn't delusional. She was... broken. Just like me. Maybe worse.

There was a desperation in the way she looked at me, like I was the only thing keeping her tethered to the world. It terrified me. She was holding on so tightly that I could feel the weight of it pressing into my chest, suffocating.

"You're wrong," I said finally, my voice quieter than I intended.

She shook her head, a soft, bitter laugh escaping her lips. "You always say that."

"Because it's true. I'm not what you think I am. I'm not—"

"You are," she interrupted, her voice sharper now. Her grip on my face tightened, her nails digging in just enough to sting. "You don't see it, but I do. You're gentle. You're kind. Even when you're cruel, you're still the kindest person I've ever known."

She was smiling, but there was something unsettling about it. It didn't reach her eyes, and her voice wavered just enough to betray the cracks beneath.

"I don't deserve you," she said suddenly, the words tumbling out like a confession. "But I want you anyway. Isn't that selfish?"

I didn't answer. What could I say? That I didn't deserve her either? That I didn't even know if I wanted her?

She leaned her forehead against mine, her breath warm against my skin. "You're all I have left," she whispered. "If you ever leave, I—" She stopped herself, biting her lip hard enough that I thought she might draw blood.

The silence stretched between us, heavy and suffocating. I should have said something. Anything. But I didn't.

Instead, I reached up and gently pried her hands from my face. She didn't resist, but the way she looked at me—wide-eyed and searching—made my chest ache.

"I'm not going anywhere," I said finally, though the words felt like a lie.

She smiled again, but it was smaller this time, more tentative. "Good," she murmured.

Her fingers twitched at her sides, like she was resisting the urge to reach for me again. And for a moment, I wondered if she really meant it—if she really believed I wouldn't leave.

But then she whispered, almost too softly to hear, "I don't think I'd survive it if you did."

The silence stretched between us, but she didn't move. Her hands stayed on my face, her thumbs tracing slow circles against my skin. Her gaze was still fixed on me, unblinking, like she was afraid I'd vanish if she looked away.

"You're mine," she whispered, so softly I almost didn't hear it.

I didn't respond. What could I say to that? That I was hers? That she was mine? The words felt too heavy, too final. Instead, I reached up and gently pried her hands from my face. She let me, but the look in her eyes as I pulled away made something twist in my gut.

She smiled again, brighter this time. “Let’s not ruin it,” she said, almost cheerfully, as if the conversation hadn’t just veered into a dark and dangerous place. “The sun’s still up. We’ve got time.”

She suddenly perked up, her usual mischievous glint returning to her eyes. “Hey,” she said, nudging me lightly with her elbow. “Guess what?”

“What?” I asked, already wary of the look on her face. It was the kind of look that usually spelled trouble.

“We’re at the top,” she said, her grin widening as she gestured toward the view beyond the glass.

I glanced outside. She was right. The wheel had stopped at its highest point, leaving us suspended above the sunlit sprawl of the city below. The streets of Las Vegas stretched out in neat, shimmering lines, the buildings casting crisp, defined shadows in the late afternoon light. The sunlight reflected off glass facades, bouncing bright beams that danced on the walls of the cabin.

She pressed her hands to the glass, her eyes wide with wonder. “Wow,” she breathed. “It’s even better than I thought.”

I couldn’t help but watch her instead of the view. The light caught in her hair, making it gleam like polished obsidian. For a moment, the excitement in her expression made her look younger, almost like the girl I remembered from high school—untouched by the years and everything that had come after.

“It’s a hell of a view,” I admitted, my gaze shifting briefly to the skyline before returning to her. “Not bad for your bright idea.”

She turned to me, her grin softening into something closer to a smirk. “See? You’re not regretting this after all.”

I rolled my eyes but didn't bother arguing. The moment stretched between us, quiet except for the faint hum of the Ferris wheel. The noise of the city below was muffled, leaving us in a cocoon of sunlight and silence.

Then she broke it.

"Imagine if we had sex up here," she said, her voice casual but her eyes glinting with mischief.

I choked on my own breath. "What?"

She laughed, leaning back against the glass and tilting her head as she studied my reaction. "I'm just saying. Can you imagine it? Right here, with the whole city beneath us? It'd be... unforgettable."

"You're insane," I muttered, shaking my head, though the faintest flicker of a smile tugged at my lips.

"Maybe," she said, unbothered. "But you're the one who brought me here, so what does that say about you?"

I didn't have an answer to that—not one I was willing to say out loud, anyway. She grinned at my silence, clearly satisfied with herself, and turned her attention back to the view.

I leaned against the railing, letting the warmth of the sun soak into my skin as I exhaled slowly. The city below was alive, teeming with movement—cars, people, signs flashing even in broad daylight. It was chaotic, but from up here, it looked almost serene.

"It's so bright," she murmured, her voice quieter now. "You can see everything. But no one down there can see us."

I glanced at her, the playfulness in her tone gone. Her hand was pressed against the glass, her fingers tracing invisible patterns as she stared at the skyline. The sunlight illuminated her face, but there was something shadowed in her expression, a flicker of something I couldn't quite place.

"Do you wish it could stay like this?" I asked before I could stop myself.

She didn't answer immediately. Instead, she turned to me, her eyes meeting mine, and for a brief moment, I thought I saw something raw in her gaze. Something unguarded.

"Yeah," she said finally, her voice barely above a whisper. "Yeah, I do."

The Ferris wheel jolted softly as it began its descent, breaking the moment. She pulled away from the glass and flashed me a grin, the vulnerability in her eyes gone as quickly as it had appeared.

"But hey," she said, nudging me again, "you'd probably chicken out anyway."

I snorted, shaking my head. "You're impossible."

"And you love it," she teased, sticking her tongue out before turning her attention back to the view.

I didn't respond. Couldn't, really. Instead, I let the silence stretch between us, the city gleaming under the sun as we began the slow journey back down.

~ 25 ~

CHAPTER TWENTY-FIVE

A Different Light

We stepped off the Ferris wheel, the heat of the midday sun hitting us like a wall. She shielded her eyes with her hand, her gaze lingering on the towering structure we'd just descended from.

"That was fun," she said, her voice light, almost wistful. She gave me a sidelong glance, her smile teasing. "See? I told you it wouldn't be a waste of time."

"Sure," I muttered, stuffing my hands into my pockets. "Let's just ignore the fact that you almost chickened out halfway up."

She stuck her tongue out at me, but the usual spark of playful retaliation wasn't there. Instead, her expression softened, and for a moment, she just looked at me, her eyes searching my face for something I couldn't name.

"Hey," she said suddenly, tilting her head to the side. "Have you realized something?"

"What?" I asked, already bracing myself for whatever nonsense she was about to come up with.

"We've never actually been on a date."

I blinked, caught off guard. "What are you talking about? We've been... places."

She raised an eyebrow, her expression somewhere between amused and exasperated. "Oh, sure. Like the motel room we're staying in. Or the bar where you got into a fight. Very romantic."

"You've got a point," I admitted begrudgingly. "But does this—" I gestured vaguely to the Ferris wheel—"not count as a date?"

She rolled her eyes. "This was my idea. You don't get credit for it."

"I'm pretty sure that's not how this works," I muttered.

"It doesn't matter," she said, brushing it off with a wave of her hand. "What matters is that we've never done the whole traditional thing. You know, dinner, a movie... the works."

I stared at her for a long moment. "Since when do you care about 'traditional' anything?"

She shrugged, her smile turning wistful. "I don't know. I just... I think it'd be nice. To have a proper memory of us, you know? Something real. Something... normal."

That word. It hung in the air between us, heavy with meaning. Normal. As if that was something we could ever hope to be.

I sighed, running a hand through my hair as her words settled in. "Normal, huh? Not exactly a word I'd use to describe us."

"Exactly," she said, her voice tinged with something almost sad. "Maybe that's why it's important. Just one day where we don't have to think about... everything else."

She turned away, looking out over the strip, her hair catching in the sunlight. The way she said it—so casually, yet with a weight I couldn't ignore—made my chest tighten. I wanted to argue, to tell her that none of this mattered, that playing pretend wouldn't fix anything. But the way her fingers twisted the edge of her shirt, like she was holding on to something invisible, stopped me.

"Alright," I said finally. "Fine. A proper date. Dinner, a movie, whatever you want."

She spun back to face me, her eyes lighting up in surprise. "Really?"

"Yeah, really," I grumbled. "I mean, we're already in Vegas. Might as well make the most of it."

Her face broke into a grin, the kind that always caught me off guard. It wasn't the practiced, teasing smile she usually wore. It was real, unguarded. And for a moment, I forgot why I always tried to keep my walls up around her.

"Okay!" she said, bouncing slightly on her heels. "Then it's decided. We'll start with dinner. Something fancy. You're paying."

"Of course I'm paying," I muttered, though the corner of my mouth twitched upward despite myself. "You'd probably try to skip out on the check if it were up to you."

She laughed, the sound light and carefree, and for a second, I felt myself relax. Just a second.

"But first," she said, stopping abruptly in the middle of the bustling crowd, "I need clothes."

"Clothes?" I asked, frowning. "What's wrong with the ones you're wearing?"

She spun around to face me, walking backward with a mischievous glint in her eye. "New ones. Something special. I'll buy them with my winnings, so don't worry about that." She poked my chest lightly with her finger. "But you're not allowed to see until we're actually going out. Deal?"

I blinked at her, the gears in my head grinding to catch up. "You want me to just... what? Stand around while you go shopping?"

"Exactly!" she said brightly, like it was the most obvious thing in the world. "Or better yet, go entertain yourself for an hour. Vegas has plenty to keep you busy."

I groaned, running a hand down my face. "You're really making this into a whole thing, aren't you?"

She smirked, spinning on her heel and starting toward the nearest boutique-lined street. "Of course I am. If we're doing this date thing, we're doing it right."

I spent the next hour wandering aimlessly through the surrounding area, her parting grin etched into my mind. It wasn't like I didn't trust her to pick something reasonable—well, mostly reasonable—but the idea of her going all out for this "date" left me with an odd sense of anticipation. Or maybe dread. I wasn't sure which.

I stopped at a coffee shop to kill some time, nursing a lukewarm latte and people-watching through the window. The streets of Vegas were alive with a chaotic energy, a mix of tourists and locals weaving through the neon-lit tapestry of the city. It was a world away from the quiet monotony I'd known before this trip, and yet, sitting there alone, I couldn't shake the feeling of being out of place.

The thought of her shopping just a few blocks away brought a smirk to my lips despite myself. Knowing her, she'd probably picked the flashiest store she could find, dragging the poor salespeople along for the ride. I could already hear her voice in my head, teasing and playful, insisting that whatever she picked was "perfect."

I shook my head, draining the last of my coffee before stepping back onto the street. Time to go see if she was ready to knock me off my feet—or just knock me out with something ridiculous.

When I found her, she was standing outside one of the upscale shops, a small cluster of bags at her feet and an unmistakable look of triumph on her face.

"Took you long enough," she said, brushing a strand of hair from her face. "I was starting to think you ditched me."

"Tempting," I muttered, glancing at the bags. "So? You blow all your winnings, or are we still eating tonight?"

She stuck her tongue out at me. "I was smart about it. You'll see. Now, ready to head back and get this date started?"

"Lead the way," I said, sighing as she grabbed her bags and started walking, her energy infectious despite myself.

As we made our way back to the car, I couldn't help but glance at her out of the corner of my eye. Whatever she'd picked out, I had a feeling it was going to make tonight... interesting.

As we reached the car, she tossed her bags into the backseat and slid into the passenger seat, humming a tune under her breath. I stood there for a moment, watching her with the hint of a smile tugging at my lips. Her excitement was almost contagious. Almost.

I climbed into the driver's seat and started the engine, the faint hum filling the silence as I pulled out of the parking lot. We didn't talk much on the drive back, her fingers tapping rhythmically on the dashboard while she stared out the window, a content smile playing on her lips.

But as we neared the motel, a thought struck me—a nagging itch in the back of my mind that wouldn't go away. If she was going to go all out for this date, then maybe... just maybe, I should too.

"Hey," I said, breaking the comfortable silence.

"Mm?" she murmured, still gazing out the window.

"I'll drop you off at the motel first," I said, keeping my eyes on the road. "I've got some... errands to run."

She turned to look at me, her brow arching suspiciously. "Errands?"

"Yeah," I said casually. "If you're gonna make this a big deal, I figure I might as well... put in some effort too."

Her eyes lit up with amusement, a teasing grin spreading across her face. "Are you saying you're finally gonna try to impress me?"

"Don't push it," I muttered, feeling a faint flush creep up my neck. "Just... don't get used to it, alright?"

She laughed, leaning back in her seat. "Deal. But now I'm curious. You better not disappoint me."

After dropping her off at the motel, I found myself wandering through the neon-lit streets of Vegas, searching for something that felt right. It wasn't as easy as I thought it'd be. Every store window I passed seemed to mock me with its perfectly curated displays of expensive suits and flashy watches—none of which felt like me.

But then, tucked away on a quieter street, I found a small shop that caught my eye. The display was simple, understated. Classy. I stepped inside, the faint scent of leather and polished wood greeting me.

The shopkeeper, an older man with a sharp eye for detail, greeted me with a nod. "Looking for something specific?"

"Not really," I said, glancing around. "Something... nice, I guess. For a date."

His eyes sparkled with interest as he sized me up. "Well, let's see what we can do."

By the time I returned to the motel, the sun was beginning to dip below the horizon, casting the city in a warm, golden glow. I carried a garment bag over my shoulder, the weight of it feeling oddly significant.

When I stepped into the room, she was sitting cross-legged on the bed, her bags scattered around her. She looked up as I entered, her eyes immediately narrowing with curiosity.

"What's that?" she asked, nodding toward the bag.

"You'll see," I said, hanging it on the back of the door. "Just... don't peek."

She laughed, a soft, genuine sound that made my chest tighten. "You're full of surprises today."

"Don't get used to it," I muttered, grabbing a towel and heading for the bathroom. "I'll be out in a bit."

The water cascaded over me, warm and steady, a stark contrast to the chaos swirling in my head. I leaned forward, pressing my palms against the cool tiles of the shower wall, and let out a long breath. It felt like I hadn't had a quiet moment to myself in days, but now that I had one, I wasn't sure I wanted it. My thoughts, left unchecked, were a minefield.

What was I doing?

I closed my eyes, letting the water wash over me. Memories flickered through my mind like an old reel of film—the night at the bar, the cuts on my chest, her laughter on the Ferris wheel. She had this way of worming her way into every corner of my life, every crack in my defenses. And somehow, I hadn't stopped her. Hell, I hadn't even tried.

It wasn't supposed to be like this. She was supposed to be a mistake, a reminder of everything I wanted to leave behind. And yet, here we were. Running away together, carving her name into my skin, planning a date like we were... normal.

Normal.

The word tasted foreign, bitter. Nothing about us was normal. Not the way she smiled like nothing in the world could touch her, even when I knew better. Not the way I couldn't seem to look at her without feeling something sharp twist in my chest. Not the way she made me feel like I was standing on the edge of something I couldn't come back from.

I rubbed a hand over my face, the water dripping down my chin. Was this love? Or was it just another form of madness? I didn't know anymore. All I knew was that she was there, in my head, in my chest, in my goddamn skin. And I hated it. Or I wanted to hate it. But I couldn't.

My mind drifted to Emily, to the life I'd left behind. The life I'd ruined with my own hands. I thought I'd feel more guilt about it, more regret. But the truth was, I barely felt anything at all. The only time I felt alive anymore was when I was with her.

And that terrified me.

I let out a shaky breath, the steam in the room thickening around me. What was she doing to me? How had I let it get this far? And why, despite everything, did I not want it to stop?

I turned off the water abruptly, the sudden silence ringing in my ears. There was no point in spiraling. Not now. Not when she was waiting for me.

Grabbing a towel, I stepped out of the shower and stared at my reflection in the foggy mirror. My chest was still raw, the letters of her name standing out in angry red against my skin. I traced them with my fingers, the sting grounding me.

What had I done?

Shaking my head, I pulled on my clothes and stepped out of the bathroom. I wasn't ready for answers, and maybe I never would be. But for now, I'd let tonight be what it was—a distraction. A moment of pretend normalcy in the middle of the chaos we'd created.

I stepped out of the bathroom, the steam from the shower rolling out with me like a ghost. For once, I felt... put together. I'd shaved, styled my hair, and wore the sharpest outfit I could manage—a dark button-down, fitted slacks, and polished shoes. The kind of clothes I would've worn if I still had a life that required dressing up. It felt strange, unnatural even, but also necessary. If she wanted a proper date, I figured I should at least try.

I adjusted my cuffs, stepping into the room, and froze.

She was standing by the window, the soft light from outside casting a warm glow around her. For a moment, I thought I was looking at someone else. Her dress—it wasn't like the others. It wasn't tight or skimpy, nor was it some cheap fabric meant to lure in desperate men. It was simple, elegant. A deep navy blue that hugged her figure just enough to be alluring without being obvious. The neckline was modest, the hem just below her knees, and the sleeves fell gently over her shoulders. She looked... beautiful.

Not sexy. Not provocative. Just beautiful.

She turned when she heard me step in, her eyes widening slightly before a playful grin spread across her face. "Well, don't you clean up nice," she said, her voice teasing but her gaze lingering longer than usual. "I almost didn't recognize you."

I didn't respond right away, still taking her in. Her hair was pulled back in soft waves, framing her face perfectly. She'd done her makeup differently too—lighter, more natural, accentuating rather than covering. For the first time, I wasn't looking at the girl who worked Thursday nights at a hostess bar. I was looking at... her.

"You look... different," I finally said, my voice quieter than I intended.

Her grin faltered for just a second, replaced by something softer, almost vulnerable. "Good different?"

I nodded, stepping further into the room. "Yeah. Good different."

She spun around once, the hem of her dress swaying as she did. "I wanted to go for something different," she said, smoothing the fabric with her hands. "Figured if we're doing the whole date thing, I should at least look the part."

"You do," I said before I could stop myself. I cleared my throat, looking away. "You look... good."

Her smile widened, and she took a step toward me, her heels clicking softly against the floor. "You don't look too bad yourself," she said, her tone still teasing but her eyes sincere. She reached out, straightening the collar of my shirt with practiced ease. "I didn't think you had it in you to clean up like this."

"Neither did I," I muttered, my lips twitching into a faint smirk.

She laughed softly, her hands lingering on my collar for a moment before dropping to her sides. "This feels weird, doesn't it?" she said, glancing down at herself. "Not being... us?"

"It does," I admitted, shoving my hands into my pockets. "But maybe that's not a bad thing."

She tilted her head, studying me for a moment before nodding. "Yeah. Maybe not."

We stood there in silence for a beat, the air between us heavier than it should've been. She broke it first, reaching for her purse and slinging it over her shoulder. "Alright," she said, her usual playful tone slipping back into place. "Let's get this show on the road. Don't wanna waste all this effort, right?"

"Right," I said, following her to the door. But as I held it open for her, I couldn't help but glance back at the room, at the life we were leaving behind for one night. And for the first time in a long time, I wondered if maybe—just maybe—this wasn't such a bad idea after all.

~ 26 ~

CHAPTER TWENTY-SIX

If This Was Your Last Week

The restaurant had a cozy charm that somehow managed to feel both intimate and exposed. Warm lights hung low over the tables, their soft glow glinting off polished silverware. The hum of conversation surrounded us, a dull roar punctuated by occasional bursts of laughter. It felt too normal for us—too grounded, too far from the chaos of the past few days. It was disorienting in its simplicity.

She took it all in with wide eyes, her expression hovering somewhere between awe and disbelief. Her fingers brushed the edge of her menu, lingering there as if the sensation itself was foreign to her. "This is... nice," she murmured, her voice unusually soft, almost reverent.

"It's just a restaurant," I muttered, feigning disinterest. But the way her eyes sparkled, the way her lips quirked upward in quiet wonder—it tugged at something deep inside me. Something I wasn't ready to name.

"Yeah, but we've been eating gas station food and whatever that excuse for room service was," she teased, her lips curling into a smirk. "This? This feels fancy."

I didn't respond, letting her excitement fill the silence. The truth was, I'd chosen this place deliberately. It wasn't extravagant—far from it. But it had just enough polish to make it feel special. For her. Not that I'd ever admit it.

Her gaze drifted over the room, taking in every detail like she was committing it to memory. The way her fingers tapped against the menu, her knee bouncing slightly beneath the table—it all spoke to that restless energy she carried everywhere, like she couldn't let herself settle. She was always on edge, even in her moments of peace.

The waiter arrived, and while I rattled off my choice quickly, she took her time. Her eyes scanned the menu like it was some kind of puzzle she needed to solve. Her brows furrowed in concentration, her lips pressing together in thought as her fingers drummed lightly against the table. She was completely absorbed, oblivious to the way I studied her.

"Any recommendations?" she asked, glancing up at me suddenly. Her eyes caught mine, and for a moment, something unspoken lingered between us.

I shrugged. "Just pick something. It's food."

"Wow, you're a real romantic, aren't you?" she said, rolling her eyes. But her words lacked venom. Her voice carried that playful edge she always wore like armor. She smiled, and it was the kind of smile that could make you forget everything else. I hated how much I liked it.

When she finally ordered, the waiter disappeared, leaving us alone with the soft candlelight and the unspoken tension hanging between us. She toyed with her napkin, folding and unfolding it absentmindedly, her movements small but telling. I wondered if she even noticed how tightly her hands gripped the fabric, like she needed something to ground her.

"You're quiet tonight," she said softly, her voice cutting through the haze of my thoughts.

I shrugged again, not trusting myself to speak. Words felt dangerous in moments like this, like they might betray something I wasn't ready to confront.

"Is it the food? Or is it me?" she pressed, leaning forward slightly. Her tone was light, but there was a flicker of something deeper in her eyes—something vulnerable.

"It's neither," I said, keeping my voice even. "I'm just... thinking."

"About what?" she asked, tilting her head. Her hair fell to one side, catching the warm glow of the candlelight. It made her look softer somehow, less like the chaotic force she usually was and more like the girl I'd known before everything went wrong.

I hesitated, glancing down at the table. "I don't know. Life. Stuff."

"Stuff," she echoed with a small laugh. "That's vague even for you."

I managed a half-smile, but it didn't reach my eyes. "What do you want me to say?"

"I don't know." She leaned back in her chair, her fingers still toying with the napkin. "Something real, maybe."

Her words hung between us, heavy and unsettling. I wanted to say something, anything, to fill the silence, but nothing felt right. Instead, I let my gaze drift to her hands, to the way her fingers fidgeted with the fabric as if she needed the distraction.

"I guess I'm not good at real," I said finally, my voice quieter than I intended.

She looked at me then, her eyes searching mine, and for a moment, I thought she might push. But she didn't. Instead, she smiled—soft, understanding, and entirely disarming.

"That's okay," she said. "Neither am I."

Her words were simple, but they hit me harder than they should have. It was the honesty in them, the way she said it without pretense or expectation. For the first time that night, I felt like we weren't just two people running from our pasts—we were two people trying to figure out if we even had a future.

The restaurant buzzed with soft conversation and the occasional clinking of glasses, but the world outside our table may as well not have existed. She'd been fidgeting with her napkin for the past ten minutes, folding and unfolding it, her fingers moving like restless birds. The soft, warm light caught on her face in the most inconvenient way—making her look softer than she had any right to. That light carved her out of the chaos we'd been living in, as if she belonged here, like this—a version of her that shouldn't exist and yet did.

"What's with the face?" I asked, breaking the silence. I needed a distraction from the way the sight of her was messing with my head.

"What face?" she shot back, glancing up with faux innocence, her eyebrows raised in playful exaggeration.

"That one. The one you're wearing right now," I muttered, leaning back in my chair and gesturing vaguely. "You look like you're about to burst into song or something."

She grinned at that, her teeth flashing white against the red of her lipstick. "Maybe I am. Got a problem with that?"

"Yes. You'd sound terrible."

Her gasp was dramatic, her hand flying to her chest like I'd stabbed her. "You know, for someone who claims to be so emotionally detached, you're surprisingly rude."

"Emotional detachment and honesty are not mutually exclusive," I said, deadpan, reaching for my water glass.

Her eyes glinted with amusement as she leaned forward, propping her chin in her hand. "Ah, so it's honesty now. What's next? Kindness?"

I snorted. "Don't push it."

She studied me for a moment, that teasing smile softening into something quieter. "You're in a good mood," she noted. "Relaxed. I like it."

I shrugged, trying to play it off. "Don't get used to it."

The waiter arrived with our entrees, breaking whatever odd moment had just passed between us. Her plate was set down in front of her, and she poked at the food like it might bite her. Her brow furrowed in exaggerated concentration. "Okay, not gonna lie, this is way too fancy for me. What even is this?"

"It's food," I said, cutting into my own dish. "You put it in your mouth, chew, swallow, and repeat. Not complicated."

She rolled her eyes, leaning back with her arms crossed. "Wow, thanks for the lesson. I'll treasure this knowledge forever."

"You're welcome," I said, smirking.

She stuck her tongue out at me, but the moment she took a cautious bite, her expression changed entirely. Her eyes widened, and she let out a soft moan of appreciation. "Oh my God. This is amazing."

"See? And you were acting like I dragged you to a torture chamber."

"Yeah, yeah," she said, waving me off with her fork. "Don't get cocky. You're still the guy who almost forgot to disinfect his chest."

I raised an eyebrow. "You're the one who put it there in the first place."

Her smile faltered for just a split second, her gaze flicking downward. It was so fast I almost missed it, but it was there—an uncomfortable reminder of how fragile this whole thing was. For a moment, the air felt heavier between us, the weight of everything unspoken pressing in. She recovered quickly, though, forcing out a laugh.

"Well, maybe I just wanted to mark my territory," she teased, the grin returning to her face, though it didn't quite reach her eyes. "You're mine now, remember?"

I nodded, letting the moment pass. "I guess I don't have much of a choice."

"Damn right you don't," she said, sticking a forkful of food into her mouth triumphantly.

The conversation meandered after that, dipping into lighter topics as we finished our meals. We teased each other about our high school days, trading memories like they were currency. She brought up the time I'd tripped over my own feet during a track meet, complete with a reenactment involving a salt shaker and her napkin as props.

"And you just *face-planted*, right in front of everyone!" she said, laughing so hard she could barely get the words out. "I thought I was going to die of secondhand embarrassment."

"Yeah, well, at least I didn't fall asleep in the middle of a study session and drool all over my notes," I shot back, leaning forward with a smirk.

Her jaw dropped. "You're never letting that go, are you?"

"Never," I confirmed. "I'm taking that one to the grave."

Her laugh was brighter and more genuine than I'd heard in a long time. It wasn't the sarcastic chuckle she used to deflect, or the forced giggle she sometimes wore like a mask. It was real, unguarded, and it did something to me. It made something in my chest tighten—a feeling I couldn't quite name. It wasn't love. Not yet. But it was something dangerously close.

Her laugh lingered in the air, warm and infectious, pulling me out of my own head for a moment. It was strange how easy she made it seem—how effortlessly she could fill the space between us with something that felt so alive. I found myself watching her more than I should have, the way her shoulders shook with laughter, the way her fingers idly toyed with her glass, the way her eyes sparkled when she caught me looking.

The waiter appeared with dessert menus, interrupting the quiet rhythm we'd settled into. She reached for hers, flipping it open with exaggerated care, as though deciding between desserts was a life-or-death situation. Her brow furrowed in mock concentration, and she tapped her chin dramatically.

"What do you think?" she asked, holding the menu out to me. "Chocolate cake or crème brûlée?"

"Neither," I replied dryly. "Go for the fruit tart. It'll match your personality—sickly sweet and impossible to digest."

She gasped, clutching the menu to her chest as if I'd just insulted her entire family lineage. "Excuse you! I am perfectly digestible, thank you very much."

I raised an eyebrow, smirking. "Is that the hill you want to die on?"

"Absolutely." She grinned and flagged the waiter, ordering both the chocolate cake and the crème brûlée just to spite me.

"You're ridiculous," I muttered, shaking my head.

"And yet, here you are," she teased, leaning forward with a smug smile. "Still stuck with me."

I didn't respond, but I didn't look away either. The truth was, I didn't mind. Not her ridiculousness, not her impulsiveness, not the way she turned every moment into something memorable. It was exhausting, sure, but it was also... grounding. Like she was the only thing keeping me tethered to whatever this life of mine was supposed to be.

The desserts arrived, and she practically lit up, her eyes widening in delight. "Oh my God, look at this! It's so fancy. I almost feel bad eating it."

"Don't let that stop you," I said, picking up my fork. "You have zero impulse control anyway."

"True," she said brightly, diving into the chocolate cake without hesitation. "But hey, that's what makes life fun, right?"

I watched her for a moment, the way her eyes closed as she savored the first bite, the way she hummed softly in approval. She had a way of making even the simplest things feel significant, like every little moment deserved its own spotlight. It was unsettling, how easily she could pull me into her world, how much I wanted to stay there.

As we worked our way through dessert, she suddenly set her fork down and looked at me, her expression turning uncharacteristically serious.

"Imagine if this was the last week of your life," she said softly. "Would you regret it?"

The question hit me pretty hard. Why would she ask that? I took a moment, before I answered. "I would have regrets, yes. But not from this last week. Perhaps not leaving with you sooner."

Her eyes widened slightly at my response, her lips parting as if she wanted to say something but didn't know how. She looked at me for a long moment, her expression unreadable. Then, she smiled. It wasn't her usual mischievous grin or the teasing smirk she often wore—it was softer, quieter. Almost sad.

"Really?" she asked, her voice barely above a whisper.

I nodded, swallowing the lump in my throat. "Yeah. I mean... I've made a lot of mistakes. Hurt people. Lied to them. But if I had one thing I could do over, maybe... maybe it would've been this. Leaving everything behind, starting over. I don't know what's coming next, but for once, it doesn't feel like I'm just... wasting time."

Her gaze dropped to her hands, her fingers nervously twisting the edge of the napkin. She didn't speak for a moment, and the silence stretched between us like a thread pulled taut.

"What about you?" I asked finally, my voice rougher than I intended. "If this was your last week... would you regret it?"

Her fingers stilled, and she looked up at me, her eyes shining with something I couldn't quite place. "I don't know," she admitted. "Maybe. Maybe not."

"That's not an answer."

She tilted her head, a small smile tugging at the corner of her lips. "I guess it depends on how the week ends."

There it was again—that undertone, that shadow in her words that hinted at something darker, something she wasn't ready to share. It made my chest ache, though I wasn't sure why.

"Stop being cryptic," I muttered, trying to lighten the mood. "It doesn't suit you."

She laughed softly, but it didn't reach her eyes. "You think so?"

"I know so."

For a moment, we just looked at each other, the weight of her question still hanging in the air. Then she leaned back in her chair, crossing her arms with a mock pout.

"Well, if this is my last week, I'm going to make it count," she declared. "Starting with dessert."

I raised an eyebrow. "You already ordered dessert."

"Then I'll order more," she said with a defiant grin.

Her ability to shift moods so quickly would've been impressive if it wasn't so unnerving. I couldn't tell if she was genuinely carefree or if it was just another mask she wore to hide what was underneath. Either way, I didn't push. Maybe because I was afraid of what I'd find if I did.

She flagged down the waiter and ordered something ridiculously indulgent, her enthusiasm drawing a laugh from the older man. When he walked away, she turned back to me with that same bright smile, as if the heavy conversation we'd just had never happened.

"You're crazy," I said, shaking my head.

"And you're an asshole," she shot back. "But that's why we work."

Her words hit me harder than they should've. I wanted to argue, to deny it, but I couldn't. Maybe she was right. Maybe that was why we worked—because I was predictable, and she was anything but.

As the waiter returned with her dessert, I watched her dig in with childlike delight, the shadows in her eyes momentarily forgotten. For a while, I let myself forget them too. I let myself enjoy the moment, the sound of her laughter, the way she looked at me like I was the only thing that mattered.

But deep down, I knew it wouldn't last. It never did. And I couldn't shake the feeling that her question wasn't hypothetical—that she was counting down to something, even if I didn't know what.

~ 27 ~

CHAPTER TWENTY-SEVEN

Less Gray

We didn't talk much on the way back to the motel. The silence wasn't heavy, but it wasn't exactly comfortable either. It felt like we were both lost in our own thoughts, the high from the date fading as reality crept back in. She leaned her head against the window, watching the city lights blur past, her reflection staring back at her with a kind of wistful detachment.

When we got back to the room, she immediately flopped onto the bed, kicking off her shoes and stretching out like she owned the place. "Let's watch something," she said, reaching for the remote.

"Sure," I muttered, shrugging off my jacket and loosening my tie. The idea of sinking into mindless entertainment for a while was more appealing than I cared to admit.

She flicked through the channels, pausing on a romantic comedy that I wouldn't have picked in a million years. But I didn't protest. Not tonight.

As the movie played, she scooted closer to me, her head resting on my shoulder. It was the kind of scene you'd find in one of those picture-perfect stories—boy meets girl, they cuddle up, and everything is fine. But it wasn't. Not for us. I could feel the tension in her body, the way she shifted every few minutes like she couldn't quite get comfortable. And I wasn't any better. My arm hung awkwardly around her shoulders, like I didn't know what to do with it.

The movie droned on, and we stayed like that, two people pretending to be normal. Pretending that we belonged here, in this moment, like we weren't running from everything.

"Do you think people actually live like this?" she asked suddenly, her voice soft and almost drowned out by the TV.

"Like what?"

"Like... this." She gestured vaguely at the screen, where the couple was sharing some overly sentimental moment. "Happy. Together. No drama, no baggage. Just... normal."

I didn't know how to answer that. So I didn't. Instead, I tightened my arm around her, and she sighed, leaning into me.

Eventually, her breathing evened out, and I thought she'd fallen asleep. But I was the one who drifted off first, lulled by the soft glow of the screen and the weight of her against me.

When I woke up, the TV was still on, casting flickering shadows across the room. The bed beside me was empty. I blinked, trying to shake off the fog of sleep, and spotted her sitting at the desk by the window. She was hunched over, her hand moving rapidly across a piece of paper.

I watched her for a moment, the scene feeling strangely surreal. She looked different in the dim light—smaller, more fragile. Like if I said the wrong thing, she might just... vanish.

She suddenly stopped writing, her hand hovering over the paper as if she wasn't sure what to do next. Then, with a sharp sigh, she crumpled it up and tossed it into the trash.

"What are you doing?" I asked, my voice still rough from sleep.

She jumped, clearly startled, and turned to face me. "It's nothing," she said quickly, her tone too casual.

I frowned, sitting up. "Didn't look like nothing."

"It wasn't important," she insisted, brushing a strand of hair behind her ear. "Just... something stupid."

I could've pressed her. Part of me wanted to. But the look in her eyes stopped me—the kind of look that dared me to pry, to break whatever fragile truce we had right now.

"Alright," I said, forcing a shrug. But the pit in my stomach didn't go away.

She stood, stretching like nothing had happened, and gave me a tired smile. "Hey, can we change hotels?"

"What?" The question caught me off guard.

"This place is getting boring," she said, waving a hand around the room. "And I want somewhere with better room service."

I stared at her, trying to gauge if that was the real reason. She tilted her head, her expression unreadable, and for a moment, I thought about saying no. About staying here, where things were familiar—even if it was just for a little longer.

"Fine," I said finally. "We'll look for something in the morning."

Her smile widened, but there was something about it that felt... off. Like it didn't quite reach her eyes.

The morning sunlight streamed through the motel room's cracked blinds, painting uneven stripes across the dingy walls. As I loaded our things into the car, she leaned back in the passenger seat, her feet propped up on the dashboard, humming some tune I didn't recognize.

She directed me through the streets with a casual ease, her finger darting out occasionally to point the way. It felt aimless, like she didn't really know where she wanted to go. Maybe she didn't. Maybe that was the point.

After driving around for a while, she finally perked up, leaning forward with a grin. "There! Let's go there!"

I slowed the car and glanced at where she was pointing. My stomach sank. The motel was the definition of rundown. Faded paint peeled off the walls, and a rusted sign buzzed faintly, the flickering neon letters spelling out "Vacancy" like some cruel joke. The parking lot was half-full of beat-up cars that looked like they hadn't moved in years.

"You can't be serious," I muttered, pulling into the lot reluctantly. I parked in front of the building and gestured toward it. "This place looks like it's one step away from collapsing."

"But I would feel much more comfortable in this one," she said, her voice oddly soft.

"Are you for real?" I stared at her, then back at the motel. The place screamed "bad idea." It was the kind of spot you'd see in a crime show, the backdrop to drug deals and illicit affairs. A place where no one asked questions because they didn't want to know the answers.

The thought made me glance at her. She was already unbuckling her seatbelt, her expression unreadable.

"I'll go take care of the room," she said, sliding out of the car before I could stop her. "Wait right here."

"No, I'll come with you—"

"No, that's alright." She waved me off, flashing a quick smile. "I want to do this on my own."

I frowned, watching her disappear into the front office. Do this on her own? What the hell did that mean? Was she trying to prove something? That she didn't need me? That she could handle this life we'd thrown ourselves into? She was already an adult; she didn't need to prove anything to me. But I held my tongue and waited, gripping the steering wheel tighter than I needed to.

She returned about five minutes later, a small key dangling from her fingers. "Room 107," she announced cheerfully, as if we'd just booked a five-star suite.

I grabbed our bags from the car, following her to the door. She pushed it open, revealing a room that was every bit as bleak as I'd expected. The walls were a dull, lifeless gray, the carpet stained and threadbare. A single bed sat in the center, its thin blanket worn to the point of transparency. The air smelled faintly of mildew, with an undercurrent of something sour that I didn't want to identify.

She spun around and spread her arms. "Ta-da! Our new home!"

I dropped the bags onto the floor, glancing around. "It's... something."

"It's perfect," she said, flopping onto the bed with a grin. "See? The mattress isn't even lumpy."

"That's your standard?" I muttered, raising an eyebrow.

She ignored me, stretching out and kicking off her shoes. "Let's go to a bar or something!" she said suddenly, propping herself up on her elbows. "It's on me!"

"But we literally just got here," I pointed out, gesturing to the bags at my feet.

"And?" She tilted her head, her grin widening. "You're not gonna tell me you're tired already, are you? Come on. Let's have some fun. Like yesterday."

I sighed, rubbing the back of my neck. She had a way of making everything sound so simple, so easy. Like none of it mattered. Maybe she was right. Maybe it didn't.

"Fine," I said eventually. "But don't blame me if you regret it later."

"Deal!" she said, springing to her feet and grabbing my arm. Her enthusiasm was infectious, even if I didn't want to admit it.

As we stepped out into the sun, I found myself glancing back at the room. The cracked walls, the flickering light overhead. It was a far cry from where I thought I'd be in life, but somehow... it felt fitting. Like this was exactly where we were supposed to be.

"Let's have fun every day from now on," I wanted to say. The words hovered on the tip of my tongue, but I swallowed them down. I didn't know why I always held back, why I always forced myself to play things a certain way. Maybe I was afraid of what they'd mean—of what they'd make real.

But as she tugged me toward the car, her laughter ringing in the air, I couldn't shake the feeling that, for now at least, this was enough.

The day stretched on like an endless road, the two of us weaving through the city without any real destination. We stopped here and there—at a diner for lunch, a thrift store where she tried on ridiculous hats just to make me roll my eyes, and a tiny bookshop that smelled of old paper and nostalgia. But something unspoken lingered between us, an undercurrent of tension that neither of us dared acknowledge.

It started small, like most arguments do. We were walking through a crowded outdoor market, the kind of place where vendors shouted over each other to hawk their wares. She was darting from stall to stall, her eyes lighting up at every trinket and oddity, while I hung back, feeling out of place in the chaos.

She stopped at a stall selling cheap jewelry, picking up a silver bracelet and holding it up to the light. "What do you think?" she asked, turning to me with a smile.

I shrugged. "It's fine."

Her smile faltered. "Fine? That's it?"

"What do you want me to say?" I muttered, shoving my hands into my pockets. "It's a bracelet."

"It's not just a bracelet," she said, her voice rising slightly. "I'm asking for your opinion."

"And I gave it," I snapped. "It's fine. What more do you want?"

Her expression shifted, hurt flashing in her eyes before she turned away, setting the bracelet down. "Forget it," she said quietly.

The tension between us thickened, coiling tighter with every step we took through the market. She walked ahead of me, her shoulders stiff, while I trailed behind, feeling a strange mix of guilt and frustration. I hadn't meant to upset her, but the words had come out sharper than I intended. Maybe sharper than I realized.

Finally, she stopped in the middle of the street, turning to face me. "Why do you do that?" she asked, her voice low but charged.

"Do what?" I asked, though I already knew.

"Push me away. Every time I try to get close, you shut me out," she said, her eyes searching mine. "Do you even want me here? Or am I just some obligation to you?"

The question hit harder than I expected, and for a moment, I didn't know what to say. The market around us seemed to fade, the noise dimming to a dull roar. I opened my mouth, but no words came out. What was I supposed to say? That I didn't know? That I was just as confused as she was?

"I don't... I don't know," I finally admitted, my voice barely audible. "I'm trying, alright? But I don't know how to do this. I never have."

Her lips pressed into a thin line, and she looked away, her jaw tight. "You make it really hard to believe that sometimes," she murmured.

We stood there in silence, the weight of her words hanging between us like a storm cloud. I hated the look on her face, the way her shoulders slumped like she was carrying the world's disappointment. And I hated that I was the cause of it.

"I'm sorry," I said quietly. The words felt clumsy, inadequate, but they were all I had. "I didn't mean to... I'm just—" I stopped, running a hand through my hair. "I'm sorry."

She didn't respond right away, her gaze fixed on the ground. For a moment, I thought she wouldn't forgive me. That this was the breaking point, the moment where everything between us finally cracked beyond repair.

But then she sighed, looking up at me with tired eyes. "I forgive you," she said softly. "But you need to figure out what you want. Because I can't keep being in limbo like this."

I nodded, the knot in my chest loosening slightly. "I'll try," I said. And I meant it, even if I wasn't sure where to start.

The tension between us lingered as we left the market, neither of us speaking as we wandered aimlessly through the city. The sun dipped lower in the sky, casting long shadows across the streets, and the weight of the argument slowly began to lift. It wasn't gone entirely, but it was bearable.

She was the one who broke the silence, her voice cutting through the quiet like a blade. "You know," she said, her tone lighter now, "you're really bad at apologizing."

I glanced at her, the corners of my mouth twitching upward. "Yeah, well, you're really good at making me feel like I have to."

She smirked, nudging me with her elbow. "It's a talent."

By the time the sun had set and the city was alive with neon lights, the air between us had softened. We drove around for a while, the car's headlights cutting through the darkness, until she suddenly perked up, her eyes sparkling with mischief.

"Let's go to a club," she said, her grin wide.

I shot her a skeptical look. "A club? Really?"

"Come on," she said, leaning toward me with that playful glint in her eye. "We've done the Ferris wheel, the restaurant... Let's do something fun."

I hesitated, my grip tightening on the steering wheel. The idea of a crowded, noisy club didn't exactly appeal to me, but the excitement in her voice was hard to ignore.

"Fine," I said finally, sighing. "But if it sucks, I'm blaming you."

She laughed, clapping her hands together. "Deal. Now let's go have some fun."

The city lights blurred into streaks of neon and gold as we drove through the bustling streets. The hum of the engine filled the silence between us, a low, steady sound that kept me grounded as my thoughts spun in circles. She sat next to me, her head resting lightly against the window, her reflection in the glass almost ghostly in the dim light. The tension from earlier had faded, but something unspoken lingered, hanging heavy in the air.

I gripped the steering wheel tighter, stealing a glance at her. She wasn't fidgeting or filling the quiet with her usual chatter. She just stared out at the city passing by, her expression unreadable. It bothered me, that stillness. Like she was pulling away, retreating somewhere I couldn't reach.

"If it helps..." I started, my voice breaking the silence.

She turned her head slightly, looking at me with curious eyes. "What?"

"I do care about you," I said, my words slow, deliberate. "You're not an obligation, and I want you around. To be honest..." I hesitated, the weight of the admission pressing down on me. "These last few days have made me feel more alive than I have in years."

Her eyes softened, the faintest smile tugging at her lips. "Really?" she asked, her voice quiet, almost disbelieving.

"Yeah," I said, keeping my eyes on the road. "I don't know what it is about you, but... you're different. You make things... less gray."

She let out a small laugh, the sound warm but tinged with something I couldn't quite place. "Less gray, huh? That's not exactly romantic, but I'll take it."

I shrugged, a smirk playing at the corners of my mouth. "Don't push your luck. I'm not exactly the poetic type."

She shifted in her seat, leaning closer to me. "You know," she said, her voice soft but teasing, "you're really bad at this whole 'emotional honesty' thing."

I glanced at her, raising an eyebrow. "And you're too good at it. Makes it hard to keep up."

Her smile widened, but her eyes held a glimmer of something deeper, something I couldn't quite decipher. "You don't have to keep up," she said. "Just... don't run away from it."

I didn't respond, letting her words settle in the space between us. The truth was, I wasn't sure if I could promise that. Running was what I did best. But as the city lights reflected in her eyes, something in me shifted, like a crack in a wall I'd spent years building.

"Thanks," she said after a moment, her voice barely above a whisper.

"For what?" I asked, glancing at her again.

"For not letting me be invisible," she said, turning her gaze back to the window. "It's easy to feel that way, sometimes."

I swallowed hard, her words hitting me in a place I didn't know was still raw. "You're not invisible," I said firmly. "Not to me."

She didn't say anything after that, but the silence between us felt lighter, less suffocating. The city outside seemed to slow, the bright lights casting fleeting shadows across her face.

By the time we pulled into the parking lot of the club, the tension from earlier had all but disappeared. She was smiling again, that mischievous glint back in her eyes. As she unbuckled her seatbelt and reached for the door, she glanced back at me, her grin widening.

"Ready to have some fun?" she asked, her voice full of excitement.

I let out a small laugh, shaking my head. "Let's see if this club of yours is worth it."

"Oh, it will be," she said confidently, stepping out of the car. "And don't worry—I'll make sure you don't regret it."

~ 28 ~

CHAPTER TWENTY-EIGHT

Mistakes

The club was alive with music and light, the air thick with the kind of energy that made it impossible to sit still. She tugged me onto the dancefloor, her excitement infectious, and for once, I didn't resist. The flashing lights bathed her face in a kaleidoscope of colors, her smile as wide and radiant as I'd ever seen it.

"You're a terrible dancer," she teased, her voice barely audible over the music.

"Thanks for the reminder," I shot back, my movements awkward and stilted.

She laughed, leaning in close, her breath warm against my ear. "You're lucky you're cute."

"Lucky me," I muttered, though I couldn't help the small smile that tugged at my lips.

We swayed together, her arms wrapping around my neck as the crowd moved in a chaotic rhythm around us. I was stiff, unsure of myself, but she didn't seem to care. Her gaze stayed locked on mine, and for a moment, it felt like we were the only two people in the world.

"This week was the best of my entire life," she said suddenly, her voice soft but certain.

"This does look like the kind of place where you'd say something like that," I replied, glancing around at the swirling lights and vibrant colors. The music thumped in my chest, loud and unrelenting, but for once, it didn't bother me. It felt like it belonged, like we belonged.

"I'm not talking about this place," she said, her tone unwavering. "Or this city. I'm talking about you. Do you believe me?"

I swallowed hard, her words hitting like a punch to the gut. Her eyes were unflinching, impossibly sincere, and for once, I couldn't find it in me to argue. "...Yeah," I said finally. "I do."

"Good," she murmured, pulling me into a kiss that made the rest of the world disappear. Her lips were soft and warm, her touch grounding me in a way I couldn't explain.

When she pulled away, she whispered something against my ear. "But you shouldn't."

"What did you say?" I asked, pulling back slightly to look at her.

"Nothing," she said quickly, her hands fidgeting at my chest before she wrapped her arms around me again. We stayed like that for a while, swaying to the music, her body pressed against mine as the crowd swirled around us.

Then I heard a voice I hadn't expected to hear again. "Holy shit. Is that you?"

I froze, my stomach sinking. Turning slowly, I found myself face-to-face with Ethan, his grin as wide and easygoing as ever. He was dressed sharply, his arm casually draped around the shoulders of a petite woman with dark hair.

"Ethan," I said, my voice tight. "It's been a while."

"Damn right it has," he said, clapping me on the shoulder. "I can't believe it's you. And who's this?" His eyes flicked to the girl at my side, his curiosity turning to recognition almost instantly. "Wait a second... is that...?"

She gave him a small smile, tilting her head slightly. "Hey, Ethan."

"Oh, wow. High school reunion, huh?" he said with a laugh. "Man, I remember you two back in the day. And didn't I set you two up once in college?"

"Something like that," I muttered, already feeling the tension creep into my shoulders.

"It's great to see you again," he said to her, his grin never faltering. "You look... good."

"Thanks," she replied, her tone polite but distant.

"This is my wife, Bethany," Ethan said, gesturing to the woman at his side. She gave us a warm smile, her demeanor as gentle as Ethan's was boisterous.

"It's nice to meet you," Bethany said, her voice soft and kind.

"You too," the girl replied, glancing at me briefly before returning her attention to Ethan's wife.

Ethan's grin widened as he looked back at me. "So, what's the deal? You two just hanging out, or...?"

"We're eloping," the girl said suddenly, her tone light and teasing. "Didn't you hear?"

Ethan burst out laughing, clapping his hands together. "I freaking called it! Back in college, I told everyone you two would end up together."

I forced a smile, though my chest felt tight. "Yeah, well... here we are."

"Well, I'm happy for you," Ethan said sincerely. "It's good to see you again, man. Don't be a stranger."

"Yeah," I said, my voice flat. "You too."

As they walked away, I felt her fingers tighten on my arm. "That was... something," she said, glancing up at me.

"Yeah," I muttered, avoiding her gaze.

She studied me for a moment before her smirk returned, playful and mischievous. "So, did I live up to his expectations?"

I snorted. "I think you exceeded them."

Her laugh was light and genuine, and she leaned into me as we moved toward the bar. "Let's get another drink," she said, her voice bright. "This night isn't over yet."

The tension from the encounter with Ethan lingered, but her presence—her laughter, her touch—made it easier to ignore. For now.

We drank some more, the alcohol dulling the edges of my anger and sharpening the edges of everything else. The lights in the club blurred together, the music vibrating in my chest. She was laughing, her eyes glinting under the neon lights, but something about her laughter felt off. Forced, maybe. Or maybe I was just overthinking again.

At some point, I excused myself to go to the bathroom, weaving my way through the packed dance floor. The fluorescent lights in the bathroom were harsh, making my reflection look as tired as I felt. I splashed some cold water on my face, trying to steady myself, but my thoughts kept racing—circling around her, around us, around the mess we were making.

When I came back, she was standing alone near the entrance, her fingers fidgeting with the hem of her dress. She didn't notice me at first, her eyes scanning the crowd with an edge of nervousness. It was subtle, but it was there—the way her shoulders tensed, the way her lips pressed into a thin line.

"You okay?" I asked as I approached.

She startled slightly before flashing me a quick smile. "Yeah, just... you took a while."

"I'm fine," I muttered, brushing off her concern. "Come on, let's get out of here."

I hailed a taxi outside the club, the cool night air doing little to clear my head. She leaned against me in the backseat, her warmth both comforting and suffocating. I gave the driver the address to our old hotel without thinking, too caught up in the haze of the night to remember we had switched to a new one.

When we stumbled into the old room, it felt strangely familiar, like stepping back into something we'd already outgrown. She kicked off her heels and collapsed onto the bed with a dramatic sigh. I followed suit, but instead of lying down, I sat on the edge, my elbows resting on my knees as I stared at the floor.

"It was a good night, wasn't it?" she asked, her voice soft.

"Yeah," I said, though the word felt hollow. My mind was still buzzing, half from the alcohol, half from something I couldn't name.

She stood and disappeared into the bathroom, leaving me alone with my thoughts. I didn't want to think. I didn't want to feel. But the silence pressed in, and I couldn't stop myself.

It was when she was in the shower that I noticed it. A small card on the ground, partially hidden under her coat. I leaned down and picked it up, my fingers trembling slightly as I turned it over.

A business card.

The name *Henry* was printed neatly on one side. On the back, scrawled in pen, were the words *Call me.*

My chest tightened, anger flaring hot and fast. When she stepped out of the bathroom, her hair damp and clinging to her shoulders, I was already standing, the card clutched tightly in my hand.

"What the fuck is this?" I demanded, holding it up like evidence in a trial.

She froze, her eyes darting to the card before flicking back to my face. "I don't know," she said, her voice cautious.

"Don't play dumb," I snapped. "It says 'Call me.' Who is he?"

She took a hesitant step forward, her brows knitting together. "I... I don't know, babe. Where did you even find that?"

"In your coat pocket," I said, my voice rising. "Don't lie to me."

She hesitated, biting her lip. "There was a guy," she admitted finally. "While you were in the bathroom. He tried to talk to me, but I didn't want to talk to him. I swear."

"Then why the hell do you have his card?" I threw it onto the bed, the anger bubbling over. "What, he just slipped it into your pocket without you noticing?"

"Yes!" she cried, her voice cracking. "I didn't want it, okay? I didn't even know it was there!"

I shook my head, turning toward the door. "I can't do this."

"Wait!" she shouted, rushing forward to grab my arm. "Please, don't leave. Don't go looking for him. Just stay. Please."

Her desperation only fueled my frustration. I yanked my arm free, my voice cold and sharp. "Why should I stay? So you can keep lying to me?"

"I'm not lying!" she sobbed, tears streaming down her face. "I wouldn't do that to you. You're all I have."

Her words cut through me, but the anger wouldn't let go. It wrapped around my chest, tight and suffocating. "You're a prostitute," I spat, the words bitter and venomous. "How the hell am I supposed to believe anything you say?"

Her face crumpled, and for a moment, I thought she might collapse. But instead, she stepped closer, her arms wrapping around me in a desperate embrace.

"Please," she whispered. "Don't go. I need you."

Her words echoed in the room, raw and vulnerable, cutting through the haze of anger and confusion in my mind. My grip on the doorknob tightened, and for a moment, I considered just ripping it open and leaving. But the desperation in her voice... it rooted me in place. It wasn't just fear—it was something deeper, something that twisted in my chest and made it impossible to take another step forward.

I tried to move anyway, to shake her off, to ignore the weight of her words and the way her hands trembled against me. But she didn't let go. She threw everything she had into holding onto me, as if her life depended on it. It was maddening. I could feel the heat rising in my chest again, that familiar frustration boiling over.

The thought of prying her off of me, of forcing her away, crossed my mind. I almost did it. Almost. But then I caught sight of her face—her tear-streaked cheeks, the way her lips quivered as she clung to me like a lifeline. And just like that, the fight drained out of me. My anger, my frustration—it all gave way to something heavier. Something that felt a lot like guilt.

I sighed and let my hand drop from the doorknob. Slowly, I sank to the floor, my back pressed against the door, and let myself fall apart beside her. She followed suit, curling up next to me without hesitation, resting her head on my shoulder like nothing had happened. Like I hadn't just tried to leave her behind.

Her warmth should have been comforting, but it wasn't. It only made the knot in my stomach tighten.

We sat there in silence for what felt like hours, the weight of the moment pressing down on us. Her breathing slowed, evened out, but I couldn't relax. I couldn't stop the thoughts swirling in my head, the questions I didn't have answers to. Why did she cling to me so tightly? Why couldn't I bring myself to walk away? Why did it always feel like I was one step away from breaking something that couldn't be fixed?

Later, much later, I found myself sitting by the door with a half-empty bottle of champagne in my hand. She was lying on the bed, her back to me, her breathing steady and soft. I didn't know if she was asleep or just pretending to be, but either way, I was grateful for the silence.

I finished the bottle alone, the alcohol doing little to numb the weight in my chest. Before I knew it, I'd passed out on the floor, leaning against the door like some kind of sentry. A part of me thought that if she tried to leave, if she tried to disappear while I slept, I'd somehow be able to stop her.

When I woke up the next morning, my head was pounding, my mouth dry, and my body sore from the awkward position I'd fallen asleep in. But worse than the hangover was the feeling that hit me the second I opened my eyes.

I felt disgusted with myself.

I didn't remember everything that had happened the night before, but I didn't need to. The fragments that lingered were enough. The anger, the jealousy, the way I'd lashed out without thinking. I'd acted like a child, throwing a tantrum over something I barely understood. And now, I was left with the aftermath.

The sound of movement pulled me from my thoughts. I looked up to see her in the tiny kitchenette, fussing over something at the counter. She wasn't the type to cook—it was one of the first things I'd learned about her—so whatever she was doing was probably simple. Toast, maybe. Coffee, if we were lucky.

I pushed myself to my feet, my head swimming as I crossed the room toward her. I didn't know what I was planning to say, but I knew I had to say something. I couldn't just let things fester like this.

She turned around as I approached, a plate in her hands, and smiled at me like nothing was wrong. Like the night before had never happened. "Morning," she said softly. "Do you want eggs with your toast?"

Her face stopped me in my tracks.

"W-Was I the one... Was I the one who did this to you?" I stammered, my voice barely above a whisper. My hand moved on its own, brushing lightly against her forehead, where a nasty black mark had bloomed overnight. My gaze traveled lower, to the side of her lips, where a faint bruise marred her skin. Then down to her legs, noticing for the first time the way she seemed to favor one side as she shifted her weight.

"No, baby... that... That wasn't you," she said quickly, her voice too calm, too measured. But her eyes gave her away. She was lying. I could see it in the way she avoided my gaze, the way her smile faltered just slightly.

I stepped back, my chest tightening. I didn't need her to confirm it. I already knew. I remembered the way my hands had shaken with anger, the way my voice had risen, the way I'd lost control. I didn't remember every detail, but I remembered enough.

I remembered those voices in my head, the ones that always whispered to me in moments like this. The ones that told me to lash out, to hurt, to destroy. I'd tried so hard to ignore them, to push them down, but last night... Last night, I'd let them win.

I clenched my fists at my sides, my nails digging into my palms. "I'm sorry," I muttered, the words sounding hollow even to my own ears.

She stepped closer, reaching out to touch my arm. "It's okay," she said softly. "I'm okay."

But she wasn't. And neither was I.

I turned away from her, unable to meet her gaze. This wasn't sustainable. None of this was. If we kept going like this, if I kept going like this, I was going to destroy her. I'd already come so close.

Something had to change. I just didn't know if I was strong enough to be the one to make that change.

~ 29 ~

CHAPTER TWENTY-NINE

Bound by Doubt

The rest of the day started with her usual energy, pulling me out of bed with a playful tug. Her smile was bright, unbothered, but the faint bruises on her face—though carefully concealed with makeup—were impossible for me to ignore. The foundation she used wasn't quite a match for her skin tone, a shade too light, and it only drew my attention more. If I hadn't known what lay beneath, I wouldn't have noticed, but I did. And every time I saw it, guilt clawed at my chest, gnawing at me like a parasite I couldn't shake.

She didn't give me much time to wallow. "Let's get out of here!" she chirped, bouncing on her toes like a child about to unwrap a long-awaited gift. "Come on. We'll find something fun to do. I heard there's a shopping district nearby, or maybe we could hit the arcade?"

Her enthusiasm was jarring, almost abrasive against the storm of emotions inside me. I nodded absently, barely registering her words as I pulled on my shoes. The weight of my guilt, my self-loathing, pressed down on me, making her energy feel suffocating. Too light.

Too bright. Too much. I forced a faint smile, hoping it would be enough to convince her I wasn't drowning in my own head.

She clapped her hands together, her excitement bubbling over. "Perfect! Let's make it a day to remember, yeah?"

I didn't respond, only shrugged as I grabbed my jacket. She didn't seem to notice my lack of enthusiasm, or maybe she chose to ignore it. Either way, her energy didn't falter. She hummed softly to herself as she grabbed her bag, a tune I vaguely recognized from a song she used to love in high school. The familiarity of it made my chest tighten.

As we stepped outside into the warm sunlight, I found myself glancing at her again. She looked so put together, so carefree, like she didn't have a care in the world. It was almost convincing. Almost. But I knew better. I saw the way her hands fidgeted with the strap of her bag, the way her eyes darted around as if searching for something—or maybe someone. I saw the cracks in the façade, no matter how hard she tried to hide them.

"Do I look okay?" she asked suddenly, spinning around to face me. She spread her arms out, a playful grin on her lips. "Not too shabby for a girl who just rolled out of bed, huh?"

I hesitated, unsure how to answer. "You look fine," I said finally, my tone flat.

She wrinkled her nose. "Fine? That's all I get? Come on, give me something better than that."

"You look great," I muttered, the words feeling foreign on my tongue. They weren't a lie, but they felt like one.

She beamed at that, completely oblivious to the turmoil brewing beneath my surface. "See? Was that so hard?"

I didn't answer. Instead, I shoved my hands into my pockets and started walking toward the car. She followed close behind, her humming resuming as if the world around us was perfect and untouched. It wasn't. And the weight of that knowledge felt heavier with every step I took.

The first stop was a shopping district she had spotted the night before. The moment we stepped onto the bustling street, her energy seemed to double. She practically dragged me through it, darting in and out of stores with wide-eyed enthusiasm, her excitement palpable. The air smelled faintly of roasted nuts and fresh pastries from nearby food carts, mixing with the synthetic tang of brand-new clothes. She was in her element—or at least pretending to be.

She picked up trinkets at one store, spinning them in her hands as if they were treasures, and tried on hats at another, laughing when one looked particularly ridiculous perched on her head. A large, floppy sunhat almost swallowed her face, and she turned to me, her grin infectious. "What do you think? Do I look like a movie star?"

"You look like you're about to garden for six hours," I replied flatly.

Her laughter bubbled out, light and genuine. "Well, there goes my Hollywood career."

I followed behind her, trying to match her mood, trying to let myself be pulled into the moment, but my laughter felt hollow in my throat. Each joke, each teasing comment, felt like another layer of armor between us—armor I wasn't sure she even realized she wore. My eyes kept darting to her face, searching for signs of the bruises beneath her makeup, for cracks in her carefully constructed joy. She didn't falter, didn't stumble, but I knew better than to trust what she wanted me to see.

At one point, she grabbed a scarf off a rack and turned to me, her eyes lighting up with mischief. Without warning, she looped it around my neck, the soft fabric brushing against my jaw as she adjusted it. "This one suits you," she said, stepping back and tilting her head to study me like an artist examining their work. "Very debonair. Like you're about to walk into some fancy film noir scene."

I tugged the scarf loose, the sensation too intimate, too exposing. "It's not really my style," I muttered, my gaze fixed on the floor.

She frowned, her hands on her hips, but the spark of humor in her eyes didn't fade. "You don't have a style. That's the problem."

The jab wasn't unkind—it was teasing, meant to pull me out of my shell—but it hit deeper than she probably realized. I wanted to argue, to push back against her words, but the weight in my chest was too heavy. Instead, I muttered, "Let's just keep moving."

Her smile faltered, just for a second, like a crack in glass quickly smoothed over. She recovered almost instantly, her expression bright again, but I caught the hesitation, the flicker of uncertainty in her eyes. "Okay," she said softly, looping her arm through mine. "Let's keep moving."

We walked like that for a while, her arm linked with mine, as she pointed out things in the windows we passed—shoes that sparkled too brightly, dresses that looked like they belonged to another era, and quirky knickknacks she declared we *had* to buy, even if we didn't. I stayed quiet, letting her fill the silence with her running commentary, but my mind was elsewhere.

Her enthusiasm felt like a performance, like she was trying to outrun something I couldn't see. And I hated how much of it reminded me of myself.

By midday, the weight of my silence was becoming impossible to ignore. We sat on a bench in a small park tucked between the towering buildings, eating sandwiches from a nearby food truck. The air smelled faintly of freshly cut grass and exhaust, the contrast almost too fitting. She chattered on about the people passing by, spinning ridiculous stories about their lives and relationships. A man in a suit walking a tiny dog became a millionaire trying to reconnect with his estranged daughter. A pair of teenagers sharing earbuds were secretly spies using music to communicate in code. Normally, I would've played along, maybe even tried to one-up her with a more absurd idea. But today, I couldn't summon the energy.

"You're really quiet today," she said eventually, her tone soft. Her voice cut through the din of the city like a thread pulling me back to the moment. She set her sandwich down, her hands resting lightly in her lap as her eyes searched mine. "What's going on?"

"Nothing," I said automatically, the lie coming too easily. I took a bite of my food to avoid her gaze, the bread dry in my mouth.

She didn't buy it, not for a second. "It's not nothing," she said, her voice a touch firmer now, like she was trying to peel back the layers I'd wrapped around myself. "Is this about last night?"

I didn't respond, which was answer enough.

She sighed, leaning back against the bench and crossing her arms. The shift in her posture was subtle, but I felt it like a physical weight. "I told you, I'm fine. You didn't do anything wrong."

"You don't know that," I muttered, the bitterness seeping into my voice. My fingers tightened around the sandwich wrapper until it crinkled in protest.

Her brow furrowed, her eyes narrowing slightly. "What's that supposed to mean?"

"It means..." The words twisted in my throat, jagged and unwieldy. I stood abruptly, pacing a few steps away before spinning to face her. "It means I'm bad for you. That's what it means."

She blinked, caught off guard, her expression unreadable for a moment. "What are you talking about?"

I ran a hand through my hair, the frustration boiling over into every word. "I hurt you," I said, my voice rising, drawing the attention of a passing couple. "And if we keep doing this—if I keep doing this—it's going to get worse. That's what I'm talking about."

She stood too, closing the distance between us with deliberate steps. Her gaze locked onto mine, steady and unflinching. "You didn't mean to hurt me," she said softly. "That matters."

"No, it doesn't!" I shouted, the words slicing through the quiet park. A pigeon flapped away from a nearby bench, startled by the sudden noise. "It doesn't matter what I meant. What matters is that I did. What matters is that I will. Because that's what I do. I break things. I break people."

Her lips parted slightly, her eyes glistening as she tried to process my words. For a moment, I thought she might cry, but she didn't. Instead, she took a shaky breath and held her ground. "You're wrong," she said quietly, her voice trembling but resolute. "You're so wrong."

"Am I?" I demanded, my voice cracking under the weight of my own emotions. "Look at us. Look at me. Do you really think this is going to end any other way?"

She didn't flinch, didn't back down. Instead, she stepped closer, her hand reaching for mine. I almost pulled away, but her grip was firm, grounding, like she was tethering me to the earth.

"You don't get to decide how this ends," she said firmly, her voice steady despite the tears threatening to spill from her eyes. "You don't get to decide what I deserve or what I'm willing to risk. That's my choice. And I choose you."

I stared at her, the words catching in my throat. My chest was tight, my head spinning with everything I wanted to say but couldn't. "You shouldn't," I said finally, my voice barely above a whisper.

"But I do," she said, her tone softening, her thumb brushing lightly against my hand. "And nothing you say is going to change that."

The silence that followed was heavy, charged with unspoken words and fragile understanding. I wanted to argue, to push her away for her own good, but I couldn't. Not when she looked at me like that, like I was something worth saving.

Her grip on my hand tightened, her fingers trembling slightly. "Don't look at me like that," I muttered, my voice strained, barely audible over the distant hum of the city.

"Like what?" she asked softly, her brows knitting together in confusion.

"Like I'm worth something." The words slipped out like poison, bitter and cutting, aimed more at myself than her. I couldn't meet her eyes anymore, not when they held that unwavering, painful belief in me. "Emily looked at me like that too. Don't lie to yourself like that. Look what it got her."

The weight of my words settled between us, heavy and suffocating. Her expression faltered, the light in her eyes dimming for just a moment before she stepped even closer, her hand cupping my cheek.

"You're not worthless," she said, her voice quiet but firm. "You've just convinced yourself that you are."

I pulled away from her touch, shaking my head. "You don't know what you're talking about."

"I know more than you think," she replied, her tone softening. "And I know that pushing people away doesn't make you stronger, or better, or safer. It just makes you lonelier."

Her words stung because they were true, but I couldn't let myself admit it. Not yet. "Maybe that's what I deserve," I said bitterly, shoving my hands into my pockets.

"And maybe that's what you've told yourself for so long, you've started to believe it," she countered. "But I don't. I won't."

She stepped back, her hands dropping to her sides as she exhaled shakily. "You're not some irredeemable monster. You're just... human. And humans screw up. We hurt each other, sometimes without meaning to. But we also have the choice to try and be better."

I stood there, staring at the ground, her words swirling in my head like a storm I couldn't control. She wasn't wrong, but that didn't mean I knew how to accept what she was offering.

"Why are you still here?" I asked finally, my voice quieter now, almost defeated.

"Because I see you," she said simply. "Not the mess you think you are. Not the mistakes you've made. I see you. And I care about you."

I clenched my jaw, my hands balling into fists in my pockets. "You shouldn't," I whispered, my voice breaking.

"But I do," she said, stepping forward again. This time, she didn't try to touch me, didn't force herself into my space. She just stood there, close enough to feel her presence, to hear the steady rhythm of her breathing.

I stared at her, her words hanging in the air like they were supposed to mean something, like they were supposed to fix something. But they didn't. They couldn't. She was wrong—so painfully, naively wrong.

"You don't get it," I muttered, shaking my head. "You think you do, but you don't. I will hurt you. It's not a question of if—it's when. It's inevitable."

Her eyes softened, the glimmer of defiance still lingering, but her smile faltered. "You're wrong," she whispered. "You don't have to hurt me."

I scoffed, the bitterness in my chest bubbling up like bile. "That's the thing. I don't want to. I never want to, but it doesn't matter. It happens anyway. It always happens."

"Because you let it," she shot back, her voice rising just enough to catch me off guard. "You let yourself believe you're broken, that you're incapable of anything else. And you use that as an excuse to keep people away."

I wanted to snap back, to deny everything she was saying, but the words died in my throat. She wasn't wrong. Not entirely. But that didn't make it any less infuriating.

"You're just going to get hurt," I said finally, my voice low and strained. "I don't want to be the one to do it, but I will. That's what I do. I break things. I break people."

She stepped closer, close enough for me to feel the warmth radiating from her skin. Her gaze never wavered, her expression softer now, but no less determined. "And what if I'm okay with that?"

I flinched, the weight of her words hitting me square in the chest. "You shouldn't be."

"But I am," she said simply, her tone unwavering. "Because I don't care about the risk. I care about you. Even if you don't believe you deserve it."

I clenched my fists, my jaw tightening as I forced myself to look away. "You're making a mistake."

"Maybe," she admitted, her voice quieter now. "But it's my mistake to make."

The silence between us stretched out, heavy and suffocating. I wanted to push her away, to say something cruel enough to make her leave, but I couldn't. Because as much as I wanted to believe I was doing it for her, I knew deep down it was for me. It was easier to stay broken than to try and be better. Easier to drive her away than to face the terrifying possibility that she might actually mean what she said.

"I don't believe you," I muttered, finally breaking the silence. "I can't."

She nodded slowly, as if she'd been expecting that answer all along. "That's okay," she said softly. "I'll believe enough for the both of us."

~ 30 ~

CHAPTER THIRTY

One Last Night

The drive back to the motel was heavy with silence. She sat beside me, staring out of the window, her hands fidgeting in her lap. Her usual energy was gone, replaced with something quieter, something darker. I didn't know what to say to her, or if I should say anything at all. My thoughts were a mess, looping endlessly back to that bruise on her face, the limp she tried to hide, the way she still clung to me like I was the only thing keeping her upright.

We pulled into the motel parking lot, the gravel crunching beneath the tires. She didn't wait for me to say anything, simply got out of the car and walked toward the door with a determined stride. I followed her, keeping my eyes on her back, trying to read her body language. She unlocked the door and pushed it open, stepping aside to let me in.

Inside, everything felt smaller, more suffocating than it had before. The air was heavy with the stale smell of cigarettes and cheap cleaning products. My eyes immediately landed on the bags in the corner. I made my way over to them, rifling through until I found her phone and mine. I gripped them tightly, like they were lifelines.

"Sorry," I muttered, not looking at her. "I need to do something alone. Wait for me here, will you?"

She didn't answer. When I finally turned to face her, she was staring at me with an expression I couldn't quite place—an odd mix of sadness, defiance, and something darker. Her eyes held mine, and for a moment, I felt like I was looking at a mirror. Her darkness met mine.

I tried to brush past her, but she moved to block the door, her arms outstretched. "Move," I said, my voice sharper than I intended.

"Say..." Her voice was soft, almost a whisper. "Do you love me?"

"I don't have time for this," I snapped, my grip tightening on the phones.

"Answer me," she said again, her tone firmer now. "Do you love me?"

I clenched my jaw, feeling the tension coil in my chest. "I said move," I growled, raising my hand instinctively, not even realizing what I was doing until it was too late. But she didn't flinch. She didn't cower. She stood her ground, unblinking, unafraid. Her gaze cut through me like a blade.

"Do you love me?" she repeated, her voice quieter this time, but no less insistent.

I felt trapped, cornered by her question and my own guilt. My voice was low when I finally spoke. "...Yes. I do."

Her lips curled into a smile—not the bright, mischievous grin she usually wore, but something darker, something that sent a shiver down my spine. "Enough to throw your life away for me?" she asked.

"Yes," I said without hesitation, and I meant it. God help me, I meant it.

Her smile faded, replaced by a look I couldn't quite decipher. She stepped aside, letting me move toward the door. I was halfway there when her voice stopped me in my tracks.

"Let's go back to the other hotel room," she said, her voice steady but soft. "Let me have one last night. Then you can do whatever you want."

I turned to face her, confused. "What are you talking about?"

"One last night," she repeated, her gaze unwavering. "No fights. No guilt. Just... us. That's all I'm asking."

I didn't know what to say to that. Part of me wanted to argue, to push back, but another part of me—the part that was so tired of fighting, so desperate for something to hold onto—nodded instead. "Okay," I said, my voice barely above a whisper.

Her expression softened, and she stepped closer, taking the phones from my hands and setting them down on the nightstand. She reached for my hand, her fingers lacing through mine. "Thank you," she said quietly, her voice trembling just slightly. There was something in her voice, a weight behind those two simple words that sent a chill down my spine.

She tugged me back toward the bed, her grip firm but not forceful. I followed her without protest, my thoughts too tangled to resist. When we sat down, she leaned into me, her head resting against my shoulder. The closeness was warm, almost suffocating, but I didn't pull away.

"You know," she said softly, tracing patterns on my hand with her fingers, "I think this might be the happiest I've ever been."

"That's not saying much," I muttered before I could stop myself. I regretted it immediately, but she only chuckled.

"Maybe not," she admitted, her tone light, almost teasing. "But still... I want to thank you."

"For what?" I asked, my brow furrowing.

"For giving me something worth remembering," she said, tilting her head to look up at me. Her eyes were wide and unguarded, shimmering with something I couldn't quite place. "If I had to pick one moment to freeze in time, it'd be this one. Right here. Just us."

I swallowed hard, unsure of how to respond. Her words felt too final, too heavy, like she was carving them into stone. I forced myself to laugh, the sound awkward and hollow. "You're being dramatic," I said, shaking my head. "It's just another night."

"Is it?" she asked, her voice barely above a whisper. She sat up, her fingers still intertwined with mine. "Sometimes... sometimes, you just know when something's going to be the last time, you know? The last good thing."

"Stop talking like that," I said, frowning. "You're making it sound like you're dying or something."

She didn't respond right away, just gave me a small, sad smile. "Sorry," she said after a moment, leaning in to press a soft kiss to my cheek. "I didn't mean to ruin the mood."

But she had, and we both knew it.

The night stretched on in fragments, each moment tinged with an edge of something I couldn't name. We ordered room service, and she insisted on feeding me bites of her dessert, laughing every time I grimaced at the overly sweet taste. She made me lie on the bed while she curled up next to me, humming softly under her breath. Every move she made, every word she spoke, felt deliberate, like she was trying to etch herself into my memory.

"You know," she said at one point, her voice quiet and thoughtful, "I think everyone has a moment they'd want to live in forever. If you could pick one, what would it be?"

"I don't know," I said, turning my head to look at her. "I don't really think like that."

"Try," she urged, her eyes locked on mine. "Just humor me."

I hesitated, my mind racing through the chaos of my life. "Maybe... maybe right now," I admitted finally, the words slipping out before I could stop them.

She smiled at that, but there was something brittle about it, something that made my chest tighten. "Good," she said softly. "Me too."

We didn't say much after that. She curled up against me, her head resting on my chest, and for a while, the room was filled with nothing but the sound of her breathing and the faint hum of the air conditioning. I stared up at the ceiling, my thoughts circling back to the way she'd smiled, the way her words had lingered in the air like a shadow.

When her breathing evened out, I turned my head to look at her. She looked peaceful, almost fragile, like she might disappear if I closed my eyes. My hand moved on its own, brushing a strand of hair away from her face.

"I don't understand you," I murmured, the words barely audible.

She stirred slightly, her lips curving into a sleepy smile. "Good," she mumbled, her voice thick with exhaustion. "That's what makes it fun."

I stayed awake long after she drifted off, the weight of her body against mine both comforting and suffocating. There was something about the night that felt wrong, like the air was too still, too heavy. I couldn't shake the feeling that I was missing something, that she was keeping something from me.

But I didn't ask. I didn't want to know.

I fell asleep with that thought lingering in my mind, the pit in my stomach growing deeper.

I woke slowly, the weight of her head on my chest anchoring me to the bed. Her hair spilled across me like a dark curtain, her breaths soft and even against my skin. For a moment, I stayed still, letting myself feel the warmth of her, the way her body curled so naturally into mine. But the weight in my chest grew heavier with every second. I knew what I had to do.

I shifted, careful not to disturb her, but even the smallest movement caused her to stir. Her head lifted groggily, her eyes blinking slowly as she woke. "Mmm... what're you doing?" she murmured, her voice thick with sleep.

I swung my legs off the bed, sitting on the edge as I reached for my clothes. I didn't answer her. I couldn't.

"Hey," she said, more awake now. She sat up, the sheets pooling around her waist, her sleepy confusion replaced by something sharper. "What's going on? Where are you going?"

Still, I didn't respond. The silence hung heavy between us, and I could feel her gaze burning into my back. When I finally turned to look at her, the smile she wore every morning had vanished, replaced by something raw and vulnerable.

Her body moved before her mind could catch up, and in a flash, she was on me, her arms wrapping tightly around my neck as she tackled me back onto the bed. "Don't go," she whispered fiercely, her lips pressing frantic kisses against my face. "I love you. I love you. I love you."

I grabbed her shoulders, gently but firmly pushing her off me. "I'm sorry," I said, my voice low and strained. "There's something I need to do alone."

Her arms tightened around me, her voice cracking as she whispered, "Please don't go..."

I closed my eyes, trying to steel myself against the ache in her voice. "...Sorry, but I can't," I said softly. "What I'm about to do is because I love you."

She stilled, her body trembling against mine. Her teeth sank into her lip, hard enough that I almost expected it to draw blood. When she finally lifted her head to meet my eyes, her expression was something I'd never seen before—caught between hope and despair, a smile that couldn't fully form.

"You said it," she whispered. Her voice wavered, and tears glistened in her eyes. "You finally said it..."

"Ahh... I—" I started to say something, anything, but the words died in my throat. What could I possibly say to make this better? To make this easier?

She shook her head, cutting me off. Slowly, she untangled herself from me and stood, walking to the door. Her hand rested on the handle for a moment before she turned it and pulled it open. "Go," she said quietly, her voice barely above a whisper. "I'll wait."

I hesitated, my feet rooted to the floor as if the weight of my decision had finally caught up to me. But I forced myself to move, stepping toward her. As I passed through the doorway, I glanced back, catching the look on her face—a mixture of resignation and something deeper, something darker. If only she knew how much I loved her. How much I would've done for her. That's exactly why I had to do this.

"Babe?" Her voice called me back just as I was about to turn the corner. "Could you buy me some tampons while you're at it?"

I froze, turning to look at her in disbelief. "What?"

She smiled at me, that same teasing smile she wore when she wanted to get her way. As if none of this had happened. As if it was all just another moment in the chaotic story of us. "Please~? I kinda need it, y'know..."

I sighed, running a hand through my hair. "Can't be helped, I guess," I muttered, waving her off as I turned to leave.

She didn't wave back. She just stood there, watching me go, her smile unchanging. It wasn't until I turned the corner that I let out a breath I hadn't realized I was holding. What was she...?

The pit in my stomach grew heavier with each step. Something wasn't right. But I shoved the thought aside, focusing on the task at hand. If I stopped now, if I let myself think, I might lose the resolve to do what needed to be done.

~ 31 ~

CHAPTER THIRTY-ONE

Goodbye

I debated taking the car, my hand brushing against the keys in my pocket. But the thought of sitting behind the wheel, alone with my thoughts, felt unbearable. I needed the movement, the rhythm of walking, to calm the racing in my chest. Maybe it would help untangle the knot in my stomach, or at least keep me distracted. Leaving her felt like ripping a piece of myself away, and every step I took only made it worse. But I had to. It was for her sake. Or maybe it was for mine. I couldn't tell anymore.

The streets were quieter than I expected, but the noise in my head made up for it. My mind churned with questions, doubts, fears. Was I doing the right thing? Was there even a right thing? The thought of her alone, waiting for me back at the motel, gnawed at me. I imagined her curled up on the bed, her face pressed into my pillow, her smile wavering as she waited for me to come back.

Would I?

I stopped, leaning against a lamppost, and rubbed my face with both hands. The thought of leaving her felt like walking into an abyss, but staying felt even worse. If I stayed, I'd ruin her. If I left, she'd crumble. Or maybe it was the other way around. I didn't know anymore. My heart felt like it was tearing itself apart in my chest.

I needed to focus. Find a payphone. That was my plan. I didn't want to call from her phone or even mine. If things went south, it was better to leave no trail. The problem was, finding a payphone in this day and age felt like searching for a relic from the past. It took ten minutes longer than I'd anticipated, every moment dragging my anxiety higher. By the time I found one, my hands were shaking.

I pulled her phone from my pocket, scrolling through the contacts until I found the name: Fanny. Her roommate. She'd know something, or at least she'd have her boss's number. And if I could talk to her boss, maybe I could negotiate. Maybe I could take on her debts. Whatever it took to keep her safe.

The phone rang three times before a groggy voice answered. "Hello?"

"Hi," I stammered. "Is this Rachel?"

"Yeah. Who's this?"

I hesitated. "John," I said, picking the name out of thin air. "I'm... uh, a friend of your roommate's."

"My roommate?" Her voice sharpened slightly. "Which one?"

"The one who's... traveling right now. She told me to call you."

"Oh," Rachel said, her tone lightening. "Yeah, she mentioned she was going on a trip to Vegas. Alone, apparently. Lucky her."

Alone? My stomach tightened. "When did she tell you that?"

"Friday night. She sent me an email. Said she needed a break or something. Why?"

"Did she mention anything about work? Or her boss?"

"Her boss?" Rachel sounded genuinely confused. "She doesn't have a boss. What are you talking about?"

My blood ran cold. "She doesn't?"

"Anyway, if you don't have anything else to ask, I have other things to do so..."

"Wait! I need to know one last thing!" Because the way she talked about it almost seemed as if.... I don't know why nor did I know when, but I decided to run. I ran frantically to that motel room. I had this ominous feeling... Why did she lie to me? And how? Her roommate.... To my question, she answered me this:

"*What the fuck? Prostitute? Is this some kind of sick joke or something? Sorry... I don't know who you are, but she isn't that type of woman, okay? You won't make me think otherwise! Now if you'll excuse me!*"

I stood there, the dial tone buzzing faintly in my ear, unable to move. My mind reeled with the implications of what Rachel had just said. She wasn't a prostitute? But that didn't make sense. I'd seen her work. I'd heard the way men spoke to her, the way she carried herself at the bar. She'd never denied it. Why would she lie to me? And for what?

I turned the conversation over in my head, replaying every word, every hesitation, every crack in her story. And then something Rachel had said struck me like a bolt of lightning.

"Friday night," she'd said. The night I'd taken her with me. The night this all began. How had she found the time to send an email? And why?

A sickening feeling clawed at my chest as I replayed Rachel's last words: "*She's not that kind of girl.*"

I needed to speak with her. But how could I even confront her? Why did she lie to me? I felt anger well up inside of me. *I know... I'll ignore her until she can't take it anymore. When she does, I'll force her to tell me everything. The best way to make her suffer without hurting her.*

Heh. She's so dependent on me, she won't be able to bear it for long. Soon enough, she'll tell me everything, and then she'll ask me to forgive her... with that way she always asks me for everything. Those eyes, that smile... her lips... her everything. I'll accept, of course. But she'll feel indebted to me. That's when I'll ask her.

That's when I'll ask her to—

The thought cut off abruptly, leaving a bitter taste in my mouth. My hands were trembling, my legs barely able to hold me upright. Why did I try to separate us? I didn't understand anything anymore. Why did she lie to me? Why was I that way? Why was I scared...?

I didn't realize I was running until my lungs started to burn. The motel loomed in the distance, its grimy facade like a beacon of dread. Each step closer tightened the knot in my stomach. By the time I reached the door to our room, I was drenched in sweat, my breaths coming in short, shallow gasps.

Something was off. The plastic bag on the door handle flapped in the faint breeze, its presence unnervingly out of place. My heart pounded as I stared at it, every instinct screaming that something was wrong. I reached out, my fingers brushing against the bag, but stopped short. My hand hovered there, shaking.

I opened the door, the bag still on the handle, and stepped inside.

I need to ignore her. I need to ignore her... I need...

The mantra in my head felt weaker with every step. My body betrayed me, trembling as though it had a will of its own. My breath came uneven, ragged, but I forced myself forward. Slow, deliberate steps carried me into the middle of the room, where I stood frozen, staring at nothing and everything all at once. My hands hung limply at my sides, trembling slightly, and I realized, too late, that I couldn't stop it anymore.

A choked sob broke free, and I turned my head toward the ceiling. It wasn't raining—of course it wasn't—but my mind latched onto the thought anyway, like I could convince myself that the drops falling weren't my own tears. I let out a shaky breath and wiped at my face roughly, but it didn't help. The weight pressing on my chest refused to budge, suffocating me in its quiet persistence.

My gaze fell to the table almost by accident, and that's when I saw it.

A letter.

It sat there, damp in places as if it had been caught in some invisible storm. My breath caught as I stared at it, unable to move. The edges of the paper curled slightly, the ink smudged in places, like it had been handled more than once. My throat tightened, and my legs refused to carry me closer. It sat there, so innocuous, so ordinary, and yet...

It wasn't ordinary, was it? It couldn't be. Not with how the air in the room had changed, like the walls themselves were bracing for impact.

I tried to swallow the lump in my throat, but it wouldn't go down. My fists clenched and unclenched at my sides as I struggled to will myself forward. But my body wouldn't listen. I could only stare at the letter, the puddle around it—not from rain, not from anything real.

I'm fine. I'm fine... I'm—

My chest heaved, and I doubled over slightly, gripping the back of a nearby chair for support. My breaths came out shallow and uneven, the sound too loud in the otherwise silent room. The letter waited for me, unmoving, unbothered by my hesitation.

My legs felt like lead as I stepped toward the table. Each movement was deliberate, like my body knew what I was about to face and was doing everything in its power to resist. But I couldn't stop now. Not when I was already here.

The letter was waiting for me, quiet and still, as though it hadn't already shattered the world around it. My hand hovered over it for a moment, shaking, before finally gripping the damp paper. It felt heavier than it should have, the weight of what it contained pressing down on me before I even read a single word.

'Dear Lucian. I'm sorry.'

The words stared back at me, stark against the smudged paper. My chest tightened. I almost heard her voice, soft and familiar, as though she were standing right behind me.

But I didn't want to hear it. This was fake. It had to be.

'I lied to you.'

The words blurred slightly, the ink bleeding where the page had gotten wet. A noise filled my ears—sharp, grating. It sounded like someone slowly opening and closing a badly oiled door over and over again. My jaw clenched, and I froze.

The noise was real. A rhythmic creaking, slow and deliberate, filling the silence of the room like a cruel metronome.

'But I did love you.'

My breath hitched. I couldn't ignore the movement in the corner of my vision. I couldn't ignore the shape, the shadow, the slight swaying that matched the sound. My hands trembled, the paper crumpling slightly between my fingers as my eyes remained fixed on the letter. I couldn't look up. I wouldn't.

No.

I must ignore her. I must.

The words in the letter began to swim before my eyes, but I refused to tear my gaze away. My mind spun, my stomach churned, and yet... I kept reading.

I loved the boy who stood in front of the class, fumbling for an answer, yet refusing to back down. Even when the other kids snickered, you stood there with your fists clenched, your face red, and your words stuck in your throat. You were determined, even when you didn't know what to say. I wanted to encourage that boy. I wanted to cheer him on, to be the one who helped him achieve his dreams.

But you never listened to me. You brushed off every word, every gesture, like I didn't exist. It was as if I wasn't even there. So, I decided, if kindness wouldn't work, maybe competition would. If I made myself your rival, then maybe, just maybe, you'd notice me.

And for a while, it worked.

I existed solely to beat you.

I existed solely to take things away from you.

That purpose consumed me. I trained harder, studied longer, pushed myself further—all for the satisfaction of seeing you trail behind me. But the harder I worked, the closer you came. No matter how much I achieved, it never felt like enough. You always caught up, always found a way to surpass me. Even when you grew taller than me, I cried in my room for days. It felt so stupid, so petty, but it was just one more thing I couldn't keep.

I used to go to all your basketball games, sitting quietly in the stands, pretending I wasn't there for you. You were so good, so naturally talented. I hated it, but I couldn't look away. You shone so brightly, and I wanted so badly to be part of that light. But even then, I knew I couldn't match you. Not really. So, I clung to what I still had—academics. You were the sports star, and I was the smart one. Surely, you wouldn't take that away from me too.

But you did. You quit basketball, and then you came for school. You joined academic competitions, entered the science fair, and before I knew it, you were beating me at my own game. I worked so hard, but it didn't matter. You just took everything.

By the time high school rolled around, I thought maybe things would change. The science project we worked on together brought us closer. I finally had an excuse to spend time with you. It was during those late nights, poring over experiments and reports, that I discovered your home life. I saw the cracks in your perfect image, the weight you carried, and how much you hid from everyone else.

And I fell even harder for you.

I saw how you succeeded despite everything you were going through. How you could still be so gentle, so kind, even when the world wasn't kind to you. I loved you for it. But even after the project ended, you still didn't really see me. I thought, maybe if I made you jealous, you'd finally notice me. So, I got a boyfriend. Not because I liked him, but because I wanted to see if it would affect you. And for a moment, I thought it did. You kept asking about him, and I kept deflecting. But even then, you didn't see me as a woman. You saw me as an obstacle.

Then came prom. I remember the way the lights made your suit shimmer faintly as you hesitated near the edge of the dance floor. My heart raced when you finally walked over, holding out your hand. I thought, just for a moment, that I'd won—that I'd finally become something more to you. When we danced, I felt beautiful. I felt like I belonged in your arms. I let myself believe that maybe this was the start of something.

But then, during midterms, you approached me—not to ask me out, not to say anything about our dance, but to talk about grades. I thought you'd seen me that night, truly seen me, but it was just another battle for you. I wasn't a woman to you. I was a wall to climb, a goal to surpass. That's all I'd ever been.

So, I gave up. I dropped out before you could surpass me completely. I didn't want to see the day when you would take that from me too. I lied about my father losing all his money, but the truth was, I didn't need to drop out. I could've gone to college, could've built a life for myself. But I didn't want any of it. All I wanted was you.

It was so easy to approach Ethan. And the moment I explained my interest in seeing you again, he accepted quite readily. The night went on perfectly as I anticipated. Soon enough, I was alone with you. You had those eyes... the same eyes you always did. Sad eyes. I tried my best to appeal to you. Looking at you, touching you, even stumbling into you just for that purpose. I wanted you to want me. And I thought I had you.

But you refused me still.

Then I saw you with Emily.

She was beautiful, kind, perfect. She wasn't just your partner; she was your equal. I hated her. I hated how effortlessly she fit into your life. How easily she got what I had spent years chasing. I wanted to rip her away from you.

So, I found a way.

One of your clients liked to meet at a hostess bar. I begged to work there part-time, just on Thursdays. I knew you'd come eventually. And when you did, I made sure you couldn't ignore me. I changed everything about myself—my clothes, my makeup, my smile. I became someone I thought you'd want. And it worked. You finally cracked. You gave in.

From there, it was so easy.

I made up stories to stir your compassion, to make you care. I told you I was a prostitute because I knew it would break your heart. I hit myself to make you react irrationally. I played with your emotions, manipulated you, pulled you deeper into my web. And then, in Vegas, I pushed you even further.

Every time you left my side, I started conversations with strangers, knowing it would make you jealous. I dropped a fake business card, knowing you'd find it. I hurt myself again, harder this time, just so you'd think it was your fault. I wanted you to feel guilty, to cling to me even more.

And then... you told me you loved me.

I made you love me.

I took your job, your girlfriend, your peace of mind. I took everything from you. And now, I'll take the last thing you have left.

Your love.

I exist solely to take things away from you.

Let me take myself away too.

Maybe, if I do this, you'll finally be free of me. Maybe you'll hate me enough to move on. To live. To find someone who deserves you. Because I never did. I'm a liar, a fraud, a parasite. And you... you're everything I could never be.

I loved you, Lucian. More than you'll ever know.

Goodbye."

Her name was signed at the bottom: Amara. The ink was smudged by what could have only been tears. I crushed the paper in my hand, the fragile fibers crumpling beneath the pressure of my trembling fist. Frustration swelled inside me, coiling tighter and tighter, like a venomous snake ready to strike. It was unlike anything I had ever felt before—primal, all-consuming.

The rain became frantic, relentless in its rhythm, crashing over me like waves threatening to pull me under. I couldn't control it. I couldn't stop it.

My gaze drifted, almost unwillingly, to her. She was moving. Barely. A slight sway, so small it could almost have been mistaken for a trick of the dim, flickering light. But it wasn't. It was real.

It was the cord.

The damn cord around her neck.

That horrible, wretched thing pulling her away from me forever.

My legs felt like lead, yet I stumbled closer, each step heavier than the last. My vision blurred—not from tears but from the torrential downpour inside my own mind, drowning every rational thought. I wanted to touch her, to reach out and pull her down, but my hands refused to move. I was paralyzed.

I opened my mouth, but the words wouldn't come. A thousand things raced through my head—accusations, apologies, pleas. Memories flashed like lightning: her laugh, her smile, her stupid, beautiful teasing. Every moment with her collided at once, a kaleidoscope of emotions too tangled to unravel.

There was so much I needed to tell her. So much I should have told her before it came to this.

But only one thing escaped my lips, raw and broken.

"You liar..."

My voice cracked, barely audible above the storm raging in my chest. It wasn't enough. Nothing I could say would ever be enough.

Her lifeless form swayed gently, like she was mocking me even now. Or maybe it was my own mind, playing tricks on me, desperate to believe she'd move on her own, that she'd look at me with those sharp eyes and call me an idiot one more time.

But she didn't. She never would.

And it was all my fault.

The weight of that realization crashed down on me, and I fell to my knees, the crumpled paper still clenched tightly in my fist. The ink smeared, waterlogged from the relentless storm pouring from my eyes. My shoulders shook as I lowered my head, staring at the floor, willing it to split open and swallow me whole.

"You stupid liar," I whispered again, the words barely audible now, like a prayer to a god who had stopped listening long ago.

The rain inside me didn't stop. I knew it wouldn't.

Not now. Not ever.

About the Author

Gracie Banks was born on November 4th, 2003 and raised among the wide skies and quiet forests of Montana. She later moved to Washington during her senior year of high school—a transition that marked a new chapter in both her life and her writing journey. As a proud transgender woman, Gracie writes with emotional depth, empathy, and a belief in finding truth through fiction.

Her love of storytelling began early, shaped by the books that filled her childhood: *Harry Potter*, *Percy Jackson*, *The Hunger Games*, *Divergent*, and *Heroes of Olympus*. By sixth grade, she knew she wanted to be a writer—and now she's making that dream a reality. Currently working on six novels across multiple genres, Gracie's debut, a psychological drama with dark romance elements, is set to release on **May 5th, 2025**.

While fantasy and science fiction are her literary home, her stories are always grounded in character, emotion, and the blurred lines between light and shadow. One of her next projects, *Fabrics of Reality*, blends post-war dystopia with eldritch horror and is expected to be completed within the next year.

When she's not writing, Gracie can be found swimming, hiking, or slinging spells in Dungeons & Dragons campaigns with her closest friends. She's a cat person at heart (though she still loves dogs), a devoted anime fan, and an enthusiastic gamer—with a soft spot for archery and anything a little bit magical.

Professional Goals

As an author, my biggest goal is to build a body of work that resonates—stories that make people feel seen, understood, or simply a little less alone. I want to explore the emotional depth of characters, create fantastical worlds that reflect real struggles, and challenge the boundaries between genre and personal truth.

In the coming years, I plan to publish across multiple genres, from high fantasy and science fiction to psychological drama and speculative horror. Each project is a new lens through which I process the world—and I want my readers to grow with me as I grow as a writer.

Eventually, I'd love to branch into screenwriting and game narrative design, blending storytelling with visual and interactive media. But no matter the format, my mission is the same: to tell stories that stick with you.

My Writing Philosophy

Every character I write carries a piece of me. Whether it's a fragment of my past, a quiet fear, or a hope I've barely dared to voice, my stories are built on a foundation of lived experience. I don't just invent characters—I understand them, because in some way, I've *been* them.

I believe that the most powerful stories come from an honest place. That's why I write with intention, grounding even the most fantastical worlds in emotional truth. My own journey—its joys, traumas, transitions, and questions—shapes the people I write and the stories they tell.

By blending that personal core with imagination, I aim to create characters who feel real, flawed, and alive. Because in the end, stories aren't just escapes—they're reflections.

Fanfiction & Early Works

Before publishing original fiction, I honed my craft through fanfiction—a space where I could explore characters, experiment with style, and grow alongside a passionate community. You can still find my works on FanFiction.net and Archive of Our Own under the username **geegeepow**, where I post stories inspired by the worlds and characters that shaped me.

Fanfiction was my training ground, and I still value it as a form of storytelling that's deeply creative, personal, and full of heart.

In fact, some of my original characters that may appear in future works may even originate in my fanfiction!

www.ingramcontent.com/pod-product-compliance
Lightning Source LLC
Chambersburg PA
CBHW081141300726
48982CB00006B/1031

* 9 7 9 8 9 9 2 5 0 4 6 1 3 *